I0563554

Semmanthaka:

The Second Quest

Semmanthaka:

The Second Quest

Dr Syd K.

ZORBA BOOKS

ZORBA BOOKS

Published in India by Zorba Books, 2017

Website: www.zorbabooks.com
Email: info@zorbabooks.com

Copyright © Dr Syd K.

ISBN Print Book - 978-93-86407-33-7
ISBN eBook - 978-93-86407-34-4

All rights reserved. No part of this book may be reproduced or transmitted in any form or by any means, electronic or mechanical, including photocopying, recording, or by an information storage and retrieval system— except by a reviewer who may quote brief passages in a review to be printed in a magazine, newspaper, or on the Web—without permission in writing from the copyright owner.

Although the author and publisher have made every effort to ensure the accuracy and completeness of information contained in this book, we assume no responsibility for errors, inaccuracies, omissions, or any inconsistencies herein. Any slights on people, places, or organizations are unintentional.

Zorba Books Pvt. Ltd.(opc)
Gurgaon, INDIA

Printed at Repro Knowledgecast Limited, India

In His service in all humility

*Dedicated to all those countless nameless
devotees of Krishna who toil tirelessly in His service.*

Foreword

The tale of the Semmanthaka has always intrigued me, especially the way it has been narrated in our Hindu *Puraanas* – the fabulous properties of the gem, the way it enters the realm of humans, its subsequent disappearance, the epic quest and, its ultimate retrieval by Krishna.

In this work of fiction, I have used this very tale as the basis for a second quest, in modern times, for this immortal jewel; a jewel that yields gold on a daily basis. Those familiar with this tale from the *Puraanas* can refresh their memories, while those unfamiliar with it can enjoy uncovering it here.

The Hindu *Puraanas* are fascinating in the sense that regardless of the number of times one narrates its many scintillating tales, the readers / listeners never lose their fascination for them. This is because these tales can be interpreted in myriad ways with varied inferences and conclusions, providing stimulating exercises in intellectual flexibility and out-of-the-box thinking.

The principal characters in this second quest are Dr Shiva Baalan, a marine archeologist of repute and his assistant Dr Yogi Yaadav, who are contracted by the avid treasure hunter cum corporate billionaire, Stalin Malhotra.

All through the narrative, I have used crucial incidents from the history of this ancient land. Since it is a work of fiction, I have used an author's prerogative to tweak these incidents to suit the plot.

As a passionate lover of wildlife, I have also included descriptions of animals and natural history that go with the geographic location of where the tale takes the reader.

Of these, the episode concerning lions is based on a real-life documentary on a male coalition in a pride that ruled over vast tracts of the Saabi Sands of the Southern African wilds.

Long, long before the Lord of the Rings, there was the legend of the dazzling Semmanthaka...

Present day Dwaaraka

Somewhere off the coast of the village of Mul Dwaraka in the Saurashtrian coast...

The two scuba divers were slowly making their way over the submerged ruins of this great ancient city. The cold, five meter deep winter water was murky and visibility was just about fair, in spite of their powerful headlamps. They were swimming close to the rocky shoreline.

'*Feels marvelous to be amongst these ancient ruins, even though the visibility could be much better,*' Dr Shiva Baalan thought as he signaled a change of direction to his assistant and fellow diver Yogesh Yaadav aka Yogi.

Above the waterline, right till the horizon, the Arabian Sea was one long languid stretch of water. The calm was more like a prelude to a storm. Suddenly, there was a rumbling all along the sea floor and the waters seemed to vibrate. The two divers felt as if a mild electric current was passing through their bodies.

'*My God, what was that?*' Yogi halted his swim and looked up, just as another, more powerful tremor, rippled along the seabed, triggering more vibrations in the waters.

'Feels like an underwater quake. We'd better get out of the water quickly!' Dr. Balaan's voice crackled through the Casio bone conduction microphone as he gave the thumbs up signal for ascending.

The two divers headed for the surface pausing only to decompress. They broke water near the dive boat, which was rocking violently on the suddenly choppy sea.

Somewhere, in another realm, a giant snake slowly shifted its rumbling coils.

Two months back...

Dr Shiva Baalan, a middle-aged, 55 year old man and a confirmed bachelor, was a freelancing marine archeologist, presently on assignment for a marine salvage company called 'Deep Treasures' that specialized in hunting for submerged treasures of lore. A visibly graying man of medium height and build with a salt and pepper French beard, Dr Baalan had the mellow, roly-poly look of a content academician heading towards retirement. His assistant Yogi was a young man with chiseled features and the sleekly muscled look of a seasoned athlete. The owner of 'Deep Treasures', Stalin Malhotra, a Canadian billionaire of Punjabi descent, had contracted Dr.Baalan for treasure hunting in and around the submerged ruins of this ancient city.

Stalin was the head of a conglomeration of companies called Zamorez Inc Corp, inherited from his late father, the billionaire Zubin Malhotra. Stalin, a 60 year old childless widower, was Zubin's only scion and was named after the erstwhile Soviet leader, of whose alpha male toughness his late father was a big fan. Stalin's interest in deep sea treasure hunting had been ignited while on vacation to a Brazilian marine resort in the Atlantic. An avid and expert deep sea diver himself, Stalin had recovered a diamond encrusted silver dagger belonging to Mayan times from the sea bed, in one of his leisure dives. He had almost immediately launched the venture 'Deep Treasures' on his return to Canada; such was the impact that the ancient dagger had made on him. The artifact now proudly adorned his bedroom wall. From then on, 'Deep Treasures' had become a passion that occupied all most all of his time.

In the ten years since the launch of his company, he had successfully salvaged two blockbuster underwater treasure troves using his super submarine yacht Treasure Voyager, equipped with world class salvage equipment. His first treasure hit had been a German cargo ship which had sunk near the coast of Newfoundland during the Second World War; it had been carrying thousand 10 kg bars of gold. Stalin had salvaged 995 of those bars. Within a year of that find, he made another mega hit in the deep waters of the Pacific near the Galapagos. This was a 16th century slave ship that had sunk near the Galapagos in a violent storm and carried 50 pots filled with gold coins. The Treasure Voyager recovered 30 of those pots.

Stalin maintained complete secrecy about these two mega hits and had also rewarded his salvage crew handsomely, thereby buying their silence. He did not look for buyers for any of those treasures and they were locked in an underground purpose-built vault in a huge villa located on a Caribbean island tax haven.

Sometime last year, Stalin had set his sights on the Indian coastal city of Dwaaraka. In 1979, the renowned marine archeologist, Dr. Rao had discovered submerged ruins just off the shore of Dwaaraka; a discovery that deeply impacted the study of human history, especially with respect to India. Since then, many more archeological remains had been unearthed, in the surrounding waters as well as inland.

Besides the historical, these discoveries had also touched a deep emotional chord with the Hindus of India, who consider Dwaaraka the kingdom of Lord Krishna. But Stalin's interest in these waters had nothing to do with sentiment which, he strongly believed, was inimical to the conduct of business. The seas surrounding the land of his paternal ancestors he viewed only as a potential treasure cache. Prior to getting here, he had done an extensive study on India's marine history that stretched to very ancient times and the country's various coastal towns, especially the city of Dwaaraka and its strong mythological connections. He then sent a couple of his most trusted treasure scouts to make enquiries about any local legends/clues leading to treasures waiting to be discovered in and around those areas. Once his scouts returned, he contacted Dr. Shiva Baalan, one of the world's topmost marine archeologists.

When Dr Baalan, accompanied by Yogi, walked into Stalin's ultra-luxurious guest suite in the Treasure Voyager (lying submerged under 50 feet of water anchored somewhere near the Elephanta islands near Mumbai), he was greeted by Stalin with a firm professional handshake.

Stalin Malhotra was a man of imposing proportions - six feet six inches tall and powerfully built. His neatly trimmed, salt and pepper haircut gave him a look of a grizzled army general. And he had a booming voice to go with his appearance. After the initial round of introductions and small talk, they got down to business.

'I have heard a lot about you Dr. Baalan; a doctorate in marine archeology from Tamil University, Coimbatore, you have done extensive research and have been published in major international archeological journals. What about you, Mr. Yogi?'

'Yogi joined me only last week, Mr. Malhotra,' Dr Baalan interjected. 'He is working as a Post-Doctoral Research Assistant with me. Yogi has finished his Doctorate in Marine Archeology from Flinders University, Australia. He had just been telling me his strong gut feel we are going to hit something archeologically huge in this part of the world when you came knocking Mr. Malhotra. I hope his premonition is right.'

'You can call me Stalin, doctor. And oh, I forgot… would the two of you care for a drink? I am certainly up for one.'

'Count me in Stalin,' Dr Baalan responded with a smile. 'And you, Yogi?'

'He is a good boy Stalin. He does not drink. Let me tell you, Yogi is quite a multitalented fellow. He's a master yoga exponent and extremely proficient in Bruce Lee's martial arts style of Jeet-Kune-do. He's also a champion field hockey player... and he's only 29! Let me say that this young man has a penchant to excel in whatever he takes on.'

'Mother-lode *da puttar*, Yogi, that's pretty impressive. Tell me, how do you find the time to dabble in all these things?'

'Dr. Baalan is just being generous Stalin-sir.'

'Oh, let me also tell you Stalin, Yogi is an expert in deciphering ancient scripts. In fact, he has devised a computer program that is doing wonders in this regard,' Dr Baalan added with visible enthusiasm.

'What else can he do doctor, or what can he not do? Can this young man help me find the Semmanthaka gem?'

There was a brief moment of stunned silence.

'Stalin, I do hope you are joking. That is just stuff of myth,' Dr Baalan replied raising an eyebrow.

'No doctor. I'm dead serious and that is why I have brought you here.'

'Do you know where to look for it?' Dr Baalan could not hide the incredulity in his voice.

'Recent archeological excavations off the Saurashtrian coast strongly vouch for the fact that Krishna really did exist and he was not just a mythical figure. The submerged ruins clearly match the ancient city of Dwaaraka as mentioned in the Mahabharata. If Krishna did exist, I'm damn sure that the Semmanthaka gem existed too, and still exists in and around Dwaaraka.'

'How can you say it still exists Stalin?'

'I can see Stalin-sir's point of view Dr. Baalan,' Yogi interjected. The last location of the Semmanthaka gem as mentioned in our *Puranas* was the ancient city of Dwaaraka. There is no mention of the great gem in any text after that.'

'You have certainly got a good assistant doctor. That is exactly my line of thinking too. Which is why I want you to probe for any clues in this regard in and around the Saurashtra coast. You can start with the existing city of Dwaaraka itself. I will give you liberal funds and assistance for this exploration. But, we must move fast. We don't know when your Government will declare the submerged ruins a heritage site and put it off limits to treasure hunters like me.'

'It will still be like looking for a needle in a haystack!' Dr Baalan blurted.

'But it will not be a haystack anymore if I tell you that I have a valuable clue in hand.'

'What do you mean Stalin?'

'Give me a moment gentlemen. I'll just be back,' Stalin Malhotra hurried out of the luxury suite. He was back within the minute holding a small leather case in his right hand, which he placed on the glass table in front of his visitors.

'Take a look at this,' Stalin clicked the case open and revealed an ancient tattered leaf manuscript, written in ancient Harappan script aka Indus script. There was a crude drawing of figure holding a necklace in his hand, the pendant of which was depicted as shining like the sun.

Where did you get this Stalin?' Dr Baalan's curiosity was aroused.

'One of my archeological scouts got hold of this at an ancient Nalini Devi temple in the Rann of Kutch. This temple is situated on the banks of the big lake there. At first, I did not know what it was about. I showed it to an Indus-Harappan expert. He told me that the writings talks about a gem that has the brilliance of the Sun itself, that yields *eight bhaaras(approximately 170 pounds)* of pure gold every day – that message is followed by some figures, of which I cannot make out head or tail. Maybe Yogi can help us here. What say you, mother-lode *da puttar*?'

Yogi examined the old manuscript at some length. 'I will need some time to study it Stalin. Mind if we take it with us?'

'Sure, take it with you. I think it's unnecessary to tell you to take good care of it. I do not tolerate carelessness of any sort.' There was steel in his voice.

'I understand your concerns Stalin. We will conduct a non-destructive study of the manuscript and return it to you. We can't promise you immediate answers, I'm afraid.'

'That's why I'm giving you liberal funds and resources. Your priority should be finding the gem.'

'Well, one thing that bothers me is, how this gem, if it is for real, can produce *eight bhaaras* of gold every day? I'm not that good in physics, but I can still vouch for the fact that this violates the law of conservation of mass,' Dr Baalan looked askance at Yogi.

'Yes it seems so sir, and yet it can be easily explained,' Yogi replied. 'If you are familiar with Dr Paramahamsa Tiwari's work on harnessing energy from the void and making machines with efficiency greater than 100%, all it needs here is to further extrapolate it with Einstein's relationship between mass and energy. Even our own Upanishads talk about *Akaasha*, the ether that permeates every inch of space - this *Akaasha*, now science calls dark energy. This dark energy is the origin of everything in the visible universe. As our own Taitreeya Upanishads aver: *Akaashad vayuhu vayor agnihi agneerapaha abdhyah prithivi....* The all-pervading ether is the source of all that you perceive in the physical world. The gem is also *icchadaari,* and this means it could transmute this dark energy to any known material. It is after all the permutations of atomic and subatomic particles inside.

'Hmm...that does sound plausible,' Dr Baalan replied thoughtfully and then, looking at Stalin: 'But I'm still not sure about this project.' 'We can only confirm our involvement after researching this leaf manuscript and determining whether it holds any solid clues.'

'Alright, I will give you two weeks to explore this. For now, let's raise a toast, gentlemen,' Stalin proceeded to mix drinks for himself and Dr. Baalan.

Back at their quarters in Ahmedabad, Dr Baalan and his assistant discussed the venture at length.

'Didn't I tell you that we were going to be involved in something big when I joined you sir?' Yogi smiled at Dr Baalan through the mirror, where the latter was adjusting his collar.

'But Yogi, this is not going to be easy. We have no concrete proof that this gem is for real. How can we, as scientists, rely on mythology for direction? If my contemporaries come to know that I'm looking for Semmanthaka gem, they will think that I have gone insane!'

'But then, even Krishna was supposed to be mythical and now the archeologists are saying that there are strong indications that Krishna indeed existed.'

'But where do we start searching, even if this manuscript does tell us something. The submerged ruins are spread over a vast area and moreover, the actual ruins of Krishna's time may be lying even deeper in the seabed, making them almost inaccessible.'

'But I still say we give this a go. The equipment and funds that Stalin has promised to provide is the stuff of dreams for any archeologist. Even if we do not find the gem itself, we could make other exciting discoveries and then convince Stalin to change course.'

'That's not a bad idea Yogi, even though Stalin doesn't look like someone who will easily change course. It's just that I don't want to get caught up in mythological mumbo-jumbo and waste precious research time. But, as you say, if we come up with other exciting discoveries in the process of searching for this mythical gem, then it will certainly be worth it.'

And that's how Dr. Shiva Baalan and his assistant Dr. Yogi Yaadav began their quest for the Semmanthaka. For the next two weeks, Yogi buried himself in the manuscript to decipher the series of figures.

'I think we may have something here Dr. Baalan,' Yogi burst into the latter's office with palpable enthusiasm. 'I have examined the manuscript under a Manu Prakash foldscope for the minutest details. After running these figures through my computer program, this is what the co-ordinates say: ***The place where the wild donkey with a star on its forehead mates.***'

'Wild donkey? The only place I know that has these animals is the Rann of Kutch, which is famous for its wild ass.'

'There is also the kiang, the Tibetan wild ass, and the Gur of the Mongolian variety Baalan-sir.'

'But in our case, it must be the native one.'

'The star on the forehead; what could that mean?'

'That could mean many things. It could mean a wild ass with a unique pattern on his body or something that is implied…could be a metaphor. For that we may have to investigate the temple where this manuscript was found.'

'You're right sir. Let's go there at the earliest.'

'Yes Yogi. We will leave immediately. But before that we have to see Stalin. And by the way, the C14 dating tests on the manuscript came in just a while ago. This leaf is older than 5000 years.'

When Dr. Shiva Baalan, along with his assistant, walked into Stalin Malhotra's suite, the businessman was effusive in his praise for the work done in deciphering the old leaf manuscript. 'Mother-lode *da puttar* gentlemen, I feel there is a tangible lead here,' he put his granite hard forearm on Yogi's shoulder.

'Not so fast Stalin,' Dr Baalan quipped with a smile. 'This is again nebulous. Regardless, Yogi and I have decided to visit that Devi temple in the Rann of Kutch from where your scouts procured this old, leaf manuscript. Before that, I would like to formalize my contract with you on this project. In other words, I'm ready to sign on the dotted line, Stalin.

All your terms are acceptable to me and, of course, my assistant Yogi is also very enthused about this. He thinks this will make a good post-doc project for him.'

'Welcome aboard gentlemen,' Stalin boomed. 'Mother-lode *da puttar*, I have a feeling that this is going to be one heck of a treasure hunt. But none of this should ever go public – that's non-negotiable!'

* * *

The tires of the old battered Mahindra jeep crunched its way over the salt pans that glimmered almost white in the stifling heat of the day, on the banks of the Rann of Kutch Lake. Even though it was the beginning of the rains, there had been no showers in the past week after an initial burst heralding the season. Here and there were scattered, small herds of wild ass, which skittered away in a gallop whenever the jeep got close. Some of these exotic equines ran ahead of the jeep, easily maintaining a gap from the straining vehicle. These animals, it was said, could clock a maximum speed of 75 km per hour and were now, by all means, living up to their reputation. The pebbles thrown up by their hooves hit the windshield like bullets and ricocheted off them as the old windshield threatened to crack.

Gradually, the silhouette of a small temple, situated amidst a clump of saline vegetation, materialized in the distance. Dr. Baalan and Yogi were seated on the front seats along with Stalin's American scout, Arthur, who was the one who had procured the leaf manuscript.

'There it is, Dr. Baalan,' Arthur pointed ahead. 'There is an old resident *pujari* who gave us the leaf manuscript. It will be good if you speak to him first.'

The jeep crunched to a halt in front of the temple. A frail looking old figure was making his way out of the temple, shielding his straining eyes against the glare of the harsh noon sun reflected off the salt pan.

'Namaste *pujariji*,' Dr Baalan folded his hands in respectful greeting. The old priest greeted him with a toothless smile.

'I have come here enquiring about this,' Dr Baalan pointed to the leaf manuscript. The old man looked at the manuscript at length, and then, recognizing Arthur, he motioned the visitors inside.

The interior of the temple was cool and comforting the compared to the sweltering heat outside. The idol of the Goddess was in white marble decked out with a few flowers. The old priest had just performed ablutions to the deity with watery milk and honey. He sprinkled the collected ablutions on his guests from a brass jug with a spout and then, offered it to his guests along with a few flowers and tulsi leaves. Yogi was the first one to reverentially accept the ablutions (also called *theertham*) in his right palm and sip it slowly without slurping. The others followed suit.

The *pujari* indicated that they sit in a corner on a brownish weather-beaten rug. He then went back to wipe the deity dry with a cloth, deck it with silk and garlands and place *kumkum* on its forehead. Next he took a few pieces of camphor on a brass plate, ignited it, performed the *aarti* and brought it to his visitors. Yogi again led the way by placing his palms over the fire, before placing them on his eyes and again, the others followed. Dr. Baalan placed a 100 rupee note on the brass plate.

The old priest placed the leaf manuscript in front of him on the deer skin mat and was soon lost in contemplation. After what seemed a long while, he slowly opened his eyes and motioned to Dr Baalan to come closer. He then spoke to the archeologist in chaste Hindi.

'Indeed the animal that is mentioned lives in these parts. In fact I have seen this particular type of wild ass a couple of times.'

'Could you then tell us its exact whereabouts sir?' Dr. Baalan felt his pulse raising.

'Nearby there's a tiny creek that runs into the lake, which is a prime breeding area for these wild donkeys. A stallion with a star on its forehead dominates the area with its harem. I would say that this stallion is a very special breed and part of a prime lineage of wild donkeys. I have heard these star marked stallions mentioned right from the time of my great grandfather who lived to the ripe old age of 98. For ages, the creek has been their territory where they brood their mares and sire calves. The creek is just short of a kilometer northwest of here. You can't miss it. Moreover, this is the beginning of the breeding season for these animals and you seem to have come at the right time.'

The visitors immediately rose on cue from Dr Baalan and folded their arms in veneration to the old priest. They then boarded their jeep and headed northwest towards the direction indicated by the priest. Within minutes, they sighted the creek, its waters sparkling like blue glass in the shimmering sunlight. There were wild ass herds scattered all around and it was quite a difficult task to hone in on a single animal with a star on its forehead. Dr Baalan took out his binoculars and casually surveyed the area abutting the creek. After almost an hour of scanning, the archeologist saw him: the stallion was shaking his head with a tinge of arrogance, redolent of his topnotch physical condition. His wet face released a shower of silver water droplets as he moved his face vigorously from side to side. He now made his way back from a drink at the creek towards the shade of a cluster of trees. His harem and calves were waiting for him. The stallion painted a picture of prime magnificence. His creamy skin gleamed and the white star on his forehead was as discernible as the noon sun. He was huge by wild ass standards and an embodiment of leg strength: legs that could launch him on powerful gallops as well as crack the skull of an adventurous predator or a rival stallion, with one kick of the hind pair.

'I think I've got him,' Dr Baalan exclaimed.

Star-face was conceived on this very patch of the Rann about seven years back, when his mother mare had delivered him wet and slimy, covered in his fetal sac. She had proceeded to eat the sac and free him from his translucent slippery cage. Within minutes he had stood on his feet as was vital to his kind, and began following his mother in ungainly trots. His father, the prime stallion, in whose harem of ten mares the newborn calf's mother belonged, also had an identical star on his forehead, a star legacy that had continued down the ages. The calf had swiftly grown into an adolescent juvenile and he was immediately ejected out of the herd, by his father. Star-face then spent the next few years on the fringes, where he built his strength and matured as a full grown adult male. Then he challenged an old stallion in battle and took over his herd in a swift decisive fight. In the next few years, he slowly inched his way back to his father's territory. By this time his father had passed away from old age and his mares had been absorbed into other herds.

In the next few seasons, Star-face adroitly defended his harem from the amorous intentions of rival juvenile males hell-bent on making their own genetic mark on the next generations of wild ass. In almost all these fights, the stallion established his dominance very fast and sent his opponents galloping away into the vast wastes of the Rann. But today was going to be different. The four year old male, who had just bloomed into his prime, made his intentions clear by challenging Star-face. Instinctively, Star-face circled his mares protectively, shook his head and bared his teeth, powerful incisors that could inflict painful and deep bites on rival challengers. He then proceeded to ignore the challenges of his rival. But this rival was not going anywhere.

He shook his head in defiance and began to snort and strut, displaying the power of his legs to Star-face. That was enough for the latter and he walked up to his challenger with a swagger. The two males then began to circle each other, gauging each other's strength and condition. They then closed in on each other. The challenger tried to get a biting hold on Star-face's flank, but the prime stallion avoided it deftly and inflicted a powerful resounding kick to the shoulders of the challenger, the thud of which carried audibly to the human being watching them engrossed, in the Mahindra.

The challenger brayed in pain but stood his ground. After a brief respite, the circling started again and then, the challenger struck with a powerful bite on his opponent's hind quarters. Star-face jumped away in pain and then pivoted on his forelegs to launch a powerful kick directed at the challenger's face. The challenger swerved gracefully to avoid the kick as those powerful legs swished past his face. He then inflicted another bite on Star-face's rump which tore off the skin. The blood started to flow immediately. This had never happened in Star-face's previous fights with other rivals. The rivals started circling each other again and suddenly they rose in unison on their hind-legs and locked each other with their forelegs, their mouths trying to get a painful biting hold on the other. Then they separated with their forelegs viciously kicking each other. The circling resumed again. Once again they rose on their hind legs and the same process started again. This went on repeatedly till Star-face introduced a variation that comes only with fighting experience, which the juvenile challenger lacked.

The seventh time when they separated after rising on their hind legs and locking their forelegs, Star-face veered around at lighting speed on his forelegs and launched a thunderbolt of a kick directly to the face of the juvenile. Those powerful hooves of Star-face made contact with the mouth of the juvenile which such force that the juvenile's jaws broke on impact and his incisors rocketed out. The juvenile brayed in pain as he absorbed the blow and bravely stood his ground. But the battle was over and the youngster's snout was a bloodied mess. Star-face smelt blood now. He launched himself viciously at his wounded opponent attacking his flanks with powerful bites. The juvenile had no option but to run away from this onslaught. He galloped across the saltpan with Star-face hot in pursuit. Now and then the youngster launched his hind legs at his pursuer but Star-face was a wizened warrior and adroitly avoided them. After a while, Star-face gave up the chase and turned to head back victoriously towards his harem.

Dr Baalan took in this action with childlike enthusiasm.

'One heck of a stallion he is,' he remarked. 'So this is the exact place where, according to the old manuscript, we can expect to find more clues.'

'Could I get to see him closer Dr Baalan?' Yogi asked with a smile.

'You sure can Yogi. But our next task is set out for us. According to the leaf, there is some kind of a clue in this area. But again, that will be like searching for a needle in the haystack. Before we do that, we need to take some photos of these beautiful animals and the magnificent landscape.'

'I'm already on it sir,' Yogi quipped.

'Good job Yogi,' Dr Baalan marveled at the way his assistant anticipated him. Yogi was turning out to be one of his finest assistants to date.

'Arthur and I will explore the area near the creek with metal detectors. Yogi, I also want you to take high resolution photographs of anything that you think looks interesting or out of the ordinary.'

'Alright sir.'

The trio meticulously went through the area in their typical archeological grid approach. The scan was widened to include the opposite side of the creek. But soon they ran out of steam, as well as time. The sun continued to beat down on them mercilessly and they had to take frequent breaks. Darkness fell. They decided to spend a few more days in the area. That night, they slept in the forecourt of the temple under a cool starry sky after having a dinner of dry *chappatis* and *bhaaji* provided by the *pujari*. The old man also provided cots and blankets and soon the three were blissfully asleep.

They were back at the creek the next dawn after a breakfast of fruits, nuts, and milk. Star-face and his harem were still there but they had shifted a bit to the west. The equines maintained a safe distance from the humans and looked at them warily even as they were slowly growing accustomed to their presence. So the three were struck with profound disbelief when the old *pujari* suddenly made his appearance and walked straight up to Star-face. The stallion and his harem made no attempt to move. The *pujari* then patted the stallion's forehead and fed him a mixture of jaggery and puffed rice out of his aged palms. Then the old man walked away with a smile, motioning the threesome to continue with their tasks.

The sun was now getting stronger. Many stones and pebbles ended up in a blue plastic sack. These would be meticulously studied at Dr Baalan's laboratory. Finally, the second day ended too, with the sun going down in a glorious hue of orange across the Rann's western sky. That night the Rann took on another hue of magnificence under the light of the full moon. After another ten days of searching for archeological clues, the threesome returned to Dwaaraka.

'Nothing out of the ordinary in all this,' Dr Baalan remarked as he meticulously poured over the pile of pebbles and rocks that they had collected so far. 'Makes me wonder whether this leaf manuscript is indeed for real.

If it is a genuine clue, then we need to conduct excavations in this area for which we certainly need the permission of the Archeological Survey of India (ASI) and, very possibly, the permission of the wildlife board too as this area is a sanctuary for wild ass. For ASI permission, we need solid indicators from our initial exploration that this area indeed warrants an excavation and I'm afraid that they are not going to accept an ancient leaf manuscript found in a temple as a valid argument. We may be even become the butt of jokes among our fellow archeos because of this. Even in the unlikely event of ASI granting us permission to excavate, I'm not sure that the wildlife board will take kindly to our intrusion into the habitat of this endangered wild ass species.' Two weeks had now gone by and the research had made no headway. Moreover, they were due to report to an eager Stalin Malhotra in a couple of days.

'On the flip side sir, we got some fine photographs of the wild ass, especially of that star faced stallion, that will make even National Geographic go green with envy,' Yogi quipped as he held an image of Star-face in his hand.

'Magnificent animals these are, and all efforts should be made to conserve them.' Dr Baalan peered at the image over Yogi's shoulder. Well it is time for lunch Yogi. Let's drop this for now. I'm really hungry.'

'OK sir.'

They stepped out of Dr Baalan's lab and headed towards a nearby Udupi eatery that served the best *dosas* and *idlis* in town. Once inside, Dr Baalan called the waiter and ordered a plate of *rava dosa* while Yogi settled for his favorite *idli sambar*. The two archeos were happily munching away when Yogi suddenly shot up from his chair.

'I think I may have found a clue and it was right in front of us all this time,' Yogi rushed towards the exit followed by an excited Dr Baalan.

'What the hell Yogi? Can you tell me about it?'

'Sir, can you please take care of the bill and join me at the lab. I'll explain then.'

Dr Baalan entered his lab with his heart beating fast. 'Tell me Yogi, where's the clue?'

'Here it is and it was all the time right here,' Yogi flipped an image of Star-face towards Dr Baalan. 'The clue is staring at us in this very photo. That star and the other spots and patterns on the neck of the animals are very likely ancient symbols and could pack a story.'

'You tell me. You are the expert in cracking this kind of stuff.'

'I have fed the scrambled patterns into my computer program along with the already present symbols on that leaf manuscript and will get an answer soon. Let's also remember that my software code only gives us a probability. My program is based on Dr Mohan Rao's outstanding research in this regard.'

The next few minutes felt like an age for Dr Baalan as he stared at the computer screen. Finally the output file was created and Yogi gave a print command. The laser printer immediately went to work with its typical humming sound. Then it stopped. There was no paper. 'Darn! Why does this has to happen just when things get really exciting?!' Dr Baalan rushed towards the stack of blank A4 bond papers stacked on the wall shelf at the far end of the room. He then fed the printer with a sheaf to get the printing restarted.

'There could be something here sir,' Yogi scanned the printout in his hand. 'It says that *the sea by the kingdom of the great temple holds the gates to the sun.*

'The sea by the kingdom holds the gates to the Sun… hmm, interesting indeed Yogi. Here "the sun" could very well mean the gem, given that the gem was initially given to Satrajit by the Sun God himself. "The kingdom" must be the ancient city of Dwaaraka, which has indeed a great temple by its shore. Could this mean that the gem could be buried somewhere in the sea near Dwaaraka?'

'Quite possible sir. But where exactly do we start looking? The area is vast and the chances of finding a particular object are small.'

'Hmm...but what about scouring the waters of the temple shore?'

'That won't be a bad idea sir. We have to start somewhere after all.'

'Alright, let's get going on this. But at first we have to talk to Stalin.'

The two were in Stalin's marine office within the hour. Dr Baalan debriefed the latter meticulously, right from their visit to the Rann, up until Yogi's finding of a possible clue.

'Mother-lode *da puttar* doctor! So what are you waiting for gentlemen? You have the full blessings of Deep Treasures to launch a dive-search in the area that you reckon that you could get further clues from.'

That was how the two archeos found themselves in the thick of a treasure hunt in the cold and murky waters off the seas of Dwaaraka. It was now their 25th consecutive day of searching and they had come up with nothing. Moreover, the rumbling of the seabed had put an abrupt end to their search. As Dr Baalan pulled himself aboard the dive boat, along with Yogi, his face wore a disappointed look. They had gone back and forth over a vast area in a thorough grid search.

'The waters were particularly cold today sir,' Yogi slowly pulled off his scuba mask.

'Indeed they were Yogi and moreover the rumbling below was definitely from underwater tremors.' Dr Baalan ran his wet hands despondently over his grey hair. 'We better get to the shore now. I don't think that we are going to find anything more here.'

Yogi was already tuning in to the coastguard. Warnings were being issued about a series of mild underwater tremors that began off the coast of Dwaaraka and continued all the way to the south along the west coast.

'I have a feeling that we should search the land along the coastline too, sir. We know that what is land today, could well have been the sea in ancient times.'

'Once again, we don't know where to look.'

'We could start by exploring the area around the temple.'

'I'm not too convinced that we are heading in the right direction Yogi. But we can give it a shot. Before that we have to talk to Stalin again.'

Stalin Malhotra was not in the best of moods when the two archeos brought him up to date regarding the search. He wanted the two to search the seas for a while longer. It took a lot of convincing by Dr Baalan to convince the big man to change tracks.

'Alright Dr Baalan. You may start exploring inland. But I warn you that my resources are not infinite. If we are not able to come up with something in the next couple of months, we may have to abandon this project.'

'I can see where you're coming from Stalin. But, I do have a hunch that the land will yield better clues.'

The next six weeks were spent in a rigorous archeological survey of the land surrounding the temple, especially along the coast line. But the search party could come up with nothing of value, except some trivial artifacts which were regardless, collected, labeled, and stored.

'I think we are hitting a dead end here Yogi,' Dr Baalan spoke to his assistant as he sat in his chair reading the day's newspaper. 'Nothing short of an underwater excavation will give us tangible leads.' His cell phone began to ring. It was his security man Raam Singh, whom Dr Baalan had employed to guard the lab and its premises, especially in his absence and during the night.

'Sir, there is a boy here to see you. He says it is urgent.'

'Ask him what his name is and where he comes from.'

'The boy says that he comes from Kutch and his name is Kisan. He says he is the grandson of the temple *pujari*,' Raam Singh replied.

'Send the boy in Raam Singh.'

A scrawny fourteen year old with big, eager black eyes made his appearance at the door.

'Sir-ji namaste,' the lad spoke after an initial hesitation. 'My grandfather wants you to immediately come with me to Kutch to his temple. He says that he has something of utmost importance to tell you. At the same time, he also told me that only you and your assistant are to come and moreover, he does not want this visit of yours to be known to anyone else.'

'May I ask you young man, what it is that he wants to tell me? I'm a very busy person and have lots of work to attend to.'

'I'm afraid sir-ji that I can't give you a reason as I myself have not been told what my grandfather wants to tell you. All he wanted of me was to ask you, on his behalf, to come.'

Dr Baalan and Yogi looked at each other. 'Why don't you ask your grandfather to talk to us on the phone regarding the matter before we come there to meet him,' Dr Baalan put his arm around the boy's shoulder. 'Listen *bête*, we are very busy at this point of time.'

'Grandfather told me that this matter can only be revealed to you in person. It concerns whatever you had come looking for during your earlier visit.'

Dr Baalan and Yogi exchanged looks again. 'Why don't we make a fast dash there and return? Maybe there is something worthwhile in what the *pujari* has to say,' Yogi interjected with visible enthusiasm.

'Something of archeological value I hope, Yogi,' there was a hint of sarcasm in Dr Baalan's voice. 'Already we have a meeting scheduled with Stalin in a couple of days - a meeting that is going to decide the future of this project.'

'That's why I feel that we should make an urgent dash right now. Let's give this an outside chance.'

'Alright Yogi let's do it. But we have to get back in time for the meeting with Stalin. The meeting can't be postponed as Stalin is returning to Canada for a brief while. He is, therefore, insistent that we meet before he leaves. Moreover we also have a sticky situation here. How can we keep Stalin in the dark about this intended visit if this information given by the *pujari* concerns this project? We will surely be violating one of the clauses in our contract.'

'Let us tell Stalin only after we hear what the *pujari* has got to say. If the info is of no value then we don't even have to tell him about this. Also, we will make sure that we are back here in time.'

'The *pujari had* better tell us something worthwhile and not some mythological stuff!'

'But sir, many things that were supposedly myths are proving to be facts, in recent excavations.'

'I don't have problems with facts Yogi. That is what we archeos are always looking for, aren't we? The last thing I want now is another dead-end clue like the one we got off the star faced wild ass stallion.'

'I see your point boss. Regardless, I feel intuitively that we must give this a shot.'

The two scientists along with their young visitor immediately took to the road in Dr Baalan's car. By the early hours of the morning, the following day, they were sitting on a deerskin mat in front of the *pujari* at the temple.

'OK *pujariji*, we are here as you had wished. Now please tell us what you wanted us to hear.'

The old man closed his eyes in lengthy contemplation. Then he got up and motioned his guests to follow him. He picked up a big oil lamp and led them to a room behind the main sanctum in a corner. The heavy teak door was secured with a big padlock. The *pujari* singled out a big iron key from a bunch strung to his sacred thread. He then slowly pushed open the door revealing a dark musty room. At the corner of the room, there was a pile of enormous brass pots. The *pujari* made his way gingerly through the gaps between the pots and then placed his hands on an iron knob on the wall and twisted it clockwise. There was a grating noise in response and suddenly, the floor at the corner of the room parted revealing a series of stone cut stairs leading down to a narrow, ancient pathway.

'Follow me,' he spoke softly to his visitors. 'You are the first set of people other than me and my guru Jaarra *baaba* to be aware of the existence of this secret passageway. Nobody outside knows this pathway, not even my family.'

'Jaarra *baaba*?' Dr Baalan interjected.

'Yes Dr Saab, as I had told you, he is my guru and a very wise ascetic. In fact we are actually on our way now to meet him. Many people know him as Jaarra *baaba* in this area. He is said to be close to 100 years of age, some say even older, but it is very hard to guess his age as he is very agile and sharp. It is actually *baabaji* who intends to meet you and tell you something. That is why I wanted you to come here in person. *Baabaji* rarely speaks to others. If he has to say something, you can rest assured that it is something of great importance. Somehow, he came to know of your earlier visit and he immediately asked me to summon you here.'

'Don't tell me that we have come all this way to see a *baaba!*' Dr Baalan muttered to himself.

'I just have one humble request for both of you,' the old priest continued. 'Please be extremely respectful in the presence of the *baaba* and talk only if he asks you to. The *baaba* actually prefers silence.'

The pathway was straight and almost 500 meters long. There was a faint sound of running water somewhere far below. At the far end, they could see dim blue light struggling through the dusty darkness. As they neared the light source, they could discern an altar of some sort. On the stony steps of the altar was seated a man with matted locks and a very long flowing beard, adorned in loose white robes that gave him a Gandalf-like appearance.

'This is the great Jaarra *baaba*. I will leave you two here as per *baaba*'s instructions,' the *pujari* whispered faintly as he motioned Dr Baalan and Yogi to sit on the bottom-most step and then silently made his way back up the corridor, leaving the two alone with Jaarra *baaba*. The *baaba* was lost in meditation and almost thirty minutes ticked by before he opened his eyes and spoke to Dr Baalan who was, by then, seething with impatience.

'*Harihar-Shiv-Shambho,* what has been spoken has now started happening. You are here now Dr Baalan and Mr. Yogi because of that,' the *baaba* spoke in heavily accented Hindi mixed with English.

'I can sense your impatience Dr Baalan,' the *baaba* continued. 'Do you hear the distant sound of running water coming from somewhere way below. Actually, it is one of the rivulets of the great underground river Saraswathi, flowing under the very ground you sit. This rivulet feeds into the Rann of Kutch Lake from below. I know of the controversy amongst you archeologists about the existence of this ancient river. Believe me, it exists. But what I'm going to tell you now is more out of this world and is of monumental significance to humanity and the planet as a whole: A planet that is now being increasingly threatened by the dark forces of greed, commercialism, terrorism, and of course environmental degradation. And… there is even a much bigger darker force threatening this globe, which will be revealed to you in due course. That's why I insisted that no other persons, other than the two of you, come to this secret place. The last thing I want is the presence of a fortune seeking treasure hunter because what I'm going to tell you is greater than the greatest of treasures. As Radheyshyam *pujari* has already told you, only two people, me and him, know of this place and now this makes four of us,' the *baaba* halted his speech and closed his eyes.

'So Dr Baalan,' the *baaba* began at length, 'a distinguished career in archeology and, in fact, one the top names in the world in marine archeology in this part of the world. A bachelor who went through a bitter case of love failure – as you could not marry the woman you loved. I know everything about you and also about your precocious assistant, Dr Yogi.'

'That's not hard these days when all kinds of information is available on the net,' Dr Baalan thought with a touch of anger. He was seething inside that the *baaba* had the audacity to speak about his private life.

'Ah, Dr Baalan, sorry to have spoken about your love life. Also, I'm not internet savvy as you may like to believe - I have never touched a computer in my life. So you can banish that thought from your mind, Teddy Bear.'

Dr Baalan reeled visibly. How the hell was the *baaba* reading his thoughts? But what shocked him even more was that the *baaba* had addressed him as Teddy Bear. How could the *baaba* be aware of a childhood pet name that his father had affectionately bestowed upon him - a name which was a family secret? This was certainly not something that was on the net. Moreover, he was the only surviving member of his family. 'Just impossible!' he whispered inwardly.

'*Harihar-Shiv-Shambho*! Nothing is impossible Dr Baalan. "Teddy Bear", in your case, springs from the word *baalu*, meaning bear, which was the short-form of your name during your childhood days.'

'And what else do you know?' Dr Baalan muttered inwardly.

'Everything Dr Baalan, everything… and I know everything about your assistant too by the grace of *Harihar-Shiv-Shambho*. I also know that you are a fan of the late Osho and that you think that my voice resembles his,' the *baaba* smiled gently.

'I've to remind myself that this *baaba* somehow can read my thoughts. I'd better stop thinking.' Dr Baalan was by now totally stumped.

'Don't stop thinking. In fact, thinking is bread and butter to an eminent researcher like you. But for now, listen to what I have got to say. As they say, leave your mind uncluttered.' Jaarra *baaba* continued in his mellifluous voice: 'First of all, I want both of you to take a deep breath, relax and set your minds free. I want both of you to take in what I am going to tell you without any prejudice. Any questions you may have, I request you to reserve for the end. I was anticipating your visit, going by what my great and respected Guruji in the Himalayas had told me last year. I had actually gone there to see him when you had come visiting here for the first time. Guruji could see your visit in his vision and immediately asked me to get back here and meet with you. And of course, he had also mentioned your client Stalin Malhotra - what he does for a living and for what he has currently contracted you. Guruji is adamant that there are no vested commercial or personal interests to be involved, especially with what I am going to show you.' The *baaba* slowly reached up for a long wooden box positioned on the top of the altar. He brought it down reverently and rested it on his lap. He then opened the lid gently. A peacock green halo emanated from inside the box. The *baaba* closed his eyes in prayer and then brought forth a long tube like object that glowed like a firefly of peacock green luminescence. '*Harihar-Shiv-Shambho!* I'm holding in my hands, one half of the flute of Krishna.'

Dr Baalan and Yogi looked at each other with disbelief.

'I know that both of you are filled with disbelief. But this is just the beginning and I want no prejudice here; just open minds. And yes, the archeologist in you would demand evidence that this broken flute indeed belonged to Krishna eons back. Let me tell you doctor, that the material of which this flute is made of is something you will not find anywhere on this planet. In fact, it comes from the highest of the worlds, *Gau-loka.* Here doctor, you may touch and feel it, but with a sense of deep respect. Remember, if there is even a tinge of moral decay in your heart, you will find that you will be unable to hold this. The material of the flute is *Shuddha-saatvik* with not even a hint of karma, unlike the material matter on this planet, especially these days, which is tainted either by environmental pollution or dark human intentions.'

Dr Baalan, still in the thrall of disbelief, gingerly reached out to touch the half-flute. The moment his fingertips graced it, he felt a huge jolt of electric energy go through his body and pulled back in reflex.

'*Harihar-Shiv-Shambho!* That tells me that your karmic debts are high, doctor as expected of all ordinary mortals. The more karma a human has, the bigger the jolt of energy he/she will feel. Just close your eyes with deep prayer to Krishna and chant the karma dissolving Mahaa Mantram... HARE KRISHNA HARE KRISHNA KRISHNA KRISHNA HARE HARE. HARE RAAM HARE RAAM RAAM RAAM HARE HARE. You can only hold it as long as your lips and mind constantly chant this mantra. I know doctor that you are not very religious, but I also know that you do believe in a higher power. So take my words on faith. In the meantime, I ask Yogi to come forward and touch it.'

Yogi reached out with his usual reverence towards the half flute. Even before Jaarra-*baaba* had indicated, he had already begun chanting the Mahaa Mantram silently. He felt a burst of static go through him as he made contact but he did not move his hand away. The current seemed to grow in energy and Yogi's entire body started trembling. Seeing this, Dr Baalan became concerned. But, the very next moment, Yogi's body began to relax as he felt a wave of sheer bliss pass through his body. He had never felt anything like this before in his entire life and now he did not want to let go.

'OK *bete*, that's enough for now. This feeling of bliss is very addictive; a bliss for which great yogic masters strive for decades to even have an ephemeral taste. You and Dr Baalan are so, so blessed that you are the chosen ones. Even Radheshyam-*pujari* has not had the honor so far and neither does he know about the flute's presence here. Now if Dr Baalan feels ready, he can come forward too.'

Dr Baalan was now more intent on finding out whether chanting the Mahaa Mantram would work. He once again reached out to feel it. There was a big jolt of electricity again, but this time he did not pull back his arm. His lips were constantly chanting the mantra in spite of his body trembling with the current. The trembling lasted thrice as long as that of Yogi's but Dr Baalan did not let go. Streams of sweat flowed from the back of his ears before he felt himself completely relaxing and going into a state of blissful ecstasy. It was as if there was nothing more to existence other than this feeling. Then Jaarra *baaba*'s voice brought him back to the present. Suddenly all his doubts had seemed to have vanished.

'*Harihar-Shiv-Shambho!* You have been touched by Krishna's magic, whether you would like to believe it or not. Rest assured that you two will never be the same after this. You will find that your thoughts and actions become clearer compared to what it has been all along and you will find a new sense of energy charging through your body for the rest of your lives.'

It took a while for Dr Baalan to mentally recover from that experience. For now, there was a sense of awe building up in him.

'I will tell you more doctor, so please sit down,' Jaarra-*baaba* put the half flute back into its box and placed it gently in its original station. He then folded his hands and bowed before the box with deep reverence before turning back to Dr Baalan and Yogi. 'You see doctor, this is just one half of Krishna's flute, the part which was held close to his lips. Now you may rightly ask me as to what has happened to the other part, the distal one. That is precisely what I'm going to talk to you about.' The *baaba* took a seat on the stony steps.

He once again closed his eyes and resumed at length, 'Doctor, we are all souls moving endlessly through the ocean of time, periodically halting at islands called *janmas* (births). Once our stay in a particular island comes to a close, we leave that island and swim towards the next and this cycle continues interminably for all unliberated souls. By the power of earthly *Maaya*, we forget the memories of our past island when we enter a new one. The reason I'm talking to you about this concerns my own journey in this ocean of time. I have come in touch with these halves of Krishna's flute in a total of four *janmas* including the current. In two of those four *janmas*, including the current one, I have come in contact with both halves of the flute. In the other two *janmas*, I have come in contact with only one of the parts.

Now you may ask as to how I know about these previous *janmas*. It is only by the grace of my Guruji that I know these facts and now I'm telling you what he revealed to me. It is only because of this knowledge of my past lives that a humble college professor of chemistry, Dr Shreedhar Yaadav, ended up becoming the Jaarra *baaba* that you see in front of you today. And now, I'm going to chronologically tell you about these four past lives because these lifetimes were instrumental in shaping the course of this great ancient Hindu land of *Bhaarath-varsh*.'

'*Harihar-Shiv-Shambho*,' the *baaba* once again went into a long trance before he resumed.

'The story begins sometimes towards the end of the *Dwaaparyug* when I was Jaarra the hunter in the verdant forests surrounding the ancient city of Dwaaraka.'

And in that other-worldly realm, the giant snake once again stirred in its coils, opening eyes that glowed like pink diamonds. Once again a chain of feather mild tremors began off the coast of Dwaaraka and continued down south to the Konkan shoreline, before petering off.

Jaarra, the hunter- The mighty dissolution

It was dusk as I waded through thick cover; bow and arrow slung over my right shoulder and a knapsack on my left. I could feel the cold blade of my hunting knife secured to my thighs with antelope hide. I had just fine tuned my bow and sharpened my knife that morning. This I did after I had woken up from the makeshift bed, on the bough of the huge banyan tree, in the deepest recesses of the forest. You see, I had been away from my family consisting of my wife and five children for almost seven days, in search of Sheval – the king of the jungle fowl. This time, I had promised my family that I would not return till I brought back the mighty rooster alive. Almost the size of a dog, Sheval was a legend in these parts. His feathers were emerald green and he had a ruby red crown on his head. He was exceptionally strong, fierce, and had razor sharp talons which he used effectively against rival roosters who dared to eye his flock of twenty hens and their chicks. There were numerous stories about Sheval's valor and prowess and I had experienced this myself, first hand. Twice in the past, I had almost captured him, but he had somehow escaped in the last moment. In those instances I realized that the bird was also highly intelligent. You see, Sheval was a prize catch for all hunters. One particular king had even announced a prize of 1000 gold coins for anyone who succeeded in trapping the rooster fowl alive. I had a livid scar below my right eye, after my last encounter with Sheval. I had somehow sneaked up on him from behind and was going to throw my net over him when he sensed my presence at the very last moment, turned and flew into my face with a fierce crow. His talons narrowly missed gouging my right eye. But this time, I had a change of strategy, just this morning.

I was not going to use my nets or even my bow and arrow. This time, I was going to use the catapult that I carried in my knapsack, a catapult that could fire darts whose tips where laced with a very potent herbal sedative that could even put an elephant into slumber. My plan was to dart Sheval and take him home alive. Consequently, I had been searching for him all these days in the jungle and only the day before, I had come across the spoor of his alpha-hen, which meant that I was on the right track. And as expected, I came across one of his emerald green feathers tucked away in a nearby bush. But even if he was nearby, hunting jungle fowl is an extremely difficult prospect for even the best of hunters. First of all, these birds are always hyper-alert and bolt at the slightest sound. Moreover, they are very agile and even take to short distance flights rocketing away from danger. They also have very keen eyesight and can discern the slightest moments by hidden predators. That they had survived as a species in these jungles for eons was a testimony of extreme caution.

I immediately hushed my gait and walked on velvet steps, just like a tiger stalking deer. If Sheval and his flock were nearby and heard even the slightest sound of my approach, they would be gone at lightning speed and it would be very difficult to re-track them.

After almost an hour of tracking like a ghost, I finally came to the edge of a clearing where I could see Sheval and his flock of hen and chicks feeding on worms and insects in the grass. Almost instantly I froze, lest these hyper alert fowl detect my presence. Very gingerly, inch by inch, I slowly went down on all fours and flattened myself on the ground with the intention of getting into range for my catapult shot. I did not want to miss him this time around. It had, after all, been a long wait for me.

As the minutes passed, I began, very slowly, crawling towards the spot which I had identified as a place from where I would fire my dart. But I did not anticipate what was going to happen next. There was a sudden flutter in the skies above and I looked up in time to see a ferocious crown eagle swoop down on one of the chicks in Sheval's flock. The hens shrieked hysterically as they scrambled in different directions with the rest of their chicks. But Sheval did not retreat going against the usual behavior of his kind, especially when it came to attack by a deadly raptor like this, which yielded no quarter.

In fact Sheval went a step further, launching himself in the air and meeting the raptor head on just as he was about to close in on the targeted chick. There was a flurry of feathers as the two birds embraced in a tangle and tumbled like a ball to the ground. The crown eagle was completely blindsided by this act of Sheval. In his innings so far, he had never met a fowl that had taken the attack back to him. The usual reaction was to evade and escape. Both birds now regained their feet and squared against each other with their wings spread. The eagle squawked shrilly in anger while Sheval clucked back in equal fury. The standoff continued for a while before the eagle turned around and took flight. But Sheval was limping now and that was when I saw the streak of red on his emerald green breast. The claws of the eagle had made its mark during that brief fight. I could not help wondering about the courage of this bird and that made me want to capture him even more. In the meantime, the targeted young chick had managed to escape in the direction of the rest of the flock.

In all that commotion, I had managed to get within range and now I slowly brought my catapult to aim. After a brief moment I fired but somehow the rooster turned in my direction in the last moment and detected my movement while firing the dart. He swerved in an instant and my dart swished harmlessly past his head. The next moment, he turned and darted off. I jumped to my feet and started to chase the birds - I was not a bad runner either, but the fowl was too quick for me. After about a few yards, he suddenly rocketed to his typical low level flight and flew off into thick cover. I stopped and threw up my hands in utter frustration. Another chance to get Sheval had been wasted.

I was tired now and badly needed a drink of water. There was a stream in the direction where Sheval had escaped and that's where I headed too, with disappointment sour in my mind. After walking a fair distance through thick cover, I suddenly halted. I could not believe my eyes. I could see a part of Sheval's emerald green body through a gap in the trees in the distance. I immediately reckoned that the bird must be significantly injured by the eagle talons and that is why it had not bolted very far off like fowls generally do. This was my one chance again and this time I was determined to get him. Once again I quietened my stride and slowly inched forward, keeping myself low to the ground. I had once again got into range when the air was filled with the most bewitching music, the sound of a flute. I had never heard such blissful melody before and I lost myself in it for a while, yet my eyes were still focused on my target. In a way, the music seemed to guide my aim as I stretched my catapult, ready to release the dart, when, suddenly the music stopped, releasing me from my trance. There was a hushed silence all around. At this precise moment I released the sling and the dart was off, searing towards the target. In the next instant, it hit home and I threw up my hands in sheer ecstasy as I rushed towards my prey. Surprisingly, the target had not moved even after being hit which itself was highly unusual. 'Had the eagle's wound already claimed Sheval?' I wondered disappointed. What was the point in capturing him dead after all this? Regardless, I hurried towards my target, breaking cover and rapidly increasing my strides.

My jaw dropped in total surprise and shock as I came into full view of the target: It was not Sheval that I had hit, but a fellow human. And I had never seen such a magnificent specimen in front of me. He was sitting on the branch of a tree with a splendid flute in his hand which was, no doubt, the source of the ethereal music I had heard, just a short while ago. The dart had penetrated the peacock green *uttareeya* (upper garment) that this extraordinarily handsome, dark blue-skinned man with extremely magnetic eyes, had adorned, and burrowed deep into his heart. I could see the blood flowing from his chest and yet there was a serene smile on his face and he made no attempt to staunch the wound with his hands. He seemed, very much, to be a man of noble lineage, perhaps even of a royal one.

'My friend Jaarra,' he spoke in a soft voice and I was stunned to hear him say my name as we had never met before. 'I was expecting you in this very circumstance as this was all preordained; my impending death at your hands - a clearing of karmic debts.'

'Oh what have I done *yajmaan*? I mistook you for a jungle fowl.' I felt distraught and deeply ashamed of my act. I had always taken pride at my prowess as a hunter and had never before erred in identifying and discerning my quarry. Yet, now, I had fatally injured this noble human being by mistake. I was instantly reminded of King Dasharatha of *Tretaayug* and how he had killed Sraavan, mistaking him for a deer while on a royal hunt.

'You can do nothing Jaarra. It was preordained that you mistake me for a bird. Anyway my time has come to depart this planet. So be in peace and do not fret over this.'

'May I know who you are *yajmaan*? You are one of the most forgiving humans that I have ever met. Can anyone forgive the person who is responsible for taking his life?'

'I'm Krishna, King of Dwaaraka,' the man replied with a smile. Once more I was speechless. Yes, I had heard of the mighty Yaadava king of Dwaaraka and his legendary exploits. But being a forest dweller who had never ventured out of the woods his whole life, I had never seen my King in person, even though I roamed his very forests.

'Forgive me my King,' I immediately collapsed on my knees. 'Oh what have I done?' I began to tremble and lament. Krishna was very beloved of all his subjects. Now these subjects would never forgive me if they came to know that I was the one responsible for his death.

'Arise my dear Jaarra. As I have told you that it is not worth lamenting about what is previously ordained. Moreover, I have an important task for you to do. This will be your atonement. I want you to climb to the very top of this tall tree and look west. You will get an uninterrupted view of the city of Dwaaraka. You have to tell me what's happening there.'

'Yes my lord,' I stammered and I immediately climbed the tree. Positioning myself gingerly at the highest branch that could hold my weight, I looked west. As King Krishna said, the magnificent city of Dwaaraka and the blue sea were part of the view. They looked splendid in the red halo of the setting sun. For a while, I was lost in its splendor, until suddenly, the ground shook violently as if the tree was being uprooted. With great difficulty I maintained my balance. But the city looked as if it was empty and bereft of life and I wondered why. I had always heard of Dwaaraka as a place full of life and zest, one of the prime reasons being its perpetually young and lively, King Krishna, whose valor and exploits were legendary. It rankled no end that this same King was sitting helpless below, on the ground, because of me. I looked down and King Krishna still lay there, looking up at me with a smile.

'The city looks very empty my lord,' I spoke loudly. 'It feels dead. I mean I see no one on its streets, not even an animal or a bird.'

'Doesn't surprise me Jaarra as they are busy killing each other, inebriated with liquor as they are and they are also completely blind to the fury that is going to visit them soon. Anyway, these things too were ordained.'

I was a bit surprised at the sense of resignation in his tone. But then, in what other manner would a dying man speak? I still could not bring myself to acknowledge the fact that the King was dying because of me. My thoughts were interrupted by a cloud of dust on the horizon. It was a lone rider and he was galloping in our very direction.

'A horseman is riding this way my King and he is coming very fast.'

'Yes, that is Shatamanyu Yaadav, one of the junior commanders in my army. He is coming here on my instructions, riding my very own horse Hamsashwa.'

Then the King picked up his flute again and held it to his lips. Even while in the throes of being mortally wounded, the music that he created was sheer bliss and once again I was entranced. It was said that even the animals and the birds stood still whenever King Krishna played his flute and now, I couldn't agree more. The sound of the thudding hooves of the approaching rider brought me back to the present. In a short while a handsome young man riding on a milk white stallion of equal magnificence came to a halt near our tree. The agile young man vaulted to the ground and rushed towards King Krishna. There was look of profound shock and indignation on his face as he beheld his wounded and dying master.

'My Lord, what happened and who did this to you? Tell me my Lord and I'll cut his body into a thousand pieces with my sword!' Shatamanyu rushed to the tree where Krishna was seated.

'Compose yourself Shatamanyu and stay down. There is no need for you to come up. I'm comfortable here. I'm touched by your concern for my welfare but let me assure you that my time has come as was ordained.'

'But master....' the young warrior protested.

'Calm down my son. Where is the level-headedness for which I have chosen you for this huge responsibility that is coming your way? Isn't it the same level-headedness that has kept you from participating in that orgy of internecine bloodbath that is being orchestrated by our Yaadav clan?'

'Yes master, I understand. But I can't bear to see you this way.'

'Believe me Shatamanyu. I'm actually in a very happy state of mind as I have accomplished whatever I had set myself to do in this lifetime. Now, I have only one more task left, which you and Jaarra will have to fulfill after my passing.' King Krishna then looked up and motioned me to come down with that blissful smile of his. I hesitatingly started my descent. I wondered how warrior Shatamanyu would react if he came to know that I was the one responsible for the King's current predicament. Once level with King Krishna, I once again beheld those magnetic eyes that had depths beyond the comprehension of even the greatest of seers.

'Shatamanyu, this is Jaarra, a hunter in these forests. As it has been ordained, both of you are going to play an important role for the future of this great land of *Bhaarath-varsh*,' King Krishna placed his flute on his thighs and held both its end with his hands. The next moment, the flute had broken into two halves.

'These two halves of my flute will shape the destiny of this great nation of *Bhaarath-varsh* and indeed of the whole of humanity in the *Kaliyug*, that has just now begun. I want you Jaarra to take the frontal half, the one I hold close to my lips when I play, to an abandoned Devi temple about 30 *yojanas* north of here. This temple is located in the village of Nalini on the banks of a lake, which is fed by one of the rivulets of Saraswathi. The temple goddess is known as Nalini Devi. You, Jaarra will take this half of the flute and hide it in a secret underground cavern below the temple.

The posterior chamber of the temple contains the entrance to this cavern. There is a protrusion on the wall which you will have to turn clockwise in order to get to the passageway which will lead you to the cavern. Once you place your half of the flute in the cavern, you are free to resume your life. I swear you to complete secrecy in this regard! Yes, there are exceptions to this hard and fast rule. The secret can be broken whenever Dharma is in extreme danger and I emphasize the word extreme. The flute halves will come to the rescue of Dharma in these extreme situations. It will be as if I have taken an avatar and rectified the grave situation. But note the words 'extreme' and 'grave'. It will not work for ordinary dangers. If it is used for all and sundry situations, then it will be akin to disrupting the workings of *Kaal* and interfering with the laws of Karma and this I absolutely do not desire.

The flute half itself will indicate to you the gravity of the situation. If the flute glows with an intense peacock green halo, it means that it is the right time to intervene and save Dharma. This secret should be revealed only to worthy individuals of great integrity and character. But even these individuals will forget about the flute half and its works completely, with the passage of the danger. All this is just a mechanism that I have put in place to keep things under control. Mankind can never be fully trusted; especially when greed and lust for power overtakes them.

You Shatamanyu, will take the distal half of my flute and gallop as fast as the wind, eastwards, where you will go to the city of Paatali. Here, you will settle down and begin a new phase of your life. When your time comes to leave this earth, you will pass on the mantle to your son and he will, in turn, to his son and so on. You and your posterity will have one son in every generation to carry the mantle forward. Your future generations too will maintain secrecy under similar conditions, till the day comes for the rejoining of the halves.

That will not happen till the ordained time in the *Kaliyug*, about 5000 years from now, when the very future of mankind will come to a knife's edge. Till that time Shatamanyu, your progenies, shall be the custodians of the distal half. In your present state, as conditioned souls, you will not be able to touch my flute. You have too much negative karma. But if you sincerely think of and pray to the highest power in this universe, you will be able to touch it at least for a while. Please remember that any evil thoughts or intentions will render you unable to even approach it - should you somehow succeed in touching it, a thunderbolt will pass through your body, quite likely killing you.'

King Krishna then produced two long thin rectangular boxes in his hands and gave one each to Shatamanyu and Jaarra. 'The flute halves will always be housed in these boxes when their services are not required by *kaal*. The boxes insulate their powers and anyone can touch them without any harm coming to them. And they should be in their boxes ALWAYS, unless their services are required,' he added with another beatific smile. He then handed the box containing the distal half to Shatamanyu, who in turn held it prayerfully to his eyes and placed it into the saddle pouch on Hamsashwa.

I was completely lost for words. How can a simple hunter like me, who has never known anything beyond these forests, be entrusted with such a huge responsibility that could affect the future of mankind? I thought I was actually in the middle of a dream. Then I looked at the young warrior standing on

the ground below and our eyes met. Even he looked a bit
out of his element. At that point the ground started shaking
with such intensity that I lost my balance and started to fall
off my perch on the tree, but for King Krishna's gentle but
powerful hands that grasped me in the nick of time. This
was the seventh or eighth time this had happened in the last
few days even though the earlier ones were much milder in
comparison the present one. The horse Hamsashwa neighed
hysterically and reared up on his hind legs. Shatamanyu,
who had fallen to the ground, somehow raised himself and
grabbed the reins of the horse trying to calm him down. The
tremors stopped as suddenly as they began. All this time
King Krishna was seated calmly with that evergreen smile
that seemed never to leave his lips. Blood was still flowing
from his wounded heart but that did not seem to affect him
in any way.

'The time has come to bid goodbye. Now Jaarra, I
want you to immediately jump down and go along with
Shatamanyu - head for the top of that hill to the East. Wait
there for the next two days before you part ways and go
about the task that I have given you.'

'But my Lord, you will be alone here and that too in this
injured state!' Shatamanyu protested.

'Don't lament for those that are fated to depart. My time
has come. You are a warrior Shatamanyu, conduct yourself
like one. I command you as your King. Take Jaarra and these
halves of my flute with you immediately and gallop as fast
as you can. Hamsashwa gallops like the wind. But even that
may not be fast enough. Get going NOW!!'

I took one long, last look at King Krishna and folded
my hands in a deep *pranaam*. Very reverently I accepted the
box containing the proximal half of the flute which my King
placed in my hands. I could feel a strong charge of guilt going
through my entire body and I began shaking from head to
toe. My King placed his hands on my head in response and

my trembling ceased immediately and I could feel a wave of bliss go through me. He then gently motioned me with those heavenly eyes of his to go forth. That smile of his was indeed bewitching and would never leave my heart. I jumped down and hopped on to Hamsashwa's back, seating myself behind Shatamanyu. Fleet as an arrow, we headed eastwards.

The ground shook a couple of times again, with lesser intensity, but the stallion seemed unperturbed. However, I grew very nervous and let out a cry as the horse leapt over a small stream. Shatamanyu motioned me to hold on to him tightly, which I did gratefully. We were now out of the thick woods onto a grassy plain. The hill was still some distance away and I wondered why King Krishna had commanded us to rush to the top. I was to get the answer as we neared the hill.

Hamsashwa thundered across the plains and I was impressed at the consistently furious pace that this stallion could maintain. It seemed as if his hooves were floating above the ground. Shatamanyu had still not coaxed the maximum speed out him. Suddenly the ground shook again, accompanied by a roaring sound. I turned around slowly to investigate and my heart almost stopped. I could see a blue mountainous wall rushing towards us from the horizon. It was almost the size of the hill that we were supposed to ascend, and dwarfed the tree tops of the forest that we had left behind. At first, I could not make out what that moving mountain actually was. And then it struck me with horror: It was a mountain of water, a monster of a tsunami. 'Faster, faster!' I screamed. 'We have to make it to the top of the hill as fast as we can!' Shatamanyu too turned for a quick look and I could see his eyes grow big with shock.

'By *Shambo*, we have to fly,' he coaxed the stallion with the reins. The equine responded and soon it was galloping at maximum speed. I turned around once again. The wall of water had obliterated the forest and was now thundering across the plain. 'Faster, faster!' I yelled. Shatamanyu goaded the stallion once again, who in turn, summoned another burst of speed from the depths of his soul. A thick lather of sweat was building on Hamsashwa's back and streamed down our legs. The ground abruptly began to slope steeply upwards as we reached the base of the hill. The horse would certainly find the going tougher as he had to climb and maintain pace. But the stallion did not slow down a whit. I turned to take another look at the approaching mountain of water. It was certainly travelling faster than us.

Hamsashwa kept thundering ahead even when the gradient became punishing. He had a dynamo of a heart and kept chugging on. I could now hear the roar of water getting close and I did not dare to look back.

It was a race against death and my heart was pounding. Just as we reached the top of the hill, the water sloshed past us at knee height. The force of the water was so powerful that all of us (men and horse) were instantly dragged along as it rushed over top of the hill. For a moment, I thought that that we would be swept over the far edge, half a furlong away; however the strength of the water petered out before we reached the edge and then started receding, leaving us thankfully behind. The stallion came to an exhausted halt and we instantly alighted and turned around to look. Our mouths fell agape with total incredulity. There was nothing but water all over and as far as the eye could see till the horizon to the west. The sea had completely wiped out the city of Dwaaraka and the forest where we had been just a while back. Hamsashwa's dynamo legs had certainly saved us. That was when I suddenly remembered King Krishna. 'What could have happened to him?' I wondered with trepidation.

Shatamanyu was standing beside me with his hands on his thin hips. The warrior had a forlorn look in his eyes. I could see his eyes going moist as his lips lamented faintly,

'O my Lord, we have lost you.' And for a long while both of us stood like that in mournful silence. Moreover, there was a deathly pall all around. Even the insects had become mute. Then Shatamanyu turned to face me forcing a stern look on his face. 'I have to journey further eastwards to Paatali as the Lord commanded me to. As for you Jaarra, I do not know how you are going to make the journey to the temple, which is at a northerly direction from here. With all this water, I even wonder whether the temple has been spared. You may have to wait here till the water recedes completely. And I do not see that happening any time soon Jaarra.'

Shatamanyu continued after a lengthy pause, 'By the way, I do hope that your family was not in the forest when the sea swallowed it.' That was when it hit me like a shock. In all this, I had completely forgotten about my poor family who were living in the forest. Suddenly, I collapsed to the ground overcome with terrible sorrow as I realized that there was no way my family could have survived this tidal onslaught.

'No, no!' I bawled as tears coursed down my cheek in streams. Shatamanyu placed a sympathetic hand on my back and I immediately turned around and clasped it hard as I shook with sorrow. I cried for a long time till there were no more tears left in me. All this while, Shatamanyu stood by my side. I could see that he had tears in his eyes too. 'I too have lost my family Jaarra,' the brave warrior choked. 'But we have to move on and complete our tasks given to us by our Lord, no matter how much difficult it is for us now. I'm sure that the Lord has a higher purpose in his mind when he gave us our tasks. Don't worry, I will wait by your side till the water recedes and personally take you to the temple of Nalini Devi which, hopefully, has not been affected by the sea.'

Thus the two of us waited on the hill for almost twenty days. We subsisted on wild berries that we foraged from the forests on the leeward side of the hill. The water finally receded but the city of Dwaaraka was completely lost to the sea. The forest that the sea had washed over earlier was now visible again. But it was not a forest anymore. All the trees were torn off at their roots and were strewn over a very large area. I could see scores of dead birds and animals littered all over. The whole area painted a bleak picture of desolation.

My tears welled up again as I remembered my family. Once again, Shatamanyu placed his arms on my right shoulder as if on cue, and let me sob my heart out. I was so grateful that the warrior had decided to give me company. Even more so when on the tenth day of our waiting, we were attacked by a gang of thugs in the forest. But Shatamanyu dealt with them with aplomb. His fighting technique with swords in both hands mesmerized me. It felt as if the swords were dancing as they whirled in circles in his powerful hands. The fight was short but intense and brutal and within minutes, the heads of all the thugs rolled off their bodies. It was time to move on.

We got back on Hamsashwa and started on our journey to the temple. For a long while we continued along the coast (as it bent north-eastward and ran along the Gulf of Kutch) before we took a detour inland towards our intended destination. Prior to arriving at this detour, we passed the present day towns of Jaamnagar, Jodiya, and Malia. The sea had taken a huge toll, destroying property and lives all along the path we had taken this far. Even when we detoured inland, the scale and intensity of the devastation remained. It took us many furlongs eastwards to arrive on relatively unmolested land. And then we turned northwest. Finally, after many days of riding, we reached our destination near the Rann of Kutch Lake. Thankfully, the tidal wave had petered out far back from the lake and consequently the abandoned Nalini Devi temple stood there unharmed.

The temple was completely empty and there was not even a priest present. After offering our prayers at the sanctum to the golden idol of Nalini Devi, we proceeded to its posterior chamber located at the backmost part of the temple. With great difficulty, we found the knob almost inconspicuous on the wall. Shatamanyu turned it clockwise and waited. Nothing happened. Suddenly there was a grating sound as the ground in the corner of the room parted, revealing the entrance to the cavern. It was pitch dark inside the passage. Consequently, Shatamanyu returned to his horse to get the oil rag torch that he always carried for emergencies and now its orange glow revealed the way.

We slowly went down the passage and reached the cavern. There was a stone altar in the cavern and I sat down on its steps with a sigh of relief. Shatamanyu also sat beside me with a deep sigh of relief. Half the mission had been accomplished thus far. But suddenly, the cavern was filled with an unearthly growling sound and we immediately jumped up. The sound was coming from the altar itself. I grabbed the flame torch from Shatamanyu and swung around to illuminate the altar in order to get a better look. Two glowing embers of amber stared back at us. For a while we could not make out what it was. Then a grey wolf like shape emerged ever so slowly. The red ambers were obviously the eyes of this creature. Slowly we were able to discern the entire creature - those mighty jaws and deadly canines. My blood froze. I had never seen a creature like this throughout my hunting life. It was a giant of a wolf, almost the size of a male lion. The size of its paws and its claws were out of this world. It was crouched on the altar with its ears flattened back, looking at us with murder in its eyes.

My hands very stealthily moved towards my bow. It was evident that the creature would be upon us any moment. Suddenly Shatamanyu sprang to his feet and, with a war cry, unsheathed his twin swords, one in each hand. In that darkness the blades gleamed like lightning as they caught the light of the flame torch. The creature appeared surprised and slunk back into the darkness. We searched for the creature, shining the torch all around the cavern, but it was gone. However, I was not convinced. I continued to hold the bow in my hand with the arrow ready.

'The creature has gone away. Maybe there is another secret way out of this cavern,' Shatamanyu turned around to face me. 'Maybe we should check to see whether this is indeed the case.' But there was another blood curdling growl and I could see the giant wolf's silhouette looming behind Shatamanyu, ruby red eyes glowing. The next moment the wolf was airborne launching himself at the young warrior, who in turn was completely taken by surprise and had no time to react. My hunter's instinct took over, goaded by a compelling sense of self-preservation and the next moment, a poison tipped arrow had rocketed out of my bowstring. It streaked through the intervening space and buried itself into the heart of the creature in midair. But that did not stem the momentum of its leap completely.

Shatamanyu jumped forward instinctively in avoidance but that was not enough to prevent the forepaws of the creature from tearing through his back. The young warrior grunted in deep pain as he doubled over. The giant wolf fell on the floor of the cavern with a thud and twisted in its death throes before finally becoming still. My concerns immediately gravitated towards the young warrior. He was now crouched on his knees, his face a grimace of pain. It was then that I noticed his bloody, torn up back. The flesh was hanging out in a huge chunk and one rib was visible. The injury looked grave. He needed immediate attention.

I grabbed his arms and coaxed him to his feet. Then, putting his arm around my shoulder, we went back slowly up the passageway back to the temple, which was still empty. Once there, I made him lie on his stomach on one of the deer mats. From the medicinal pouch that I always carried with me, I removed some herbs and crushed them to a thick paste.

I applied this paste liberally over Shatamanyu's wounds. The wounds were really deep and could get septic. As the hours passed, he began rapidly developing a fever as the infection took hold. His body temperature shot up considerably and he slipped into fever induced delirium, moaning incoherently. Concerned, I immediately placed a wet cloth over his forehead and tended to him. At the same time, I started working on his wounds, to clean them up. With a red hot knife, I removed the pus that had started to form.

The claws of the wolf had indeed carried poison and being a hunter, I was very well aware of the danger from these kinds of wounds - I had been raked on my thighs by a leopard ten years ago. Shatamanyu had now become almost unconscious and could not even feel my hot knife as it singed the periphery of the major wound. For the next couple of days, nothing seemed to improve but then on the third night, his temperature shot up even higher and the wound looked even more lurid, leaving me extremely worried.

And then I did the strangest thing without attributing any logical reason to it. It was as if I was guided by an invisible force. Chanting the HARE KRISHNA Mahaa Mantram with utmost devotion, I took my half of King Krishna's flute out of its box. It was glowing peacock green as I gingerly placed it on Shatamanyu's wound. The young warrior moaned as his body immediately started convulsing as if a wave of current was going through him. After a short while, I pulled the flute half away from him and his convulsions immediately stopped. Astonishingly, the wounded area began showing the initial stages of healing. The white pus like appearance of the exposed flesh was now turning to a healthy red. I kept repeating this process and by the end of the seventh time, Shatamanyu regained consciousness, his full body drenched in sweat. His fever had also stabilized. But he was still very weak as the blood loss, consequent fever, and infection had almost killed him.

Shatamanyu tried to sit up, but then, flopped weakly onto his stomach and fell into a deep sleep almost. I knew what I had to do next. I placed the flute half back in its casing and immediately went out of the temple in search of food. I shot down a couple of pheasants near the lake with my darts and cooked them over a fire built up from dry leaves and twigs. There was one small problem. I could not take the meat inside the temple. Therefore, I had to somehow bring Shatamanyu outside. Surprisingly he was able to get up and walk back with me, albeit slowly. I was amazed at his quick recovery.

The young warrior Shatamanyu's wounds were completely healed in three days' time and it was time for him to move eastwards to Paatali.

'Thanks for saving my life,' Shatamanyu firmly grasped my hands as he sat astride on that stately steed Hamsashwa.

'You have to thank our King's flute for that.'

'Regardless, without you it would not have been possible.'

'But it was because of me, you were compelled to come here in the first place, to be attacked by this ferocious beast Shatamanyu.'

'The Lord above has his own equations in all this Jaarra. Let me bid goodbye to you now. I'm sure you will do your utmost to implement our beloved King and Lord's last wish and I too will strive to do this, till my last breath.' The warrior jumped up on his horse, removed the box containing his flute half from the saddle pouch and reverently touched it to his forehead before placing it back.

Hamsashwa reared up magnificently on his rear legs and then was gone like an arrow eastwards, leaving a cloud of dust in his wake, as his hoofs thundered across the salt pan. I felt a tinge of sorrow to see this great warrior leave but then I composed myself. A higher duty beckoned as ordered by my King Krishna. And here ends the first part of the story of my life as Jaarra the Hunter.

'That was very interesting to say the least,' Dr Baalan spoke, breaking the spell that the narrative had cast. 'I knew that Krishna met his end at the hands of a hunter, but this is the first time I'm hearing the intricate details.'

Harihar-Shiv-Shambho Dr Baalan. And now I will speak to you of another life where I came into contact with the other half of the flute which the warrior Shatamanyu took with him for safekeeping. In that life, I made the acquaintance of two towering personalities of this great land.'

Satyavaan Yaadav – The Revolution

Around the year 320BC, I Satyavaan Yaadav, was almost 20 years old. In fact, my lineage could be traced directly to the great warrior, Shatamanyu Yaadav. I was living in a small town called Ambara, which was situated on the outskirts of Magadha. When my ancestor Shatamanyu had first arrived from the West, he had gone straight to the city of Paataliputra. Here he settled down as a low profile tiller of land; his only intention being safeguarding his flute half. Over the generations, my ancestors moved out of the big city and finally settled down at my birthplace of Hasthaamba, a small village to the north of Ambara. Three consecutive seasons of failed rains and drought had brought me to the town seeking my fortune. Here I took work as an assistant to a grain merchant.

My task was to take care of the orders and deliver them to the customers. Business was good, especially during these times of drought, but the political, social, and economic situation of Magadha Empire was worsening by the day. The main reason for this was our vain and wicked monarch Dhana Nanda, who had a reputation of being a miser, as well as a treasure hoarder. Moreover, he was also a very cruel and ruthless man and showed absolutely no compassion to his subjects reeling under the drought, especially the poor of the land. The words 'revolution' and 'overthrow' were whispered in some circles but remained whispers. Dhana Nanda had an efficient ring of spies all over his land and rebellion was swiftly nipped in the bud.

Recently, an unknown young man named Chandragupta, guided by a shrewd Brahmin named Kautilya, had led a failed rebellion, leading with a ragtag unit of young men. The young man and his mentor, managed to escape to the forests after suffering heavy causalities. There were rumors that they were lying low there to recuperate and launch another attack on the King.

The passing days, however, saw no respite from the drought and this was compounded by the oppression unleashed on the poor by the King's chief henchmen. One such henchman, who went by the name of Xervos, was formerly a high ranking Greek warrior in Alexander's army. He had deserted when Alexander's battle-worn troops were milling along the Ganges, contemplating the prospects of engaging in battle with the then mighty Nanda army. Alexander made the decision not to press on and turned back. But Xervos, enchanted by the land, was in no mood to follow his master and had, surreptitiously and daringly, swam across the raging torrent of the Ganges in full spate. Here he surrendered to the Nanda army and became their prisoner of war.

Xervos was a man of enormous physical strength. He issued a challenge to King Dhana Nanda that he would singlehandedly combat ten of his best soldiers and defeat them. Dhana Nanda, intrigued by the confidence of this Greek warrior, accepted the challenge.

The contest was conducted. Xervos proved that he was as good as his boast and even better. Dhana Nanda, impressed by Xervos's show of strength and prowess, immediately freed him from his prison and made him a Captain in his army. Xervos swiftly rose through the ranks to become a local vassal on the outskirts of Paataliputra - his domain included my native village of Hasthaamba.

Xervos soon proved that he was as ruthless as he was strong and the reputation of his cruelty spread far and wide, much to the delight of King Dhana Nanda, who now used him as a brutal enforcer throughout Magadha. I was unaffected by all this till the day my family's properties and land in Hasthaamba were seized by Xervos under the orders of our King, the reason being nonpayment of revenue dues over the past year.

My parents pleaded and groveled, both to Xervos as well as the King, in vain. My old parents were evicted and physically abused by Xervos and his men. They now lived in a decrepit hut in the village, completely broken in body and spirit. For my father, it was even worse. The loss of his land and property was like a stake driven through his heart, but even more bitter was the fact that the sacred family secret, the flute half of Krishna, was now with Xervos. Of course, Xervos did not know this fact and it was critical that it remain that way. My father surmised that Xervos eventually would come across the flute-half when he scoured through our possessions for things that he could loot for the King. What he would do with it was pure guesswork. He could throw it away or he could give it to the King and in both these situations, the flute-half was as good as gone. The sacred duty given to my great ancestor Shatamanyu by Lord Krishna and protected by generations of our family would now be broken. This was what broke my father's spirit and led to his untimely demise.

As I pondered over options to retrieve my priceless ancestral property, I came to the conclusion that there was no way I could accomplish this alone. There was also nobody in the Nanda Kingdom who could help me to do this. There was however, one dangerous last option: seek help from Kautilya and his warrior pupil Chandragupta. But where would I find them? They were supposed to be hiding in the thick forests abutting Hasthaamba from where they conducted their guerilla campaign against Dhana Nanda. From all reports, thus far they had proved to be more elusive than wily leopards. Dhana Nanda's forces had been tracking them in vain for the past one year. Obviously, Kautilya was very shrewd as well as courageous. That he had completely outfoxed Dhana Nanda's ruthlessly efficient spy network was a testimony to his own network of spies, which was also rumored to be spread all over the Nanda land.

As days passed, I grew more desperate and had no option but to wander around the jungles myself in the hope that I would run into Kautilya and his men. I set out one dawn in total secrecy toward the jungles. Once there, I started crisscrossing it in a grid, at its deepest parts. Of course, I was armed with a spear to protect myself from dangers like wild animals and bandits. Thankfully, I did not encounter any danger during my first five days there. I slept on the trees during the nights and then fed on fruits and berries. From my elder uncle, who had an avid knowledge of the jungle, I had learnt which jungle berries and fruits to eat and which to leave alone. Another couple of days passed without any event before I ran into big trouble.

It was around mid-afternoon on the eighth day when I encountered a small band of three heavily armed Nanda soldiers. They were obviously looking for Kautilya and his men. The leader of the band was surprised to see me in the deep forest and immediately wanted to know what I was doing there. I concluded from the manner of his questioning that he suspected me of being one of Kautilya's men, or even worse, one of his spies. That surely meant instant death. I had to quickly come up with a viable excuse. I had not anticipated that I would run into Nanda's men and my desperate brain cast about hither and thither for a plausible excuse. Finally I told the leader that I was out in the forest to look for a very rare medicinal herb in order to tend to my uncle's grave illness. The leader was not buying any of it. I embroidered my tale with complete work and home details, yet he remained unconvinced. He had made up his mind that I was one of Kautilya's spies and I knew what was in store for me.

King Dhana Nanda had issued orders for spot execution of any suspected spy without even a mock trial. Lots of innocents had paid with their lives for this draconian decree. Now it was my turn - hands bound behind me, I was made to kneel at sword point. Then one of the men positioned himself behind me, his sword ready to slice through my neck. I gritted my teeth and closed my eyes, bracing myself for the death blow. It was prayer time now. My only regret was that I would fail in my familial duty of protecting Krishna's flute half. Moreover, there was no one to take care of my old mother once I had gone. I fervently prayed to Lord Krishna. Our *shaastras* tell us that a man will never be reborn who takes Lord Krishna's name in his dying moments.

Suddenly, there was a whizzing sound and I cringed inwardly thinking it was the sound of the sword heading for my neck. But the next moment, I heard three long drawn painful *Aaaaaaaahs* one after the other. I opened my eyes and saw that the three Nanda soldiers were on their knees with arrows embedded in their chests. Another three arrows whizzed into the soldiers' heads, finishing them off. I looked around me and could see no one. There was a rustle of dry leaves to my left. I turned towards the sound and a young man armed with a bow and a quiver of arrows appeared, walking towards me.

'Who are you and why are you here in this part of the jungle. If you give me an unconvincing answer, I'm afraid that I will have to kill you myself,' he spoke sternly. Since this young man had killed Nanda's men, I surmised that he could potentially belong to Kautilya's rebels. I decided that I would tell him the truth regarding my objective. I had to take my chances.

'O great warrior, first of all let me thank you from the bottom of my heart for saving my life. If you had not come here, I would have been dead for sure. Let me now tell you who I am and what I'm doing here. I'm Satyavaan Yaadav of Hasthaamba and I have come here in search of the great Kautilya and his valiant protégé Chandragupta, with the intention of joining them in their struggle against our tyrant king Dhana Nanda.'

The young man's eyes went over me at length before replying: 'How am I to believe you Satyavaan? You could also be Nanda's spy and this entire thing could have been a set up to plant you amongst us and reveal our location to his army.'

'You have to believe me young warrior because I also detest King Nanda and the atrocities he perpetrates on his subjects. This I swear on the life of my old mother who has suffered because of him. Moreover, there is another very urgent matter for which I have to secure the services of the great Kautilya. So please young warrior, take me to him.'

'I'm afraid that I cannot do that.' The young man looked over me with raised eyebrows. 'You have to go back to your home. First of all, I'm still not convinced about you. Moreover, it is too dangerous for a civilian like you in the jungles: wild animals, the elements, and of course the constant threat of being ambushed by Nanda's men. So please take my advice Satyavaan and go back. I will personally escort you to your village.'

'Sir, please believe me. This is a matter of life and death for me and more importantly the restoration of my family honor. I cannot but meet Kautilya. I also would like to join you in your struggle. I am fed up of life under the tyrant Nanda,' I pleaded.

'No way! You have to go back Satyavaan,' the young warrior replied fiercely.

'Then you better kill me because I'm not going back. Life has no meaning for me with my family's honor at stake.' I was getting desperate.

The young warrior again looked over me again, but this time his eyes softened a bit. 'Look it is a big risk for me because we have been strictly warned by Kautilya not to take in strangers without properly vetting them. If I take you directly to him, the great man will be furious. I have the highest respect for Kautilya and will not do anything to contravene my orders. I'm afraid I cannot take a chance on you. So it is better for you to go back.'

'Then kill me here,' I was defiant. 'But you will have the blood of an innocent man on your hands.'

'Alright, alright,' the young warrior threw up his hands in despair. 'I will take you to him. But remember that Kautilya is very, very shrewd and nobody can fool him. If you turn out to be a spy, you will surely lose your life. As for me, I will fall in my leader's eyes and lose my entire honor.'

'You will not regret it young warrior; that is my final word to you.'

'Alright then, follow me,' the young warrior was still reluctant.

I followed the young man through thick jungle in complete silence. We had now entered its thickest part and the going was perceptibly slow. There were lots of twists and turns in the path and I wondered whether this was to actually confuse me. At many places, I felt that we had doubled backed. But then, I did understand the young warrior's predicament. Obviously, he was taking a big risk by bringing a completely untested stranger to where Kautilya and the rest of his group were hiding. It was evident that he worshiped Kautilya and held him in deep respect. But then, so did most in the Nanda kingdom.

We stopped to rest for a brief while under a majestic teak. The young man offered me some juicy berries from a bag slung over his left shoulder and this I received with eagerness as I had not eaten for a while. He also offered me water from his animal skin pitcher. I felt refreshed and stretched my wary muscles. Suddenly, the young warrior held my hand tightly and motioned me to freeze. Deathly silence followed till I heard a faint rustle above me. I tried to lift my head to take a look at the source of the sound but was immediately dissuaded by a mighty squeeze from the strong palms of the young warrior. Again silence followed, broken by a light growl and faint thud. The next moment, a magnificent male leopard landed on the ground just a few feet ahead of us. My blood froze instantly as those amber eyes bored into us and for a while, time stood still. I anticipated that the cat would spring on us any moment. But, it just turned away, totally uninterested, and slunk into thick cover in a smooth velvety gait so typical of its genus. There was not even a sound of a broken twig, unlike us clumsy humans. I was still frozen with fear when the young warrior shook me and motioned that it was time to leave. We had obviously rested under the arboreal lair of a leopard.

We continued on our way, executing so many zigzags that I completely lost all sense of direction. Dusk was fast approaching with the light fading every minute. Suddenly, I saw a small clearing ahead of us in the distance. That's when it happened: I felt something like a thin thread brush my legs below my knees, followed by a deafening snapping sound and a rush of air. The next instant I saw the young warrior turn like lightning and rush towards me as if to push me away. I took the full brunt of his charge and fell sideward to my right. There was a swooshing sound as a huge wooden board studded with rapier sharp nails smashed into the warrior's back. I went numb with shock for a long while before I could gather myself. The young man was still standing there impaled on the wooden board. Blood was now oozing out of his mouth and he made a weak gurgling moan that betrayed his unbearable pain. Then, his head drooped down and he was gone. My entire body trembled with fear as well as rage. I had walked accidentally into one of the gruesome traps laid out by Dhana Nanda's men and the young man had saved me, but killed himself in the process.

Tears scalded my cheeks as I wept uncontrollably. I should have died instead of this brave soldier of Kautilya's. I was completely lost and, more importantly, I did not know what to do next. It was almost twilight when I got up wearily with my eyes still wet. I could not bring myself to look at the corpse of the selfless young man because of whom I was standing now without even a scratch on my body. I then started walking aimlessly towards the clearing. I didn't even care to check whether there were more traps ahead. Grief completely overpowered me.

On reaching the clearing, I forlornly looked across and perceived the top of what seemed like some old abandoned ruins, most of which was hidden in thick vegetation. The light was fading quickly and I had to tamp down my grief and find shelter for the night. The old ruins looked good for that but I had to make sure that they were not occupied by some beast. Therefore, I approached them with caution, even though my heart was still heavy.

As I approached, I discerned a faint moaning sound emanating from the ruins; the sound was distinctly human. It was as if somebody was in acute distress and pain. I hesitated, but then the sound was so insistent I had to investigate. I slowly approached the entrance of the ruins, moving aside the cut branches stacked at its entrance and cautiously peered inside. There was nothing but gloom, except for the moaning sound. My eyes strained to adjust to the darkness but could not see a thing. The moaning continued and after a while I thought I could see movement on the floor ahead. It seemed like someone was lying there. The moans abruptly ceased and there was complete silence. I gingerly took a step forward but suddenly I felt the bite of cold sharp steel at my throat.

'Do not move if you value your life,' the voice was firm and hypnotic. I immediately froze in response. 'Drop all the weapons at your disposal, including hidden ones; NOW!!'

I instantly dropped my spear, reached into my clothing for my knife and dropped it to the ground too.

'Is that all?'

'Yes, that's all the weapons I have.'

'Turn around.'

I slowly turned to face the source of this magnificent voice. My eyes took some time to readjust to the gloom. My jaws dropped as they fell on the imposing, tall, lean figure in front of me. He had long hair flowing to his waist and his eyes blazed like two amber diamonds. His body was lithe and chiseled and he looked weather-beaten - definitely a man accustomed to living outdoors. A huge sword gleaming menacingly in his hands. 'Master Kautilya!!!" the words burst from my mouth as I recognized the man and I instantly dropped to my knees, hands folded in deep respect.

'Indeed it is stranger. I'm Kautilya. But let me tell you that I'm not at all pleased to see you here, the way you seem overjoyed to see me.'

'No, no, master Kautilya, please believe me when I tell you that I'm no threat to you or your men in any manner. In fact, I see you as the true savior of this land who will liberate us from the evil Dhana Nanda. I am also no spy master, Kautilya. I was escorted here by one of your own young warriors. Alas, he is no more with us. He was impaled in one of the fiendish traps laid by Dhana Nanda's men. It was actually I who was to be impaled. But your young warrior selflessly gave up his life, and for this I will be indebted to you and your cause for the rest of my life. O master Kautilya, this is truth in its entirety.'

Kautilya stared at me at length and I felt his diamond-bright eyes boring through my soul. It was as if he was reading my inner thoughts. I had heard that Kautilya was a master of reading people's faces as well as body demeanor. He was also supposed to be an excellent astrologer.

'Can you tell me the name of this warrior who you say has given his life for you?' There was a film of moisture on his diamond eyes.

'I'm afraid he never told me his name and neither did I ask him. But I can take you to the place where this sad incident happened. It is near here.'

'Then take me there at once.'

We quickly arrived at the site of the trap. The young warrior's body was still impaled on the wooden board.'

'Kumaarasaagara my child, one of my best boys,' Kautilya cried out. There was undisguised agony in his voice. He walked up to the board, placed his arm on the head of the body and stood in deep silence for a while. Then he turned to me fiercely, his diamond eyes glowing red hot: 'You are going to tell me everything about how you met Kumaarasaagara. You are going to tell me everything about yourself, your family, and why you want to meet me. I warn you that I do not tolerate fools and what's more, I do not tolerate liars. Moreover, you have cost me one of my most able boys. So young man, you will lie to me at your own peril as I have countless ways to verify whether you are indeed speaking the truth. You are yet to convince me that you are not one of Nanda's spies. But the fact that Kumaarasaagara himself was bringing you to me, as you say, gives you some credibility in my eyes.'

'I will tell you everything master Kautilya as I had told Kumaarasaagara himself.' I knelt on the grass and once again told him my story as I had told Kumaarasaagara. I did it in painstaking detail as I wanted to earn the full extent of his trust. At many places, he stopped me and asked me pertinent questions to cross and double check my narrative, and I answered him with honesty, without no hesitation. When I finally finished, I could see that some of the hostility and anger in Kautilya's eyes abated a bit and I instantly prostrated myself at his feet. 'Master, please help me and my old mother. I beg of you to take mercy on this humble servant of yours. Nothing will give me more pleasure than seeing the evil Xervos getting punished for his cruel acts against the innocent.'

'I can understand your feelings young man, but my mission against Nanda has got nothing to do with petty revenge as many people make it out to be. It is about the reestablishment of Dharma in this land. If it was a fight only for revenge, then this rebellion becomes bereft of values. So many people are suffering in this land under the rule of Dhana Nanda and if revenge was our only motive we will need several entire lifetimes to even the score. But that does not also mean that the wicked will go unpunished.' Kautilya tossed his long matted hair over his shoulders and wiped the sweat off his brows.

'I have to rush back. If not, I may lose the best of my best boys,' Kautilya turned back towards the way we arrived. I immediately followed him. The Brahmin walked at a furious pace. He was supremely fit and agile for a man his age; he could very well have been in the seventh decade of his life. On reaching the ruins, Kautilya let out a low bird whistle. Within minutes a few of his men materialized out of nowhere.

'Yonder is the body of our beloved Kumaarasaagara. One of Dhana Nanda's fiendish traps has claimed him. I want you to bring his body here for a proper funeral. Thank God his parents are not alive to see this day. Go immediately, before the jungle scavengers start feasting on his body.'

'Yes master!' The men were off like arrows.

Kautilya turned towards the entrance of the ruins, clasped his palms tightly together and went into deep meditation. He let out a fierce sound that seemed to emanate from his very depths. It was almost like a lion's deep growl. The next instant the insides of the ruins were brightly lit by torches attached to its walls and ceiling. My jaw dropped in sheer amazement. Casting a sideward glance at me the Brahmin remarked: 'Agni Yoga,' as he entered the cave. I followed him dumbstruck.

It was only when Kautilya bent to the floor that I discerned a prone figure lying on a bed of hay and rags. It was a young man of magnificent build. He must surely be another one of Kautilya's select band. They all seemed to be endowed with spectacular physiques. His face bore a princely look reflecting royal lineage. Even when his eyes were closed, I could sense the power of his gaze behind it.

Right then the young man was moaning as if he was in deep pain. The lower half of the young man was covered by a ragged blanket. It was only when Kautilya gently removed it that I saw the hideous injury on the abdomen. His hips were completely shattered and he would never walk again.

'My God!' I blurted out.

'This is thanks to the massive pounding he has received at the hands of Xervos. My best man Chandragupta has been grievously wounded, to say the least. And I'm afraid that I'm going to lose him.'

'Is this the great warrior Chandragupta? Oh my God, master Kautilya, he is famous all over the kingdom. The one who fights with fierce courage; the one who is a thorn in Dhana Nanda's side - tell me my master, is he the same great one?'

'Yes he is verily the same Chandragupta.'

'Then we cannot afford to lose him sir.'

'Yes, I cannot afford to lose him. But there is nothing much we can do. The wound is mortal and has grievously damaged some of vital internal organs.'

'But you are the great one, master. You will surely find a way.'

'Alas, I have tried all the herbal concoctions that I know of and nothing has helped so far. Astrologically too, his stars are not in the right place now. If he survives the next few weeks, he will come out of it stronger. But as things are now, we need a miracle from Krishna himself!'

'Krishna!! You said it master Kautilya. Indeed, Krishna has the miracle and it is available right here on this Earth. In fact, it is available in this very kingdom of Dhana Nanda's. To be more precise, that very miracle is inside my ancestral home at Hasthaamba. If we get hold of that miracle, Chandragupta will be out of his predicament in no time!'

'What miracle are you talking of?' Kautilya raised a questioning brow.

'It is a family secret - a device that has been handed down to us generations ago by Lord Krishna himself, towards the end of his time in the ancient city of Dwaaraka. We are sworn to secrecy by our fathers and forefathers to not divulge it to anyone except when Dharma is in real danger. But there is another problem master. Even if I tell about this secret device, it is next to impossible to get hold of it as my parental home is in the clutches of the evil Xervos. And it is quite possible that he has taken it out of there with him and moved it to Dhana Nanda's treasury. That will make it completely impossible to retrieve. You know very well master, how the miser King guards his riches!'

'What are you prattling about Satyavaan? I can make neither head nor tail of it!'

'Master, I'm telling you that I have the miracle that can bring back our Chandragupta.'

'Is it some kind herbal concoction?'

'No master, this is a treasure, extremely invaluable and sacred.'

'You are saying that such a device can save Chandragupta? This is the kind of magic mumbo jumbo with which I have no patience!'

'It is certainly magic sir, but not of the kind that you are alluding too. Will you allow me to explain …?'

'Alright, we have nothing to lose here have we? If my dear Chandragupta can come back hale and healthy, what more do we want? Start talking!'

'But before I tell you, we need to make sure that Dharma is in real danger. This is the clause I have been sworn to regarding this article.'

'Don't you think it already is neck deep in danger my son. With all the atrocities perpetrated by Dhana Nanda and his men, the Dharma of entire *Bhaarath-varsh* is in danger. Invading forces can enslave us if things do not change quickly. You can start telling me without any hesitation.'

I cleared my throat, then proceeded to quickly brief him about my family secret without leaving out any details of the information that had been handed down to me through my paternal family tree. I told him the story where Lord Krishna had handed down one half of his flute to my great ancestor Shatamanyu Yaadav.

Kautilya had an expressionless, stone-faced look when I finished. I was not sure whether he believed my story or not. He frowned, his large forehead wrinkling into deep furrows his dark eye lashes arching upward. For a while he seemed lost in thought. Then his eyes focused on me, boring through me.

'I find it hard to believe it that you are in possession of a part of Krishna's flute. But I have heard and seen more incredible things in my life.'

'Believe me master; what I'm saying is the truth. If we can get the flute half here and place it on Chandragupta's wounds, he will be healed instantly.'

Alright, even if what you say is true, it would involve a big cost in terms of men and resources to retrieve the flute half. Especially if Xervos has taken it out of your family home and put it in his own mansion which is nothing short of a fortress. And, like you rightly pointed out, it would be next to impossible if it has gone into Dhana Nanda's possession. In both situations the flute will be akin to putting a garland in the hands of monkeys. Xervos conducts himself like a savage brute. In the last encounter, he got into a one on one conflict with Chandragupta and almost killed him by inflicting these ghastly wounds.'

'But this is definitely worth a try master.'

'Maybe.'

'Then allow me master, to go back to Hasthaamba and find out where the flute half is - whether it is still at my home of whether Xervos has removed it.'

'Alright Satyavaan,' Kautilya spoke at length. 'I'll let you go. But I'll send two of my elite boys with you in disguise, both for your protection and to make sure that you are not double dealing with us. And you will have to be quick. We do not have much time at our disposal.'

After a night's rest, I set out early the next day with two of Kautilya's elite guards. All of us were disguised as poor hermits. After travelling throughout the day with just a couple of stopovers, we arrived at Hasthaamba without any incident. It was already dark by the time we reached my house. We rested under a tree in the front of my house to observe the going-ons. There seemed to some kind of activity inside the house. I could see a few of Dhana Nanda's soldiers walking in and out. I also grew concerned for my old mother. What happened to her, I wondered. Was she still at the hut which she had moved into after she and my late father were evicted by Xervos and his men? I needed to make sure.

I approached a passerby and asked him what was going on, after introducing myself as a wandering hermit. I came to know that Nanda's men, under the command of the evil Xervos, were slowly emptying all the valuables from people's houses. My mind started racing. I had to find some way of getting inside the house. Suddenly I had an idea.

There was a secret passage leading from my house to the backyard. I had to sneak in to it immediately.

I turned to the two elite guards and asked them to follow me. We took a circuitous route to the backyard. There was small trap door there, with a hidden knob that would lead us into the house. It was very dark but I knew the backyard of my house like the back of my hand and had no problems in locating the trap door and twisting the hidden knob. The trap door opened with a loud creak and for a moment I panicked. Thankfully nothing happened and we warily entered the passage that led to one of our two storerooms. The flute half with its casing was in the sanctum of our *puja* room, in a trunk hidden behind the main idol of Goddess Devi.

As I gingerly stepped out of the storeroom, I ran headlong into one of Nanda's guards. Both of us were blindsided but the guard was the first to recover. He instantly unsheathed his sword and I grit my teeth as I raised my hands to parry his strike. But his blow froze in midair as if someone had clamped his hands. The next instant his neck was broken. I was so thankful that Kautilya's elite men had accompanied me on this mission. If not for them, I would have been dead for sure.

Immediately, we dragged the man deep into the storeroom. Here we disrobed the corpse and I donned his uniform. The dead guard was thankfully about my own girth and his uniform fit me perfectly. I then walked back into my house, my heart pounding lest I was found out. I walked straight to the *puja* room. A voice boomed behind me, 'Make it quick. I do not think that there is any money or any artifacts worthy of our king in this house.' It was surely another of Dhana Nanda's guards.

Without turning around, I mumbled: 'You go ahead; I will take a final look.'

'Alright, but hurry! We have got many houses in this village to search.' The guard walked past me without a backward glance. I immediately rushed to the sanctum and found, to my intense relief, that it had not been violated. The trunk containing the flute half was there as it had always been. As my father had taught me, I closed my eyes and reverentially chanted the HARE KRISHNA Mahaa Mantram in my mind as I lifted the lid of the trunk, retrieved the flute half with its casing and tiptoed to the storeroom and back into the passage.

'I'm going to hide this behind some bushes outside, to be retrieved later. Please do not touch the box for any reason whatsoever. Also, you two get out of here using the cover of the night. Wait for me near the edge of the forest. I will join you there before dawn. I want to meet my mother and enquire about her health. She has not heard from me for a while and may be really worried.'

'Alright, we will wait for you, but you have to come to us by dawn else we will have to come looking for you as per our master Kautilya's orders. Actually, we are not supposed to let you out of sight.'

'Even if I do not get to meet my mother, I will still be there before dawn. You have my word on that. Now please leave immediately. Staying here any longer will be fatal for all of us.'

I hurried back into the house and then walked out of the main entrance. The other guard was waiting for me. Thankfully it was dark which was why the guard did not recognize anything out of place.

'We got orders that there will be no more searches tonight. It is time for us to retire.'

'You go ahead. I have to meet a close relative who lives here. I will join you shortly after midnight,' I replied again in a low voice.

'You know it is against the rules to meet relatives whilst on guard duties.'

'Could you please make an exception tonight? This relative of mine is very sick and he may not live long.'

'Alright, just for tonight. Report back at our tent after you have finished your visit. We have to be back here early tomorrow and get back to the search.'

I hurried to the hut where my mother was supposed to be staying but it was empty. Where could she have gone, I wondered. Then it struck me. My uncle (father's cousin) stayed nearby and she could very well be there as my father had been especially close to this cousin when he was alive. When I got there, I was relieved to find my mother as much as she was relieved to see me after a long time. But they (mother, uncle, and his family) were surprised to see me in a Nanda soldier uniform. How could a person who despised Nanda and especially, his tyrant soldiers, now be working for him, they wondered. I took my mother aside and explained to her as to how I ended up in this hated uniform. I also swore her to secrecy - to keep the main reason of my visit away, even from my uncle and his family. For now, it would just suffice for them to know that I had only come to visit her in a disguise that I had managed to steal from a nearby camp of Dhana Nanda's army.

'Son, you have to be extremely careful,' my uncle advised with a look of apprehension on his old wrinkled face. Nanda's spies are teeming all over the place and if you get caught, they will swiftly put you to death after inhumanely torturing you. I hear that the latest mode of torture is boiling you alive in hot water. Be well aware that Xervos is a beast of a man, famous for extreme torture of his captives. He quite often visits this place with his men. He also severely beats up whomever his mind fancies. He suspects people for the flimsiest of reasons. That is why son, you have to get away from here as quickly as possible, before daybreak. I also warn you not to go anywhere near your house. Your house is as good as Xervos' - like many of the other houses that he has fancied in this area and grabbed through brute intimidation and force. Moreover, it has become his place of residence whenever he visits Hasthaamba.'

'Yes uncle, I hear you,' I then paid my respects to him as well as my mother.

'Don't worry, I am safe and happy here son,' my mother assured me as I left.

Under the cover of darkness, I made it back surreptitiously back to the place where I had hidden the box and then made it to the rendezvous with Kautilya's elite at the edge of the forest. We then rushed back to the secret ruins where master Kautilya was waiting with the wounded warrior Chandragupta. On reaching the cave, I immediately requested Kautilya to ask all other men to leave the cave besides myself, Kautilya, and of course Chandragupta. I, then gingerly opened the box containing Krishna's flute half, chanting the HARE KRISHNA Mahaa Mantram reverentially. As soon as the box opened up, the flute half glowed and lit up the cave with its ethereal peacock green luminescence.

This confirmed that Dharma was in danger, just like my late father had told me. Master Kautilya was visibly struck with wonder. There was an incredulous look on his face, almost bordering on disbelief. 'I humbly present before you Lord Krishna's flute half, Master Kautilya. I will now go over Chandragupta's wounds with it, if I have your permission, Master.'

'Go ahead Satyavaan. Chandragupta's condition has deteriorated very badly. Now, only the mercy of Lord Krishna can save him.'

'Lord Krishna does not let his true devotees down Master.' I gently removed the blanket covering the warrior. Once again I was taken aback at the enormity of his wounds - his pelvis was almost smashed to pulp. It was as if his completely paralyzed legs were barely attached to his torso.

'This is with the compliments of that beast Xervos!' Kautilya spoke with undisguised anger.

I closed my eyes and concentrated on Lord Krishna, my lips chanting the eternal prayer, 'HARE KRISHNA HARE

KRISHNA KRISHNA KRISHNA HARE HARE. HARE
RAAM HARE RAAM RAAM RAAM HARE HARE.'
I then gently passed the flute half over Chandragupta's
pelvis. Nothing happened for a while. Suddenly, blue streaks
began emanating from the flute half, entering his body. In
the next few moments, the smashed pelvis began regaining
its original shape. The copious bruises on his chest also
disappeared without even a faint scar. Chandragupta, who
had been moaning deliriously until now, went completely
quiet - the only sounds were of his deep breathing. There
was an aura of peace and radiant energy on his visage. He
was now sleeping very peacefully.

'One of the greatest miracles I have ever seen in my life,
thanks to you Satyavaan, and of course, the mercy of the
Lord,' Kautilya spoke gently with a tone of ardent gratitude.
'Dharma has been saved today,' he added.

'I am so, so, so happy to be of some use to you Master.'

'You have more than proven yourself to me. Now, I'm
in your debt because you have saved my beloved Chandra.'

'It is my good fortune to be of service to you, my Master
Kautilya,' I prostrated at his feet and then proceeded to tell
him everything that had transpired at my house.

'You tell me that Xervos now and then visits and stays
over in the houses, especially the good ones that he snatches
from the subjects.'

'Yes Master.'

'You also tell me that your house is a very good one.'

'Yes Master, it is one of the best in the locality.'

'Then it is possible Xervos will stay over there
sometimes.'

'That's what my uncle told me Master.'

'Then I have a plan in mind.'

'Yes Master?'

'We will send a spy over to determine exactly when he
comes over to your house to stay. Once that is established, we

will go there in disguise and launch an ambush on him through the secret backdoor of your house. In fact Chandra will lead this mission, with you as the guide. Eliminating Xervos will be a big shot in the arm for our mission and will drive a stake through the heart of Dhana Nanda. It will, indeed, be a very dangerous mission as the Greek warrior is very cunning and of course enormously strong. He can take on ten of our elite men singlehanded. Only Chandra has the skills to deal with him, even though the last time he tried he received a near fatal lesson at the hands of this giant. That has planted seeds of self-doubt in him which I want removed. That's why I want him to confront Xervos again one-on-one.'

At dawn the next day Chandragupta opened his eyes. I was actually lying by his side with Master Kautilya on his other side. I immediately awoke when I sensed Chandragupta stirring. Master Kautilya was up too. Within moments, the young warrior was sitting up. He threw off his quilt began looking and touching his hips and waist with a look of incredulity.

'Master Kautilya, what has happened to my ghastly wounds? They seem to have disappeared and I feel completely hale and healthy. I can move my legs again! I thought that I was done after the fight with Xervos. How did my wounds disappear?'

'Ask him,' Kautilya pointed towards me and that was the first time the young warrior became aware of my presence. He looked at me quizzically, the eyebrows of his handsome face arching up.

'Let me introduce myself to you Prince and our future king Chandragupta,' I folded my arms in a *n*amaste and bowed my head. 'I am Satyavaan Yaadav from Hasthaamba and I'm here with you by the grace of my Lord Krishna. In fact, I now strongly believe that all that has transpired was meant to be.' I then proceeded to bring the young warrior up to date with my story.

'Are you saying that it is Lord Krishna's flute that has brought me back from the doors of death?'

'Have no doubts on that regard, my Prince.'

'I'm not that religious you know...but I do admit that my recovery has been nothing short of a miracle. The wounds that I received during combat with that beast Xervos were really hideous. I believed that I would die. But not only are my wounds gone, I also feel supercharged as if I had not received even a single wound!'

'Lord Krishna is indeed a master of miracles. And you should be actually thanking the Lord, my prince.'

'I told you that I'm not religious. But I'm grateful to you that I'm alive.'

'It would behoove you Chandra to be a bit more reverential to the flute of Krishna which has given you back your life, whether you believe it or not. I am also swearing you to absolute secrecy regarding this flute. You cannot reveal this even to your best friends.' Kautilya interjected.

'I will keep that in mind, Master. I'm sorry if my words sounded disrespectful in any manner,' the young warrior prince folded his hands in *pranaam* and bowed his head to Kautilya.

'Alright, now it is time to talk of our strategy with regards to Dhana Nanda,' Kautilya fiddled with his thick plaits. 'And that includes the complete annihilation of Xervos.'

'I want nothing more than to get my hands on that monster again,' Chandragupta spoke with pent-up rage.

'My child Chandra, I want you to rise above the petty notions of revenge and look at the big picture. But then, be assured that the big picture holds the image of Xervos being taken out of the equation for good. I have given a fair deal of thought to this. Satyavaan here tells me that Xervos regularly visits his home village and stays at his house. What's more, there's a secret passage in his backyard that leads straight into his house that only Satyavaan knows of. We could use that to good effect to organize an ambush.'

'Master Kautilya, I'm always prepared to be of any service to you. We can go over there with your men right away,' I replied.

'Not so fast. First of all, Chandra needs to get some good practice in mace fighting, especially in countering the brutal chain mace of that giant Xervos. The last time, he used his sword against Xervos, he failed massively. Chandra's sword broke into two with one hard blow from Xervos's chain mace and then the brute smashed his pelvis. This time around I feel that Xervos's mace should be countered with another mace. For that one needs enough practice to withstand the shock of countering the earth shaking power of Xervos's blows. And while Chandra practices here, we will send out our spies to gather information on when exactly Xervos will be visiting Hasthaamba and precisely where he will be camping every night. Using this information, Chandra will lead a select band of our warriors under the cloak of darkness, and ambush Xervos. Satyavaan will once again accompany us to guide the way.'

The next two weeks flew by like the wind as a select band of Kautilya's elite warriors, led by Chandragupta were put through a brutal regimen of mace training by the Master himself. The maces used for the training were made of granite with cast iron handles. Chandragupta, especially, was set a higher benchmark compared to others. He had to strike huge boulders with his mace a hundred times, with all his might, so that his hands would start getting used to the shock generated by the blows. This would be good preparation for the fight against Xervos. But brute force was not the sole aim of the training; developing agility was also given priority. Kautilya reasoned that in a fight with Xervos, Chandragupta's only edge was his superior speed. Xervos always won easily when it came to a straight, one-on-one contest of strength. While this was going on, Kautilya's efficient spies were meticulously gathering information without arousing the slightest suspicion. At the end of the 18th day, Kautilya's spies were back with the requisite information.

The information was very specific. Xervos was to come to Hasthaamba in three days with a troop of 100 heavily armed men and he would be staying at my house. The spies had already watched the house being readied for Xervos's stay. This was the precisely the information Kautilya was seeking. He immediately instructed Chandragupta to select a hundred of his best men and proceed in disguise to Hasthaamba.

Master Kautilya and I would also accompany these men. At the outskirts of Hasthaamba, the band would split into two groups of 95 and 5. The smaller group headed by Chandragupta, accompanied by myself and Kautilya, would proceed in stealth to my house in Hasthaamba. Once there we would sneak in through the secret entrance in the backyard and ambush Xervos. The larger group of 95 would disperse and roam the streets of Hasthaamba in disguise and try to neutralize Xervos's soldiers outside the quarters. Xervos was to be taken dead or alive, though Kautilya reckoned that it was almost next to impossible to take the giant alive. The Greek would surely fight to death rather than allow himself to be captured.

Within the next couple of hours, Kautilya and Chandragupta readied their mission. We were all to be disguised as *Naaga Sadhus*. Everyone had their swords sharpened and hidden under the saffron garb of a mendicant. Our foreheads were liberally smeared with the sacred ash and *kumkum* and our hair matted with ash paste to give us an authentic look. Only five warriors, including Chandragupta, carried the stone maces and these maces were to be carried openly. This would not arouse any suspicion because *Naaga Sadhus* were a martial group of mendicants and it was quite common for them to carry weapons. Five stone maces would not attract attention but a hundred swords certainly would.

The men set out single file, split into 10 groups, with Chandragupta in the lead and myself and Kautilya at the tail end. We moved without making any sound, not wanting to attract unwanted attention. If we were, by chance, accosted by Dhana Nanda's soldiers, we had our story ready: we were *Naaga Sadhus* and were proceeding towards the town for alms.

We reached the outskirts of Hasthaamba without incident. And then, as planned, we dispersed. Myself, Kautilya, and Prince Chandragupta, along with three of his best men proceeded towards my home. We did attract attention from passersby, including some of Dhana Nanda's soldiers. But the attention was not that of suspicion - it was one of profound reverence mixed with curiosity.

When we reached my house, we settled down on the street diagonally across the front gate and posed as if we were meditating. Very soon, a curious crowd gathered around us. Some of them prostrated in front of us and sought our blessings while others gave us food, fruits, and milk. Some of them wanted us to predict what the future held for them and their families. Master Kautilya just humored them with his charismatic smile and asked them to come back the next day, assuring them that the future would be revealed then.

The sun was going down now and the sky had turned a beautiful orange. Fruit bats emerged from their daytime roosts and the skies were filled with silhouettes of their fox heads and vampire wings. It was time to make our move. Master Kautilya gave us a hand signal which meant that we had to prepare for action. Any moment now, darkness would fall. Once again it was my job to lead the way to my house through the secret entrance in the backyard.

In another few minutes it was dark enough and I got up and slowly strolled towards my house, closely followed by Master Kautilya and Prince Chandragupta. There were a few of Dhana Nanda's soldiers posted near the front entrance of the house, but they were completely unaware of our secret motive. It did not take any special effort from us to sneak past them to the back of the house concealing ourselves in the shadows cast by trees and bushes. We expected the back of the house to be unguarded but were surprised to find two guards posted there. There was no option but to take them out swiftly and silently. This Chandragupta effected with lightning efficiency. It was the first time that I had seen him in action and his speed and skills were staggering. One moment these two guards were hale and healthy and in the next, their necks were broken like twigs. Kautilya signaled to the other three men following us. Two of them were to stay concealed in the shadows of the backyard. The two corpses of the soldiers were positioned to look as if they were still guarding their posts.

Then Chandragupta, Kautilya, and one of the men named Maana (Chandragupta's right-hand man), made our way through the secret passage to the interior of my house. The house seemed empty but there were human voices coming through the master bedroom, the door of which was slightly open. We proceeded to peek through the slit and found an enormously muscular man lying stark naked on the bed, tended to by a group of servants who were massaging him with mustard oil. It was Xervos. Even in his prone position, the colossal power and strength of his oil glistened body shone through. He was built like a prime bison. His face, with his golden locks, was strikingly handsome and yet somewhat sinister. Master Kautilya made a sign to Maana. He would now go out and alert the rest of the warriors to blindside Dhana Nanda's soldiers stationed throughout the area, while we took care of Xervos inside the house.

We waited outside the room for another few minutes. Then we heard a bird call made by Maana, which was a signal to us that the outside operation had commenced. The next moment, we stormed into the bedroom, completely surprising Xervos. The group of servants was struck dumb with terror. We allowed them to leave the room and huddle in a corner in the main hall under the guard of Maana who had, by this time, returned inside.

'Do not move Xervos!' Master Kautilya placed his sword on Xervos's throat.

'Oh, so you have returned once again with your ragtag band of young tyros. Didn't you forget the pasting that I had given your little pet puppy the last time? I thought that I had killed him with my mace. To see him alive back here again is indeed a miracle. This time I will make sure that he is dead and gone,' Xervos spoke without the slightest hint of fear.

'Amazing indeed Xervos that you speak to me as if you have us under your mercy.'

'You know old man, one shout from me and my soldiers will be here and you will be pleading for your life.'

'We have already made arrangements for that Xervos. So do not worry about that. Save your energy as you have a lot to answer for, for your murderous crimes against the people of my land.'

'Ha, ha, ha, foolish old man,' Xervos guffawed. 'I answer to none other than King Nanda, least of all to commoners like you. And King Nanda has given me a free hand to do as I please.'

'We have our ways to bring you to heel, Xervos!'

'Go ahead and try old man.'

The next few seconds were a blur as Xervos knocked the sword out of Master Kautilya's hand and sprung like a panther, lightning quick. For a man of his bulk and size, his speed was baffling indeed. In one single motion he picked up his chain mace which had been lying by the side of the bed.

'Now it's time for all of you to die. Come on old man, take me on,' Xervos snarled.

'Do not threaten old people Xervos. It does not suit a warrior like you. Take on Chandragupta, who is soon going to become the king, not only of this land but of the entire *Bhaarath-varsh*. This time, my pet puppy is prepared for you.'

'Ah yes…bring him on old fool. But don't you think that we need more room than here. We will combat each other in the hall, man to man. And I will take him on without a stitch of clothing on my body. This time, my mace will finish off the job, left unfinished in the last encounter. I will relish the smashing of each and every part of his body, old man.'

'That we shall do,' Chandragupta interjected. 'I too will wear no clothing to make it an even contest.'

'You are a foolish little boy and you will certainly pay for your temerity.'

'That we'll see.'

The two naked men now circled each other, their muscles glistening with sweat. Although Chandragupta himself was well built and tall, he was still dwarfed by the giant Xervos, whose extended reach with his mighty arms, almost touched the ceiling. The chain mace swung like a rag doll in the arms of the mighty Greek, making whooshing sounds as it swooshed past Chandragupta's face. In response, the latter ducked deftly. For a while the contest remained evenly balanced as both warriors looked for an opening. Twice it seemed that Xervos was going to hit home, but Chandragupta bent his body backwards like an arc as the mace just glazed his chest. The next moment, the young prince arched like a spring, leapt into the air and brought his mace down on Xervos's right shoulder. The giant parried it at the last moment with his right hand. The contestants again separated and began circling each other.

As the combat wore on it appeared as if the giant Greek was slowly getting the upper hand. Xervos whirled his chain mace again and moved menacingly towards Chandragupta. The latter stood his ground and allowed Xervos to move in. Suddenly, the young warrior went down on his knees, raised his mace up in the air and, foreshortening the chain reducing its radius, swung it with deadly accuracy and power eliciting a deep grunt from the giant; his face instantly becoming a bloody mess. But he still remained standing, even as the blood trickled down his huge body. Finally his knees buckled under him and he toppled face down on the ground, never to rise again.

The young warrior Chandragupta now put his right foot on the prone body of Xervos and roared a victory bellow like a tiger would, over the carcass of a prime bull gaur that it had brought down after a titanic struggle. I could literally see sparks flaming from his eyes. Such was his fervor and passion to achieve his goal. That very moment laid the foundations for the eventual victory of this rebel team over the cruel Dhana Nanda and his huge army. I was there to witness the great occasion when Prince Chandragupta eventually ascended the throne and was proclaimed king. I also saw the day when he rose to become Emperor Chandragupta Maurya. Kautilya rewarded me handsomely, then let me go back to my old mother in Hasthaamba. He also made sure that my family heirloom would always remain a secret. But that was redundant, because as legend has it, matters regarding the flute half were completely erased from even the extraordinary brain of Kautilya.

'And that, Dr Baalan, was another one of my past lives,' Jaarra *baaba* reclined on the steps with a twinkle in his eye. 'Let me add that the slaying of Xervos was a turning point in the history of our land. Had Chandragupta lost to Xervos, I shudder to think of the alternative. Now Dr Baalan, let me recount yet another past life where the Lord's flute once again saved the day for the survival of Sanaatana Dharma in this ancient land of ours.'

'Incredible Jaarra-*baaba*,' Dr Baalan exclaimed. 'Your description of events are very vivid. It is as if one is actually present there. Please continue.'

The seer graciously inclined his head: 'This happened in the year 1666 in central *Bhaarath* abutting the Deccan plateau…'

Shambhu Yaadav - The Great Escape

$\mathcal{M}$y name was Shambhu Yaadav. I was the youngest of five children (four older sisters and I) and the only surviving one. My four elder sisters were abducted, raped, and murdered by the marauding army of the barbaric Mughal Adil Shah, when he conquered my city of Vijayanagara by treachery. However, I was not yet born at that time. The old Hindu monarch Ramaraaya was our king and it was the year 1565. He fought valiantly against the invading Mughals and for a while it seemed like he would be able to contain the savage marauders. But then, treachery within his own regiments did him in and he lost valiantly to the mad Jihadi Sultan, Adil Shah. After the Mughals took control of the city, they went on a rampage. The destruction and looting lasted well over six months. The fiend of a Sultan then gave orders to torch the city and it burnt continuously for almost one year. Even the granite hills surrounding our city had cracked; such was the heat and ferocity of the destruction.

My parents somehow survived months of pillage and destruction by hiding in a small hut on the outskirts of the city. But when the city was torched, the heat became unbearable, from the mighty fires that roared constantly day in and day out. Subsequently, they escaped to central *Bhaarath*, to a small hamlet near present day Narsimhapur in Madhya Pradesh. There in the village of Sitapur, I was born in the year 1586 and grew up to live a long and fairly uneventful life. You see, the events that I am going to talk to you about happened in 1666, when I was an old man of 80.

Around the late 1620s, my old and ailing father handed me a case that I had hitherto seen in the *puja* sanctum of my house. My father had never encouraged any questions about it and had only told me that it contained a sacred item. But now, on his deathbed, he whispered slowly in my ears: 'This case contains one half of the flute of Krishna. This is a family secret my boy, and from now on, you should take good care of it. You must not reveal this to anybody but to my grandson (your son) during the last stages of your life, just like I have revealed it to you. I believe that, if not for this flute, our family would have been completely wiped out in Vijayanagara itself by the Mughals. The flute also has magical powers of healing my son, and other miraculous powers yet to be discovered. You will be pleasantly surprised by what it can do. But then, you can't use these powers indiscriminately. These powers can be used, and the secret revealed to a worthy person, only when Dharma is in acute danger of collapsing in our land. The flute will glow peacock green during those times and that's when you can summon its powers for help.'

After my father passed away, I followed his instructions and led a very peaceful and uneventful life as a land tiller at Sitapur, until that fateful day in 1666. As I told you, I was 80 years old at that time, but as fit as a fiddle.

On that day, I had gone to round up my cows which were grazing on the verdant hillocks surrounding my village. Little did I know that fate would lead me to a chance meeting with one of the greatest protectors of Hindu Dharma that history has known.

As I approached the top of the hill, I rounded a huge boulder and ran straight into a man with a straggly beard, who looked like a poor mendicant. He was very short, but his frame looked solid as a rock and he had a steely glint in his eyes. That's when I noticed a sword gleaming in his hand. For a while we took each other's measure till he finally broke the silence: 'I am traveler along with a few other friends. We are looking for some food and shelter for the night.'

My mind was racing. Why a mendicant would carry a sword, I wondered. Then it struck me. The previous evening a huge contingent of Mughal soldiers had come to the village announcing that they were looking for a band of dangerous fugitives who had escaped from Agra - anyone who helped in their capture would be heavily rewarded by Emperor Aurangzeb himself. This was actually the fourth or fifth time that soldiers had come looking for them in the last three weeks. The guards had warned us to be very cautious and keep an eye out for anything suspicious.

For a moment, I did not know what to do. Should I report them to the Mughal soldiers who were camping on the northern outskirts of the village? But something about the man in front of me struck me as noble and stately. A ray of honest courage emanated from his face. Suddenly the man clapped his hands. The next instant, seven more ragged mendicants materialized out of the surrounds.

'These are friends travelling with me and we are all very tired and hungry. We would be very grateful *daada*, if you will help us in this regard.'

'I'm ready to give you food and shelter for the night,' I replied at length. 'But you can come in only after dark.'

'Why can't we come now?'

'There are Mughal soldiers in and around the village.' I waited to see a reaction on the mendicant's face. There was not even the faintest flinch, except that his piercing eyes grew slightly wider. 'They are looking for a band of escaped fugitives from Agra and have announced a huge reward to anyone who helps in their capture.'

There was still no sign of discomfort on the man's face and in fact, he was smiling now.

'We are the very men that these soldiers are looking for *daada*. But we are not dangerous fugitives; I can promise you that.'

'Then, who are you? I need to know the truth before I render you and your friends any help. Besides it will pose great risks for me and my family. Everyone knows how cruel Aurangzeb and his soldiers are, especially to those that dare cross him.'

'I cannot tell you much now *daada*, except that I'm a fighter for Dharma; the same Dharma which is in extreme danger of getting destroyed under this beast of an emperor. You have to trust me on this. We mean you no harm even if you decide to report us to the Mughal soldiers. Please help us in the name of Lord Shiva.'

Aurangzeb was no favorite of mine either. His cruel, draconian rules, especially the hard brand of Wahhabi Sharia Islam that he enforced on the land, made Hindus like me third class *dhimmi* citizens, with absolutely no status. We had to pay a huge sum in gold coins every year as *jizzia*, which we could avoid only if we converted to Islam. Any failure to pay the tax was swiftly punishable by immediate decapitation without trial. I had seen many families convert to Islam under this duress and also a few defiant ones who paid with their lives. Since I had a small inheritance – gold, which my father had brought with him from Vijayanagara, I had somehow survived this far. But the future looked bleak to me, especially when I thought about my two children: my married son and unmarried younger daughter. It was not a safe environment for non-Muslim women. Moreover, those boyhood tales that I heard from my parents of gruesome pillage, death, and mass rape, which Adil Shah and his army had wreaked on Vijayanagara were still fresh in my memory.

'You know the courier hawks of the emperor have brought news of your escape long before you arrived here. And even if you were to safely leave from here, you will face increasing obstacles along the way.'

'We know about those courier hawks *daada*, and we have anticipated and avoided detection this far, by the grace of Lord Shiva.'

'Alright, you and your followers can come in to my house after dark. My house is the first one on the left as soon as you come down the hill.'

'We will be forever grateful to you *daada*.'

It was way past sunset when the band of mendicants softly knocked on my door. Immediately I ushered them inside, requesting them to speak in low voices and only when necessary. One never knew when an alert Mughal guard would pass by - they always kept their eyes and ears open, eager for the huge reward placed on the head of these fugitives.

Soon my guests were eagerly feasting on the humble meal of dry *rotis* and buttermilk that I offered them. It seemed obvious that they had not eaten well for a long time. After the meal, they rested on the floor of my front room, on the big frayed *chaarpaai* that I laid out for them. For a long time no one spoke until their leader addressed me in a low voice: '*Daada*, why are you living here like a slave under the tyranny of the Mughals? Just come with us. We can carry all of your family (which meant me, my son, his wife and two children, and my young unmarried daughter) on our horses, which we have left on the hill. You can live a life or honor and dignity as a Hindu in the land where I live. Even Muslims are treated as equals there.'

I did not know what to say. His offer was very tempting. I had had enough of life as a *dhimmi khafir* in a *sharia* dominated society.

'You do not have to make any decision now *daada*,' the short leader added with a smile. 'Any time in your life, if you want to come down to my land in the south, you are most welcome. I will see to it that you and your family are well settled.'

Then we all lay down to sleep. It was close to dawn when we were awoken by the sound of harsh knocks on the door. 'Open up,' the voice on the other side boomed. I instantly recognized the voice and trembled with fear. What I should do now, I wondered. I motioned to my visitors to pretend that they were still sleeping and slowly headed towards the door, oil lamp in hand. I undid the bolt with trembling fingers and opened the door gingerly.

A huge Mughal guard barged in, almost bulldozing me. I recognized him instantly even though his face was obscured by the shadows. It was Baram Khan, the right hand man of local Mughal lord, Gul Muhammad Akhtar.

'Get me some water,' he growled, gazing fiercely at me. But I knew why he had come here. For the past few weeks, he had barged in, in the same manner, and all those times his intentions were the same. He wanted my young daughter, who was considered as very pretty in our village, as one of his concubines. In return, he promised that he would pay the *jizzia* on behalf of my family, to the emperor's coffers, every year, indefinitely.

'Please sit here Khan *sahib*, while I get you the water.'

Baram Khan seated himself on the stone platform near our door, constructed for the purpose of seating visitors, and scanned the room with his large, red-rimmed eyes.

I returned with a jug of water and placed it in his huge beastly hands. He emptied it in one massive gulp. Then he looked at me with a half scowl half smile.

'You remember my offer old man?'

'I need some time to think it over Khan *sahib*.'

'I can very well get what I want by force, old man. But in your case I am making this concession out of honor.'

'I understand Khan *sahib*.'

'Don't test my patience forever. I want your answer in two days. Else, you know very well what I can do.'

'I understand Khan *sahib* and I will give you an answer by tomorrow evening.'

As he rose to leave, he threw another glance at the sleeping figures on the floor. 'It seems, old man, that you have visitors. I don't remember seeing this many people the last time I came.'

'Yes Khan *sahib*, they are relatives of mine visiting from the south.'

'Then why did you not immediately report their presence as the emperor has ordered.'

'They came in just now. I already told them they must report to you in the morning.'

'What did you say old man?? They came in now? But I was just camping there outside the village with my men and did not see anybody come in.'

I was lost for words but I gathered myself. 'They came in the dark Khan *sahib*. That is why you or your guards may not have noticed. I will surely bring them to you in the morning.'

'NO,' Khan thundered. 'I WANT TO SEE THEM NOW!! WAKE THEM UP OLD MAN. AND BECAUSE YOU DID NOT IMMEDIATELY REPORT YOUR VISITORS AS REQUIRED BY THE EMPEROR, YOU WILL ALSO HAND OVER YOUR DAUGHTER TO ME, RIGHT NOW, AS PENALTY!!,' My entire house shook with the reverberations of his voice.

'Please forgive me Khan *sahib*,' I immediately fell at his feet and embraced his giant knees tightly. But he threw me off with one flick of his leg. I perceived a streak of movement from the peripheral vision of my left eye. Even a panther did not move that quickly. Baram Khan reeled back grunting as if hit by a boulder as the short leader of my visitors rammed into him with all his might. The powerfully built Mughal lost his balance and fell backwards on the floor with an audible thud. The next instant, the mendicant leader was sitting atop his chest with a gleaming dagger in his hand. There was a muffled cry of '*Har Har Mahaadev*' as the dagger plunged into the jugular of the Mughal. The blood gushed out like a fountain and completely drenched the short man. He looked towards me. '*Daada*, we have to leave immediately as his men will surely come looking for this beast. Please come with us. If you stay back, they will wipe out your entire family. With my men and me, you stand at least a fighting chance. You can lead the rest of your life as a Hindu with dignity and respect, and so can your family. I will make sure of that.'

I was still shell-shocked by all that had transpired. But I gathered myself. Yes, the leader was right. There was nothing for me and my family here other than *jizzia*, humiliation, certain abduction and rape of my daughter, and now, death. We would have to leave with nothing but the clothes on our back. I immediately instructed my family to prepare for escape and they were even more willing than I. Soon, we, along with our visitors, were heading surreptitiously out of a small side door facing the hills. That was when I remembered the flute half. Chanting the HARE KRISHNA Mahaa Mantram in my mind, I rushed inside to retrieve this priceless family heirloom. If anything could protect us from the army of 1000 plus camped outside our village, it could be very well be this sacred object.

We moved stealthily in the pale light of dawn without making a sound and made our way to the top of the hill, single file. The fear of being caught by the Mughals infused energy into our bodies, still groggy with sleep. Soon we were mounting the horses. I clambered onto the same horse as the short leader. My son, daughter-in-law, my two grandchildren, and my unmarried daughter were carried by other riders. Soon we were off, riding in a silent trot trying not to alert the Mughal soldiers with the sounds of the thudding hooves. Now and again we looked back to see whether anyone was on our trail. But the coast was clear. We had to cover as much ground as possible and put a good distance between us and the Mughals before they discovered their dead leader. Then all hell would surely break loose. I dreaded to think what the soldiers would do to the rest of the villagers in their rage.

It was slowly getting brighter every passing minute and the eastern sky was glowing orange. We now paused at the edge of a clearing. In front of us was a stretch of open land as far as our eyes could see. In the distance we could see the pale outline of the Satpura mountain range that stood in our way like a colossal sentinel. Beyond the range, began the Deccan plateau and that was where we had to get as quickly as possible. According to the short leader of the mendicants, the heart of the Deccan Plateau was the region from where he hailed, which he claimed was the Promised Land for Hindus.

Looking from where we stood now, the shortest route to the plateau was over the mountain range. The other alternative was a circuitous route that meandered through areas heavily infested with Mughals. We had to make a dash across this vast open space over to the range. Every passing minute spelt increasing danger from behind. The short leader looked at his men and then waved his sword in the direction of the mountains. In the next instant, we were off galloping like the wind. The vast plain was uninhabited except for a few peasants that we came across now and then. This had once been the land of the Asiatic lion but now, most of the wildlife had been butchered by Mughals through their *shikaars*. We had hardly covered a couple of miles when one of the mendicants shouted, 'The Mughals are after us.' Looking behind, we saw a huge dust cloud following in our wake, at a distance. It was surely the 1000 plus army, led by Gul Muhammad Akhtar.

'Faster, faster!' the short leader urged his men to goad their steeds. The horses responded and soon they were galloping at peak capacity. A froth of sweat lathered on their backs as the horses pushed on. The mountains loomed into full view, but there was still a reasonable distance to cover. And the cloud of dust behind us was steadily getting closer.

If we did not reach the mountains first, we would very soon be within spear throwing range, and some of the ace Mughal guards were renowned for their accuracy with the javelin spear, thrown from horseback in full flight. Our horses seemed to tire but the riders urged them on. We had almost reached the foot of the range when we spotted a small wall of rock before us. If we could get behind these rocks, we would at least have some kind of cover. Now there was renewed urgency. Somehow we had to make it to that wall. Our horses had reached breaking point and any time anyone of us could go down. But these horses seemed to be of a special breed and they somehow summoned one last ounce of energy from their tiring legs. We dared not look behind to see how close our pursuers were.

Finally, we made it to the wall and one by one our horses went behind it. The horse on which I was seated along with the short leader was the last one to come around the wall - we had made it by the skin of our teeth. For, as we came around, a javelin spear narrowly whizzed past our heads and smashed into the rocks.

Now we galloped up a narrow winding pathway that snaked its way around and up the mountain. Within moments we could hear frenzied cries of '*Allah O Akbar*' from the pursuing Mughals. They were hot our heels like a pack of wolves on the scent of their prey. To our advantage the path was narrow and could accommodate only a couple of horses at a time. If push came to shove, we could turn around to face them and take them on, two at time.

Somehow, I felt supremely confident about the fighting skills of this gang of mendicants. I was convinced by the way they handled their horses that they were an elite band of soldiers and riders.

The path suddenly straightened and ascended very steeply. The horses slowed due to the punishing gradient. But after a furlong, it came to a dead end, much to our chagrin. We were left staring at a vertical wall of granite that blocked our way. We milled around in confusion till the short leader barked orders for all of us to disembark.

'We have no option but to turn around and fight our enemy. We certainly have an advantage as our enemies are downhill from us. This means we can use stones and boulders effectively. So let's prepare to welcome our pursuers. *Har Har Mahaadev!*'

'*Har Har Mahaadev!*' his followers echoed in unison and soon they were working in complete coordination collecting rocks and marking the boulders that could be dislodged and let loose on their pursuers. The hoofs of the pursuing Mughals clattered louder by the passing second and before long we could see the helmeted heads of the lead soldiers making their way up the slope towards us.

'Let them come closer,' the short leader grunted. A few moments passed then the approaching soldiers came into range. 'Now!' the short leader motioned with his sword. The next instant, a wave of boulders and rocks went crashing down the steep pathway, straight onto the approaching Mughals. The first rock took a bounce, flew up, and smashed into the chest of the first soldier, throwing him off his horse. His companion was stunned before his horse too was taken down by a second boulder. And then it was a deluge, completely taking the Mughals by surprise and throwing them off balance. They had no option but to beat a hasty, temporary retreat. The band of mendicants screamed their war cry victoriously: '*Har Har Mahaadev!*'

The short leader knew we could not keep the Mughals at bay for long. It was only a matter of time before we ran out of rocky ammunition.

'Eventually, we will have no option but to take a stand here. Two of us will wait here and stop them. You can go ahead my leader,' one of his followers replied.

'No more sacrifices for my sake. You have done enough of this service in the past and I have lost a few good men like Tanaaji and Baaji. Therefore, I will fight to the end with you. But three of us will escort this family to the safety of the Deccan while the rest of us fight.' The short leader then turned towards me. 'Three of my trusted men will take you and your family out of here to the Deccan. For this, we will try to create a diversionary opening.'

He could not have been more right as the next wave of Mughals came up the path only to be repulsed by more stones and boulders rolling down their way. But the Mughals only seemed increasingly roused after each of these attempts and kept coming back with savage zeal. Each time, they were getting further up the path. It would only be a matter of time before they got within hand to hand combat range. What's more, the band of mendicants did not have any long range weapons other than their swords. A final sword fight was thus inevitable.

'The rogues have nowhere to escape to. Do not spare anyone,' the booming voice of Gul Muhammad Akhtar carried through clearly. We had by now exhausted our ammunition of rocks and boulders and the enemy had sensed our predicament. We were about to be charged by a steady stream of Mughal guards.

Wave after wave of the charges were met with raw courage by the short leader and his men but they slowly began tiring in front of my own eyes. The warrior mendicants were trying their level best to create an opening for me and my family to escape. So far there had not been even a small window of opportunity for this. Suddenly, I remembered my father's advice and opened the box containing the flute half. The peacock green radiance took everyone's breath as the lid came off. Dharma was surely in grave danger now. I closed my eyes and began chanting the Hare Krishna Mahaa Mantram. For the next few moments, I felt myself transported to another world and became totally oblivious of the fighting around me.

Suddenly, there was an unearthly rumble followed by the sound of thunderclap. The sheer wall of granite behind us parted, revealing an opening. For a moment, I could not comprehend the implication and then it hit me.

'Come on everybody. The Lord has opened up a passage for us through the mountain.'

The short leader looked incredulously at me.

'No time to wait. Trust me. This is indeed the way.'

We entered the crack, the peacock green light of the flute half illuminating the way. We were suddenly enveloped by a sense of collective fearlessness even though the next wave of Mughals was now within striking distance. The spears and javelins whizzed past us but we did not even flinch. Then there was another loud crack behind us.

We turned around and saw that the ground had parted along the path of the approaching Mughal soldiers and we saw them falling into the chasm along with their horses. This was followed by a titanic landslide as the path behind us crumbled, letting loose a gigantic wave of rock and rubble that tore down and completely engulfed the hillside all the way down, to where the remaining Mughal army milled about restlessly waiting for their piece of action. It was over just like that. Not a single Mughal soldier or his horse survived the wall of rocks and sand that roared over them. All was deathly still.

The short leader looked at the flute half in my hands with a mixture of awe and reverence. 'What magic is that *daada*?'

'It is not magic my dear friend. It is the power of the Lord himself. The power he shows when Dharma is in real danger. And you my friend seem to be a worthy beneficiary of this miracle.'

'You have to tell me more about this *daada*, once we get to my land and you and your family are completely safe.'

'I certainly will. But none of you shall reveal this miraculous incident to anyone else outside this group. This I need you to promise solemnly.'

'You have my word *daada*, and that of my men.'

Suddenly there was a shrill cry behind us. 'HALT,' a voice boomed. It was the Jehadi Gul Mohammed Akhtar. He had miraculously survived the deadly landslide.

'You cowards, if you have any honor and guts take me on!' The Mughal shook his sword menacingly. One of the men in our band immediately jumped down from his horse to take up the challenge, but the short leader now sprang in front of him.

'This is my battle Veerya... *aai shapath*,' he moved like a leopard towards the Jehadi. The short leader then launched himself in a jump, his muscular thighs and calves acting like a spring. He deftly feinted to the left like a gazelle, avoiding the Mughal's forward rush, and the next instant he had brought his sword slicing through the air onto the helmet of the Mughal with all his might. The Mughal reeled back with disbelief as he had not expected such a move from his short opponent. Before he could gather himself, the sword of the short leader had brought the Mughal's neck under its mercy.

'Surrender or die!' the short leader roared.

'Do as you will,' Akhtar replied.

'Alright I spare you - go back to your master Aurangzeb with my message.'

'And what is your message?'

'That he will, from now on, treat all his subjects equally regardless of their faith. He will cease the cruel and unjust *jizzia* on Hindus and stop raining terror upon them. He should also halt the destruction of their temples.' The short leader pulled the Mughal back on his feet. 'Get going fast now.' He sent the Mughal on his way - the latter walking off with his head hung low by the weight of his comprehensive defeat.

'*Har har Mahaadev*!' The short leader's victory cry reverberated across the Satpuras. His men echoed his cry and rushed forward to embrace him. I embraced him too and so did my son. I was completely awestruck. I had never seen a warrior of his prowess in my entire life. To defeat Gul Akhtar in a couple of moves was no mean feat. The Jehadi was renowned for his swordsmanship as well as his brute strength. The short leader then signaled that we should resume our journey. It took us close to three hours to forge our way through the crack in the mountain; the crack dynamically closing with a grind of the rocks behind us as we rushed through.

A week later we were in the Deccan. Only when the short leader went all the way to his fortress in Raigarh and fell at the feet of his old mother Jijabhai, did I realize that he was none other than the great Maratha Chattrapathi Shivaaji. I was completely overwhelmed to say the least. Afterwards, I revealed the exact nature of my family heirloom to the great Hindu king. Shivaaji was awestruck with wonder and devotion. But I forbade him from revealing this, even to his men who had accompanied him to the North.

The flute half thus played a crucial role in the legendary Maratha king's epic escape from Agra where Aurangzeb had invited him on a friendly visit for truce, but later resorted to treachery and placed him under house arrest. Had this escape not been successful, the history of this great ancient land would surely been very much different and the very survival of our Hindu Dharma would have been put into great jeopardy.'

As promised, Shivaaji carried the secret of Krishna's flute half till it was abruptly erased from his brain. Nor did his followers talk about the miracle on the Satpuras to anyone as the incident was completely erased from their memories as well, almost immediately after we reached Raigarh. I lived the remaining years of my life in that bliss called *Hindaavi Swaraj* where Hindus like me lived with full dignity and honor without worrying about *jizzia,* and more importantly, worrying over the safety of our women folk. Even Muslims lived as full equals.

'Thus ended my saga as Shambhu Yaadav, Dr Baalan,' Jaarra *baaba* continued. Let me I will tell you the story of one more *janma* - that of Shreedhar Yaadav - which happened in 1944 and which is going to be of great relevance to you in this meeting with me….. *Harihar-Shiv-Shambho!*'

Shreedhar Yaadav – Vande Maataram

'*My* fellow soldiers of the INA,' our commander boomed. 'You know the gravity of the task that is lying ahead of us. And yet, we are here and we will never give up our just fight to liberate our beloved motherland from the clutches of the British. We are here today as one fierce spirit to take on our much stronger enemy who is also very cunning. We will never give up, even though we face heavy odds. Because, the task that we have undertaken is sacred beyond these words. We will fight unto death for this cause. And therefore, we march ahead.

Today, I have designated the regiment of Sanmat Singh, who hails from the proud community of valiant Sikhs, the community that gave us a lion called Bhagat Singh, a community that has shed so much blood for our nation, to march further west towards Nagaland and Mizoram. The enemy is sleeping and is unaware of our intentions, thereby putting the advantage of surprise on our side. Once we successfully take over the North East, it will be a serious boost of morale for us. It will also serve as a launching pad to claim the rest of our motherland. And we will not rest till we fly our tricolor in the ramparts of the Red Fort. That is my promise to you as our leader. *Jai Bhavani! Vande Maataram*!'

'*Jai Bhavaani! Vande Maataram*!' We echoed in chorus, raising our fists.

Then each of us in Sanmat Singh's regiment (we were 100 in total), beginning with Sanmat Singh himself, shook hands with our commander and embraced him. I could feel an electric charge of courage and inspiration flow into me from my commander when it was my turn. And then, when I looked into his blazing eyes, I could see the affection that he had for each of us on an individual basis. Our commander was one of those rare men whose very demeanor was inspiring; to say nothing of the vision and courage he had for a free *Bhaarath*.

'Go forth my boys and take the battle to the enemy. Be victorious!' he roared as we left on our mission. We walked in complete silence, single file, through the thick, green wilds of Burma, in the small hours of the morning. There was a sliver of a moon in the cloudless sky. We were now close to the Northeastern border of India. In another 20 km we would enter into an area of Southern Nagaland, which today is its border with Mizoram. Our plan was to take our enemy, the British, by complete surprise.

We had an advantage on our side because the British did not guard this area with serious intent. Our entry into Nagaland would then help us to lay the platform into Chittagong of pre-partition days and thence into Calcutta, the economic capital of British India. There our commander would join us with the rest of his troops and we would begin our march towards Delhi.

In spite of the weight of the task lying ahead of us, we were relaxed and in high spirits. Our march to the border was unimpeded except for one incident about 5 kms away from the border, where we had to make a detour because of an angry hissing obstacle. It was a hyper-protective king cobra guarding its nest of eggs. Fortunately, this Queen of snakes, which packed enough venom in her fangs to completely wipe out our regiment, gave us ample warning from a respectable distance, else we would have marched right over her nest resulting in loss of life for a few of us. We respectfully took a detour before we continued on.

Our destination was close now. There was a small post of the British Indian army 200 meters across the border. Getting there would not be a challenge at all for our regiment. Little did we know that we were going to be victims of a painful, insidious betrayal.

The border was now just 200 yards away and the thick jungle gave way to a clearing. We could see the small cabin which served as an outpost for the British army. It appeared to be uninhabited. Our regiment leader Sanmat Singh called a halt temporarily and we got into a huddle to discuss our next plan of action.

'There seems to be no one at the post. However, to confirm this, I am sending brother Soldier Mann Singh as reconnaissance.'

'Yes sir,' Mann Singh replied with a salute. He was one of our toughest men and had been very impressive during training exercises. Mann Singh immediately took a detour to the right and disappeared like a ghost into thick cover. After a good half an hour, he reappeared by our side just as silently as he had gone.

'Everything is clear sir. The post is deserted and empty.'

'Alright, let's move. We will march straight through the clearing and take the post. We will be there till daybreak and then move southwards towards Chittagong.'

All hundred of us formed a single line and began marching across the clearing. Our first expected skirmish with the British had seemingly ended in victory without even a single bullet being fired from our guns. This forebode well for the task ahead. Or so it seemed…

Suddenly British guns began booming all around us in the clearing, out of nowhere. We immediately fell flat on the cold dew coated grass and began firing in retaliation. We had no idea as to where exactly the enemy fire was originating from. We had been ambushed, completely blindsided (history would later record that we had been insidiously betrayed), and we had no other option but to minimize our losses and beat a hasty retreat. Our courageous regiment leader, Sanmat Singh, ordered the retreat and we withdrew, pell-mell, to the cover of the thick Burmese forests.

The assault by the hidden British forces was relentless. Mann Singh took a bullet to his forehead and his head burst up like a ripe melon. A few others were also struck down. From where I lay flat on the open ground bullets whizzed past my head. I could see the rest of my regiment, along with our leader, hurrying back to cover. I had somehow been cut off in the suddenness of the ambush and the consequent melee. Now I had to find a way to get to them.

After a brief while, I summoned the guts to get up and run. Even as the bullets whizzed past me, I took off like an antelope. I had almost reached the safety of cover on the other side when I got hit. An enemy bullet found its mark and shattered my lower spine. My legs buckled under me and I fell to the ground in a dead faint. I don't know how long I remained like that. When I finally opened my eyes, it was nearly daybreak and the guns had fallen silent. There was nothing but the green of the Burmese jungle around me. I instantly wanted to get up and rush eastwards to rejoin my regiment. It was then that I realized my true predicament. I was paralyzed from waist down. My legs were completely useless.

My throat was totally parched. I badly needed water but there was no water anywhere near. I remembered seeing a stream a kilometer to the east. I had no option but to crawl forwards, dragging my body, as thirst was killing me. Slowly, I began this painful process. Here and there thorns tore through my palms but I continued on with rest stops every now and then. It took me five hours to somehow crawl to the bank of the stream and dip my face into the water. It felt like ambrosia. I decided to stay put in that area, hoping that my regiment would come looking for me. Little did I know that the entire regiment had been wiped out in a second ambush further east.

I waited and waited for many days subsisting on wild berries and water from the stream. But my body was slowly giving up. As the days passed, I grew more and more feeble. I spent my days lying on the banks of the stream so that I could drink water whenever I was thirsty.

I passed out on the eleventh day after my injury. I do not know how long I lay unconscious till I opened my eyes to a familiar voice. It belonged to my cousin Lakhan. I was visibly shocked and my thoughts raced. I gratefully gulped the water that my cousin poured down my throat as he rested my head on his lap. Then he fed me some pieces of dry *chappati* that he had brought along with him. After munching a few pieces I asked him feebly, 'Lakhan my brother, how did you find me here?'

'You will not believe it Shreedhar - a holy man came to our house a few weeks back as I was tending to your ailing father, who has alas now expired.'

'What? Did you say, father expired?'

'Yes.'

Tears scalded down my cheeks. I felt helpless that I could not be by my father's side during his last moments. My father had been ailing for almost a year and the doctors had told us to be prepared for any eventuality.

'Once again Lakhan, how did you find me here?'

'As I told you, a holy man visited us as your father lay dying and he gave him a letter etched on a rolled piece of bark. The holy man did not say who had written the letter. But the letter clearly told us your exact location, predicted your father's death by the evening of the same day, and also instructed me to bring a precious family heirloom to you. Moreover, it said that there would be a man who would return from the east in about ten fortnights time and this heirloom is to be passed on to him. It then instructs you to go the city of Jabalpur and start a new life as a teacher in the field of sciences.'

'What unbelievable nonsense Lakhan! Just look at me and tell me how I am supposed to get back on my feet in my paralyzed state and start a new career? As far as I can see, my life is finished.'

'Good question Shreedhar. But then, let me first hand over to you the family heirloom which I have brought with me in a box. I have sworn an oath that I will not open it at any time during my journey here. Consequently, I do not know what is in the box, but I think it is something very special as the holy man had told me to constantly chant the HARE KRISHNA Mahaa Mantram all through my journey here, especially whenever I touch the box. Do you know, there was this strange tingling sensation whenever I carried the box?'

'I have a fair idea what it is Lakhan. Just pass me the box.'

I gingerly opened the long rectangular box and instantly a brilliant peacock green luminescence engulfed me. I remembered my father telling me that this luminescence happens only when Dharma is in extreme danger. I slowly curled my index finger and thumb to pull out the flute half. I could feel a tingling current surge through my fingers and I had to let go of the flute after a while because of a surging sensation of increasing current running through my body.

I realized that it had been a while since I had prayed. Here again I remembered my late father's advice as to what to do in this situation. I closed my eyes and then chanted the HARE KRISHNA Mahaa Mantram with reverence, and once again placed my hands on the flute. Now it was much easier to handle. I kept on chanting the Mahaa Mantram and after a while the sensation of the strong current died down to a pleasant tingle that, in a few minutes, became a sensation of absolute bliss. I had not realized that I had slowly gotten to my feet and was now standing strong. The numbing pain in my back had gone. I felt the base of my spine with my left hand for the bullet hole that had been the cause for all my misery. The hole had gone and I could feel only smooth, unmolested skin.

'This is a miracle! What is this object, this family heirloom of yours?' There were tears in Lakhan's eyes.

'A great family tradition and a precious gift from the Lord that I am bound by oath not to tell anyone, unless it is really required. Maybe, if the Lord so wills, it will be revealed to you in time. But for now, this is it Lakhan. We are going to stay here and wait for that man from the east as per the instructions of the holy man.'

'Ten fortnights in this jungle Shreedhar! How will we survive here for this long period?'

'I'm a proud soldier of the INA Lakhan and adept in the art of survival. I am going to stay put as I believe strongly that these instructions come from a higher source whose reasoning is beyond our comprehension. But Lakhan, you can go back home if you wish.'

'No brother. I'm going to be by your side. I will not abandon you here by yourself in these wilds of Burma,' Lakhan gave me a tight embrace.

The days passed steadily without much incidence, even though we were still wary of being spotted and captured by the British forces. As much as we hoped that our beaten INA would make a miraculous reappearance from the east, it was not to be. We subsisted on fruits and wild berries and were hungry most of the time. Yet we felt energized and filled with a strange confidence that everything would work out right. Lakhan was always by my side and I was struck by his devotion to me. I decided to reveal to him the exact nature of my family heirloom. Lakhan was stunned to say the least. But from them on, he worshipped the object every morning and evening, chanting the HARE KRISHNA Mahaa Mantram.

At the end of ten fortnights, we strained our eyes regularly eastwards to see if anyone was coming but no one came. Another ten days passed and thoughts of home began tantalizing my brain. Somehow I resisted them. It was almost the end of the 11th fortnight when we a saw a bearded figure with long unkempt hair, wearing only a loin cloth and a rag across his chest, making his way steadily through the jungle, towards us. There was a steely unhurried demeanor in his walk and even from a distance; we could see the fire of purpose in his eyes. There was a magnetic aura about him that transfixed us as he approached. He halted at a distance of about 150 meters from us and beckoned us over. I looked at Lakhan and we exchanged glances before stepping forward in unison.

'Only you,' the man pointed to me. I once again exchanged glances with Lakhan and then, motioned him to stay put. As I neared him, the bearded man turned away and motioned me to follow. After a long while he stopped and turned around to face me. I could recognize the light smile on his face. It was our supreme commander; the commander of the INA, Netaji.

'Netaji, Netaji, is that really you?? I just cannot believe it!' I was totally shocked.

'Yes soldier, it is me, Netaji. I have returned from the dead or supposedly dead.'

'What happened Netaji?' I was curious as well as concerned.

'After that tragic betrayal by one of our own men, who was a mole planted by the British, our army retreated further back east. We faced massive defeats elsewhere in Indo-China and to top it all; I was betrayed by the defeated Japanese army to the British in an unexpected and shocking prisoner exchange in the jungles of Malaysia. The British put out false news that I had perished in a plane crash, while they were actually holding me in an underground cell in Malaysia and were planning to airlift me in a Russian cargo plane to a Siberian prison in its northern Arctic wastes with the full blessings of the Russian leader Joseph Stalin. I somehow managed to escape and went into hiding for a few weeks before making for here.'

'So glad you are back Netaji. The country needs you and I'm sure you can lead us once again in spite of these temporary setbacks.'

'The country does not need me anymore soldier. In fact, our motherland will become free even without me. My life's mission from now on has taken an entirely different focus, a much higher goal.'

'I do not understand what you are saying Netaji.'

'I have come here to take that precious heirloom of yours, as per the instructions of the holy man who came to your father. It was the same holy man who helped me escape British captivity in Malaysia. In return for his help, he made me accept *deeksha* from him and made me his disciple. He told me that you would be here at this precise location and that I had to take your family heirloom with me to a remote cave in the Himalayas and spend the rest of my life there in meditation as a *sanyaasi*. This is only a cog in the bigger scheme of things soldier, which you will come to know in time.'

'So you are the person that the holy man referred to in his letter to my late father.'

'Yes, I'm verily the same person soldier. And remember, you must never tell anyone that you met me here. As far as the rest of the world is concerned, I am dead. This I command you as your leader to swear. By the way, who is that fellow with you?'

'My cousin Lakhan Netaji, who brought the holy man's letter to me.'

'You will keep this a secret even from him.'

'I will Netaji. Please rest assured about that. The letter from the holy man further instructs me to go to Jabalpur and take up a career in science.'

'Was that your passion before you joined the INA Shreedhar?'

'Yes Netaji.'

'I will spend no more time here Shreedhar. I also want you to leave immediately after you've handed over to me, your family heirloom.'

'Yes Netaji,' I placed my precious family heirloom into Netaji's hands with tears in my eyes. My lips were chanting the HARE KRISHNA Mahaa Mantram. I was pleasantly surprised to hear that Netaji too was chanting the same mantra. He received it with an immense sense of devotion and then placed his right hand on my head.

'God bless you soldier and thank you for your selfless service to the INA as well as to the motherland... *vande maataram.*'

And then he was gone... it all felt like a waking dream. I knelt down on the ground and was transfixed as my misty eyes saw him fade away rapidly into the distance. A touch on my shoulder brought me back. It was Lakhan.

'Who was that man? I saw you give him Krishna's flute half. Are you sure that he was the same person mentioned in the holy man's letter?'

'Yes, I have absolutely no doubts about it. It is corroborated by what he told me were the contents of the letter. Moreover, his real identity makes him all the more credible.'

'Aren't you going to tell me who the man was?'

'I'm afraid I cannot tell you that my dear Lakhan, as I'm bound by oath. Suffice to say that posterity will see that man as one of the greatest sons of our soil.'

Soon we crossed the border into our motherland where we melted away into a throng of people. We travelled to Kanpur where Lakhan and I parted ways. I then made my way to Jabalpur, while Lakhan headed back to my hometown. All incidents pertaining to Krishna's flute, in the forests of Burma, would be completely erased from his brain by the time he got back home.

At Jabalpur, I found a job as a part time clerk at a local post office. I also enrolled in the local University for a Bachelor's degree in Chemistry. I did not stop till I had attained a PhD. I then got a job as a professor in the same university. Between 1956 and 1986, I married and had two daughters. My wife passed away in 1979 and both my daughters got married and settled in the USA. I retired from the university in 1984 and continued there as an Emeritus. One night I had a vivid dream in which Netaji asked me to come immediately to the precincts of the Pashupatinath temple in Kathmandu, Nepal.

I immediately took the next flight out to Kathmandu and made my way to the temple. There I waited for almost ten days. On the 11th day, I was approached by a holy man whom, I later come to know, was the same person who had written a letter to my father before he died. He told me that he had been sent by Netaji and took me on a long trek through the Himalayas towards the direction of Mt Everest. After a few days of trekking at very high altitudes, during which I fainted thrice, we reached a huge secluded cave. The holy man motioned me to go inside and then walked away. I entered the cave with slight hesitation, but was overjoyed to see Netaji there in deep meditation. He had not aged a bit in the years since I had last seen him, in the jungles of Burma. He was now close to 90 years old but still looked like he was in his 50s. There was a resplendent glow surrounding his body.

I waited patiently for two full days for him to come out of his trance. Even though it was summer, there was a perceptible chill because of the high altitude. Finally, he opened his eyes and I could feel the power emanating from them like concentrated laser beams. Netaji's lips parted in a gentle smile. He recognized me instantly.

'I know that you have been waiting patiently soldier.'

'Netaji, you summoned me and I'm here.'

'Yes, I sent for you; I have further instructions.'

'Yes Netaji.'

'Now that you have admirably fulfilled the professor phase of your life it is time for you to embark on the next phase; the life of Jaarra *baaba*.'

'Jaarra *baaba*?'

'Yes soldier. The time has come for me to reveal certain things about you that you yourself do not know.'

Then Netaji patiently recounted my past lives as Jaarra, Satyavaan Yaadav, and Shambu Yaadav. I listened with rapt attention. It was an overwhelming experience for me. Netaji rose and held my face in his hands.

'It is time for *deeksha* soldier. It is the same *deeksha* my own guru gave me. My guru is the holy man that escorted you here, the same holy man that brought the letter to your father before he died. It is time for you to discard your professor role and become Jaarra *baaba*. It is time for you to step into the higher role for which you have taken this birth as Shreedhar Yaadav.'

Thus I started the process of becoming Jaarra *baaba*. After *deeksha*, for which I had to go through grueling, non-stop penance for three years, Netaji became my Guruji and that's how I have been addressing him since. He then revealed to me that the other flute half was in a temple in the Rann and that I should take custody of it. This is the very half that you hold in your hands now.

When I came here in late 1986, there was only the poor but scholarly priest Radheshyaam *pujari* in the temple. He welcomed me with open arms. The *pujari* told me that he had been informed of my arrival by a certain holy man and had been expecting me. I, in turn, told him about the secret passage under his temple and led him down this passage of which he himself had been completely unaware. Since then, I have been here for the past 25 plus years, waiting for this very day. During these past years, I have made regular trips every year to visit my Guru, Netaji. I now address him as Guruji. He is now close to 127 years of age still looks the same. He intimated to me about your visit here during my last meeting with him. He knows everything about the purpose of your visit and your current project with Stalin Malhotra. Now he says that it is time for the two halves of the flute to unite again. For this purpose you, my dear Dr Shiva Baalan, have to go to the Himalayas to meet with my Guru. Guruji has also requested for Yogi to come along.'

'I find this a bit strange. You had time all these years to reunite the flute halves. Moreover, you yourself could have taken it along with you during your annual visits. Why now and why us? What has that got to do with our quest for the Semmanthaka?' Dr Baalan asked.

'All these answers can be given only by Guruji, Dr Baalan. This has everything to do with your quest, be assured. Beyond this I cannot say anything more as my assigned task ends here. I will therefore advise you to take the next flight to Kathmandu and go to the precincts of the Pashupathinaath temple. There you will be met again by a certain holy man and he will take you to my Guruji.'

'But...'

'Dr Baalan, you do not have to complete your sentence. I can complete it for you. Deep inside your logical heart you find all this, especially the fact that Netaji is still alive and has now become an ascetic, a bit hard to believe. You also find it ridiculous that you now have to go all the way to the Himalayas to see a nonexistent Netaji, isn't it?'

'That's true, as much as I would like to believe you.'

'Ah that skeptical, scientific mind Dr Baalan, even after I have revealed so much to you. I can tell exactly how you feel as I was, myself, a student and a teacher of science. But believe me once again, that this has got everything to do with your quest. One more thing, Dr Baalan. Do not breathe a word of this to your Stalin Malhotra. As much as he is the key person behind your quest, this mission goes far beyond making an addition to someone's treasure collection.'

'What do you mean by that? I will have you know that we are bound by contract to Mr. Malhotra regarding this quest. If this journey is really connected to our quest, then it has got everything to do with my client. Not keeping him in the know will lead to a breach of contract and I do not function that way. I have a reputation to maintain you know.'

'But what is at stake here is beyond whether someone's reputation gets made or marred, something beyond this realm.'

'If this is indeed something beyond this worldly realm, then why us?' There was a tinge of skepticism in Dr Baalan's voice.

'I'm afraid doctor that this answer too can be provided only by my Guruji. Regardless, I request you to take this flute half with you to Guruji. The physical hazards of getting to his Himalayan abode are very challenging and dangerous to say the least. This flute half will protect you along the way. Moreover, this will be your calling card that will identify you when you get there. Also, do not forget to take heavy winter clothing. It is that time of the year.'

Dr Baalan exchanged a long look with his assistant. 'What do you think Yogi?'

'I say that we at least give this some consideration.'

'Alright,' Dr Baalan turned towards the ascetic. 'We may decide to do as you instruct us. But if things are not as you say, then we reserve the right to walk out of this. I'm still very uncomfortable about keeping all this from Mr.

Malhotra. This is the first time in my career that I'm not being open with a client.'

'Let me say this to put you at ease - you may choose to walk out even now and no one will stop you. The Lord does not operate that way. Even at the end of the Gita, he allowed Arjuna to do as he chose. So who am I to force you into anything? But please remember that we are after all His instruments in this mighty *Leela* that He orchestrates. Things will get done as fated even if the instruments change.'

'I get what you are saying Jaarra *baaba*. However, I will decide about this only after I get home. Please give me time to think.'

'Certainly doctor - remember, you must not reveal the secret of the Lord's flute to anyone. This will result in severe repercussions not only to you but to entire humanity. The onus is on your doctor!' Jaarra *baaba* placed the long rectangular box containing the flute half in Dr Baalan's hands.

And somewhere in that another realm, the giant snake once again shifted its coils with a colossal hiss.

The Himalayas

$\mathcal{B}$ack at Ahmedabad, Dr Baalan looked at his mobile phone screen uneasily, scanning a slew of messages from Stalin Malhotra. The earlier messages requested him to call him back and the later ones did not hide their irritation as to why the archeo was not responding. The last and the latest one commanded him to drop by his office immediately. Dr Baalan immediately called Stalin, who picked it up with a gruff hello.

'Sorry Stalin, we had gone back to the Rann for more surveying.'

'Without informing me Dr Baalan? I hope you remember the terms of our contract. It explicitly mentions that you have to keep me informed of your whereabouts as long as the contract holds good.'

'My bad Stalin, I overlooked it in the rush of things.'

'And why did you switch off your phone? At least you would have known that I was calling.'

'It would not have mattered sir, because there is no cell phone coverage at the Rann.'

'Anyway, what was it that made you rush back to the Rann?'

'Umm... nothing,' Dr Baalan replied, trying hard to conceal the uneasiness in his voice. 'We just thought that we should do another search near the creek area.'

'And did you find anything interesting?'

'Negative.'

'Maybe you should look on the other side of the creek. Anyway, keep me informed of your whereabouts from now on Dr Baalan and I want to see you both ASAP.' Malhotra did not hide the displeasure in his voice as he hung up.

'Phew,' Dr Baalan ran his hand through his hair as he shook his head at Yogi. 'This is going to be more difficult than we thought. It was just for one day that we were gone from Stalin's orbit and he is upset. I don't know how he will react if he knows the truth. Moreover, how are we going to go the Himalayas to meet this Guruji again without informing Stalin? I have never snuck around like this in my professional life before. I feel so disconcerted Yogi.'

'Relax Dr Baalan, I have an idea. Let us go to meet Mr. Malhotra in person and tell him that we need a break of a week or two in order to unwind and get a fresh perspective on our quest. This break will be an unpaid one. We can use this time to check whether this Guruji is for real or not.'

'Hmm…not a bad idea,' Dr Baalan replied at length. 'But believe me Yogi, Stalin is no fool and cannot be lied to easily. I'm a bad liar too; very, very bad in important matters. Just ask my family.'

'Leave this to me Dr Baalan. I'll handle it.'

'If he finds out somehow that we are going to Kathmandu in search of a Guruji, who could also turn out to be our long missing Netaji, all hell will break loose. Other than being angry, he will think that we have gone insane!'

'Honestly Dr Baalan, with all due respect, after all that we heard and experienced at the Rann with Jaarra *baaba*, is there any reason to be skeptical? At least, I'm not. I believe we have something tangible here.'

'My heart tells me that we should take this trip to Kathmandu, but my science-conditioned brain still rebels, Yogi.'

Yogi placed a reassuring hand on Dr Baalan's shoulder. 'Let us give the heart a chance this time… and please leave Mr. Malhotra to me.'

'If you say so.'

The following day, Yogi ambled up the ladder that led to the top deck of Stalin Malhotra's luxury submarine yacht. The yacht was now floating on the surface exposing its magnificent steel-blue hull. Malhotra was standing with his back to Yogi, facing the sea. A brisk breeze was blowing across the deck.

'So tell me Yogi, where is the good doctor?'

'Dr Baalan could not come as he is under the weather. He conveys his apologies for not being able to make it.'

'And it looks like our mission too is under the weather,' Stalin Malhotra turned and faced Yogi with a forced smile.

'It appears so Mr. Malhotra and that is why Dr Baalan and I request you to give us a two-week hiatus so that we can come back with a fresh perspective on this entire business.'

'That is a big ask, don't you think Yogi?'

'Sure sir. I understand. That is why we are not asking to be paid during this short leave.'

'You see, Yogi,' Malhotra's voice and visage became perceptibly sterner. 'Money is not an issue for a person like me. Results are what I seek.'

'Sir I understand where you are coming from and respect your point of view. But this quest is a very tough one and perhaps requires a fresh view, an out of the box perspective. For this we need a gap in the way we are reviewing how things have transpired thus far,' Yogi replied with conviction, his eyes making full contact with Stalin's steel grey ones.

'Okay, I grant it,' Malhotra replied at length. 'But I want you two back on the quest exactly two weeks from now - come sun, moon, or rain.'

'Thank you sir.'

They took the Jet Airways early morning flight the next day to Kathmandu via New Delhi. There was lot of turbulence in the air, especially in the New Delhi-Kathmandu leg of the journey, closer to the destination. Since it was bang in the middle of winter, the air cut them like a cold whiplash as they stepped out of Kathmandu airport, in spite of their heavy winter accoutrements.

From the airport, they took a cab to the Pashupathinaath temple and, as instructed, they waited at the bottom of the steps. The minutes melted into hours and still no one came. The cold was getting to them and moreover, they were starting to get hungry. There was a tea stall across the streets from the steps and the wafting aromas whetted their appetites even further. Soon they found themselves sipping some hot tea and munching *samosas*. Then it was back to their vigil at the bottom of the steps. It was almost 4 pm and yet nobody had come.

It had grown even colder and the wind was cutting through their jackets. Suddenly Dr Baalan turned, sensing a presence behind him. He was stunned because he had not seen anyone approach them from any direction. Yet, there was a bare footed hermit standing on the step above, dressed only in a loin cloth, with a staff in his hand. His body was covered in sacred ash giving it a grey color and his grey beard just melted into it. His eyes were burning red and yet there was an aura of sublime calm about the hermit.

Dr Baalan felt a warm glow emanate from the body of the hermit, envelope him and dispel the cold and shivering.

'Follow me Dr Baalan,' the hermit spoke in fluent English. 'We are embarking on a long journey by foot and it is going to take us a good two days. The place where we are heading can only be approached on foot.'

'Is that so?' Dr Baalan did not hide his consternation in his voice.

'Yes, Dr Baalan. But believe me when I say that you will get used to it. It is only the first few steps that are the most difficult. Once we get going, it will get easier. Law of inertia, doctor.'

Dr Baalan looked at Yogi quizzically. 'A hermit alluding to laws of physics. Cannot get any weirder,' he thought.

'Yes Dr Baalan. I'm a hermit who knows a bit of physics too.' The hermit sported a faint smile on his visage.

'Another mind reading fellow,' Dr Baalan muttered inwardly.

'Yes indeed, doctor, even the man that you are going to meet is one. Let me also tell you that the path will get steep and treacherous as we proceed further on our journey. Moreover, it is snowing very heavily up in the mountains. We have to watch for other dangerous situations too. But believe me when I say that you will have nothing to worry about. The flute half will protect you from all calamities. Even if we get into the direst situations, just remain calm and the situation will pass. But do not do anything foolish out of panic. Then even the flute half may not be able to save you. You see, there is a limit to even the Lord's miracles.'

'*Saadhuji*. I believe you. But I'm not as physically fit like my assistant here is, for this high altitude trek. So why don't I stay here and just send my assistant with you?'

'No Doctor sir. Without you, this journey will not happen. Once again, I tell you that you have no cause for worry. Just trust me and you will see.'

'Alright *Saadhuji*, let's go. But let me tell you that if my body starts rebelling, I will not proceed further!'

They started walking at a slow but steady pace through the crowded streets of the city. In two hours' time, they had reached the outskirts and now the scenery was becoming more and more mountainous and the path had a marked upward gradient. The layer of snow on the path, which had started out as a mere dusting gradually became thicker and, after a while, the clear crunch of the ice was heard under their hard boots. As for the hermit, he continued to merrily walk barefoot, totally confounding Dr Baalan and Yogi.

Within a couple of hours, their pace slowed as the altitude steadily increased. Now they were touching 12,000 feet and the path was getting narrower and narrower. They skirted a deep gorge; a steep wall of rock on their left and a precipitous fall to their right. It was beginning to get dark and after a while they came across a plateau where they spotted a small hut.

'We will rest here for the night,' the hermit said. The hut was empty. It was a very small structure made of bamboo poles and a straw thatch. The walls were made of crudely arranged bricks. Regardless, it was a welcome thing for Dr Baalan, who was close to complete exhaustion. There was a bit of firewood in one corner of the hut. Obviously, this was some kind of a rest house for travelers.

The hermit gathered the firewood in the center of the hut, then folded his palms together and closed his eyes. Within minutes, a bright yellow ray emanated from his palms and set alight the firewood, leaving Dr Baalan and his assistant stunned. Very soon, the hut was filled with the warmth of the fire. Dr Baalan and Yogi unzipped their sleeping bags inside the hut and almost immediately fell into a deep sleep. As for the hermit, he continued to sit beside the fire in deep meditation and he would remain that way through the night.

The light of the morning filtered through the doorway of the hut and awakened the sleeping duo. Dr Baalan stretched as he got up to a sitting position. He felt so well rested. It had been ages since he had slept so well. Besides him, Yogi began to stir and very soon he was up too. The fire was still burning. It appeared that the hermit had brought more firewood through the night even though he had not moved from his spot. There was also a kettle on the flame filled with boiling water. The hermit added a tea like powder to the kettle and the entire hut filled with a strange but very pleasant aroma. After a while the hermit pointed to the kettle and told Dr Baalan. 'Drink this and it will warm your entire body like red hot coals. You will not even need a jacket after that.'

The hermit then emptied the contents of the kettle into a wooden mug and offered it Dr Baalan.

'Drink it hot. That's when it is the most effective.'

Dr Baalan blew on the mug with his mouth before slowly lifting it to his lips to sip. The taste was very much like tea, but very strong. As the liquid entered his food pipe, he felt as if his insides were scalded by fire itself. By the time he finished, he felt like it was summer outside. He began unbuttoning the top buttons of his jacket - it felt too warm.

'I advise you to keep the jacket on to conserve heat. It will last you through the entire day as we travel through the bitter cold.' The hermit now refilled the mug and passed it on to Yogi.

The wind-chill had died down to tolerable levels this morning as they followed the hermit along a narrow path that steadily climbed upwards to 20,000 feet. The hermit himself was still clad in his loin cloth and was still chugging along like an engine without any apparent discomfiture. His footing was sure like that of a mountain goat's as he led the twosome towards a panoramic lookout from where the snowy path took a hairpin bend.

The view was spectacular to say the least; the rays of the morning sun reflected off the snowy mountain cliffs in a variety of hues and colors. Dr Baalan got so completely engrossed in the unfolding panorama that, for a moment, he forgot all his little aches and pains. For the next three hours, they kept going till Dr Baalan signaled that he would like a small break. The place where they halted was more open in the sense that the sheer cliff to their left had given way to a slope. The wind had now picked up raising the chill factor but hermit's drink was still doing its job of keeping them warm.

Dr Baalan sat down on the path and pulled out three chocolate bars from his backpack and offered one to Yogi, who sat beside him and the second one to the hermit. 'I have no taste for these modern foods. Anyway I eat only on rare occasions and cannot remember when I last ate.' The hermit politely declined the confectionary.

'You mean that you can live without food?' Dr Baalan sounded incredulous.

'Yes, you can say so. Direct energy absorption from the sun rays. This is an ancient yogic technique called sun gazing. And these days this technique has been honed further by Hira Ratan Manek'

'Amazing, indeed!'

While the archeologist and his associate munched on the chocolate bars, little did they realize that eyes were watching them closely from the top of the slope and from behind a huge rock. Actually, the unexpected presence of the humans had been sort of a distraction for these eyes because their actual focus was on the solitary bharal which was standing a hundred meters away. The humans below, save the hermit on the path, were unaware of this deadly game of hunter and prey going on at the top of the slope above them. The beautiful grey pelt of the elusive snow leopard blended perfectly into the snow, making it completely invisible to the hyper alert senses of the bharal. The hunter now regained her original focus and lowered herself to the ground as she slowly inched towards her prey. It was imperative that the hunter had to be successful this time around as she had two little mouths to feed; two young cubs waiting for her in a cave high above in the mountains. She had spotted the bharal from her lair and had determinedly made her way to her prey, expending a lot of vital energy in the process. She had not fed for almost a few days now and now she had to bring down this sure footed, wild mountain sheep. The bharal was facing away from her and was standing on an eight foot high piece of rock.

The sheep was aware of the human presence below but chose to ignore it. It had seen many such trekkers in the past and had gotten used to them. But the presence of the humans had worked to the snow leopard's advantage as it had slightly dulled the senses of the bharal. The ram did not even have the time to react as the snow below the rock it was standing on suddenly came alive. The snow leopard shot up like a rocket and clamped it jaws around the bharal's throat and they toppled together down. The death bleat of the bharal as well as a muffled roar was the only sound that carried down to the ears of the humans below.

'The snow leopard has made its hunt,' the hermit remarked aloud.

'Was that what the sound was? Where, where?' Dr Baalan immediately reached for the binoculars in his backpack.

'Up there,' the hermit pointed to the slope above them.

Dr Baalan whirled in the direction the hermit had pointed to, with the binoculars over his eyes, but could not see a thing.

'Concentrate on that spot for a while. If you are lucky, you may see her.'

Again Dr Baalan could see nothing. He was almost about to give up when his eyes picked up a faint movement on the snow. It was as if the snow had come alive. He saw a sheep like animal being dragged over the top of the slope by a grey shadow. Then they were gone, just like that. Suddenly, there was an audible groan as the snow on the slope came to life and rippled like a blanket.

'Avalanche!' the hermit exclaimed in alarm. Before he could say another word the entire snow cover on the slope came hurtling down towards the hapless humans.

'Don't panic. Just stand your ground. Nothing will happen to us. I repeat, just stand your ground.'

It all seemed to be happening in slow motion - the snow hurtling down towards them. Dr Baalan and Yogi braced for the inevitable, when suddenly the mass of snow rose up and went over the top of their heads. They could feel the air as it swooshed past their scalps and hurtled down into the valley below. It was all over in a matter of seconds; such was its speed and ferocity. It took a while for Dr Baalan and Yogi to regain their composure. The hermit was completely unperturbed.

'You have survived an avalanche. It was sure death coming at you. But the flute half saved you.'

'It was all ignited by the commotion created by those creatures above on the slope, I'm sure now, in retrospect. I could not see clearly but there was an animal that dragged a sheep over the slope,' Dr Baalan breathed hard after his near brush with death.

'That was the snow leopard; the rarest of the rarest cats. You are lucky to even get this fleeting glimpse. Many trekkers come here year after year to see this elusive animal and go back disappointed. The vibrations generated by this hunt were enough to trigger this mini avalanche.'

'You call this mini?!'

'Yes Dr Baalan. The major ones destroy everything on their path, bringing entire mountain sides down.'

'The miracle of miracles was that this avalanche just skimmed on top of us, missing us. I just can't explain the science of it. In all probability, it should have swept us along with it down to those depths there. It's all so incredible,' Dr Baalan was still shaking.

'The miracle is in your hands, - a part of that divine musical instrument.'

'Yes, now I have seen it with my own eyes. There are still things beyond the realm of man's comprehension in this universe.'

The journey for the rest of the day was uneventful. They crossed the 20,000 feet mark. Once again they came across another open area on the side of the mountain and again there was an identical hut like the one they had sheltered in the previous night. Once again, the hermit gathered a similar heap of firewood from the side of the hut and deposited it in the center. Before long the fire was burning bright and the hermit was lost in meditation. Dr Baalan and Yogi were about to lie down when the hermit spoke with closed eyes.

'Dr Baalan, are you and your assistant familiar with the legend of the Semmanthaka gem.'

'Yes to some extent I am. But my assistant, Yogi, has a more in-depth knowledge of its history,' Dr Baalan replied, startled, as he had not expected this question from the hermit. 'As it is the focus of our quest, Yogi did quite a bit of research on it, especially ancient scripture.'

'Well, I'm going to retell the story of that jewel, except now, there will be certain nuances that you may not have come across however detailed your research was. Pay close attention to me as this may yield vital clues in your quest.'

'Sure sir,' Dr Baalan quipped. 'We are all ears, especially me.'

'I'll begin this tale with a vital cog in the narrative; the lion. Indeed, the king of the jungle, or more appropriately, the king of the saltpans of the Rann played a pivotal role in the entire story of the gem.'

Some time before the Mahabharata

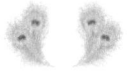

$\mathcal{T}$he male lion was close to nine years of age, past his prime and with a handsome reddish brown mane that was thick all the way to the elbows of his massive forearms. The same mane had served as padding from the mighty blows of rival males, eager to usurp his position as a pride lord which he shared with his half-brother. His eyes still had amber fire in them as he walked with a regal swagger, his open mouth revealing massive canines. And yet, he was just barely back on his feet. His hind flanks bore terrible claw rakes and those wounds were still fresh and burning; wounds that he had received just a week back. His regal gait hid the fire of hunger raging through his belly. He had not fed for close to eight days. Most importantly, his half-brother, his constant companion, was not by his side. He would walk forever alone from now on. This defiant walk of the defeated loner hid the fact that he had lost his pride, his latest litter of cubs, and his sustenance.

Just eight days ago, he and his half-brother were the undisputed monarchs of the salt pans of the Rann abutting this scrub forest. They had ruled over a pride consisting of eight lionesses and their cubs, a pride which they had wrested five years back from the then resident pride male. They had, in fact, taken over without even a semblance of a fight as the then pride male had been old and feeble. Since then, it had been five years of male lion bliss or as close as it could get to it. The alpha and beta females of the pride were expert huntresses and there was always something on the dining table in the form of wild ass or gazelle meat, even in days of paucity, as it so often happens in the salt wastes. The two half-brothers also mated with gay abandon and sired healthy litters over this time of their reign. The males also came into their own whenever it came to bringing down big game like Nilgai.

That five year reign, short by human standards but decent by male lion standards, were years of unbridled ferocity and brutality when it came to snuffing down challenges from rival males as these half-brothers enforced their will and even annexed adjacent pride lands. However, their reign had come to an end eight days back when a group of three nomadic males made their final charge after three failed attempts over the preceding months.

Actually, there were four of the nomads, their number being reduced by one, only eight days back. Before we come to that, let me tell you that three months ago, these four nomads, all of them brothers from the same litter had arrived as wary youngsters who had been rejected two years back from their own natal pride area in what is now Junaagadh. Two years, the most part of which they had spent in a mixture of trepidation, chance, skill, and even recklessness where luck could have easily gone against them. This two year period was akin to going through a test of fire, a coming of age. All this pain had made them tougher mentally. Moreover, these two passing years had tipped them into their prime with their strength on an ascendant.

Yet the foursome had hesitated when they waited at the edge of the territory ruled by the half-brothers. The boundary areas of the pride were heavily scent-marked by the pride males and told them unequivocally that they were trespassing at their own peril. The first two times they came face to face with the half-brothers, they turned tail without even a semblance of a fight. But the third time around, they had come across one of the half-brothers by himself at the edge of the pride area and that had emboldened them to stand their ground. But the half-brother, a veteran of many brutal territorial skirmishes, held his own valiantly against the three pronged challenge of the nomads. In spite of suffering a terrible claw rake on his left side, he had managed to see the fight through and even inflicted a terrible bite injury on the left forepaw of one of the nomads. The warring parties withdrew behind their respective lines but the injuries on both sides gave notice of the chink in their invincibility. Now both sides knew that the other could be beaten given the right circumstances.

The fourth time around, the half-brothers had met the four nomads head on, just nine days back. This time, the half-brothers were furious because the nomads had come quite deep into the pride land in an act of open defiance. For a long while, rival parties stared each other down ferociously, neither backing off. The stalemate was broken when the half-brothers charged the nomads with full throated roars that emanated from deep within their abdomens. The volley of roars ate into the confidence of the four young nomads and they turned tail to scamper away in four different directions. The half-brothers, however, managed to chase down and corner one of the four males in isolation. This was the same male that had been bitten in his forepaw by one of the half-brothers in the previous skirmish.

The young nomad suddenly found himself in a fight to death against two males experienced in fighting. To his credit he fought valiantly. But due to his wound, as well as being without the support of his fellow nomads, he lost ground rapidly to the relentless ferocity of the twin attack by the half-brothers. The young nomad suddenly found an opening and rushed out to clamber on a nearby tree. But he was not quick enough. One of the half-brothers jumped up from behind him and clamped his jaws on the exposed lower spine of the nomad. Instantly, the nomad flipped headlong into the ground and lost his senses. Then came the crushing bite to the skull and it was over for the young nomad.

The two half-brothers swaggered back victoriously back to their pride. Little did they know that the night would bring in another territorial skirmish. The three remaining nomads regrouped at the edge of the pride land and roared forlornly to their fourth companion who would never return. One would have expected the nomads to concede defeat, but the absence of their companion made them even more defiant. As dusk approached, the three remaining nomads marched back into the pride land roaring their challenge at the half-brothers. The response from the half-brothers was one of contempt because of their recent victory. Only one of the half-brothers ventured out into the darkness to meet the challenge.

As soon as the three nomads came into his sights, he launched himself at the threesome, roaring ferociously. Again the three brothers made an about turn and scampered back to the edge of the pride land with the half-brother hot in pursuit. The chase continued past the borders and led the lions to a dry streambed. It was here that the nomads suddenly halted their run and turned around to face their pursuer. Actually, this was a ploy executed to brilliant perfection, to split and isolate their rivals.

They charged him in unison. Now the tables had turned and the half-brother was caught in a fight for his life. Regardless, he fought valiantly as the paws, claws and canines relentlessly tore into him from all sides and slowly started to wear him down. The pride male was now hunching down and instinctively protecting his spine from getting bitten and paralyzed. But his soft underbelly was now exposed and bore the brunt of the claw rakes and bites. Blood started flowing from his underbelly and the half-brother began rapidly losing his stamina. Confident of victory, the three nomads briefly paused in their attack and rested. The half-brother had now completely lost his strength, due to massive loss of blood, and could not even get up.

At this point, the other half-brother pride male came in to assist his doomed sibling. He was immediately dispatched by a fierce three pronged attack by the nomads who had now gained supreme confidence. The nomads then returned their attention to the heavily injured half-brother and launched another volley of attacks. The half-brother was now slowly descending into a leonine coma but there was still some life left in him and he weakly flailed his paws as the three nomads launched a fresh wave of attacks. Finally, towards the small hours of the morning, with a crescent moon shining in the cloudless sky, they held him in their jaws; one his head, the second his stomach, and the third his hindquarters. After a protracted minute or so, they heaved in synergy and broke the back of the half-brother like a twig. The cracking of the spine was audible for miles in that dry wilderness.

The surviving half-brother did not return to his pride land. He somehow sensed the change of fortune and begun putting as much distance as possible between him and the rival nomads, who would now inevitably become the new kings of his pride. His innings as a pride male had come to an end and he had become the nomad.

Five years of complete dependence on his lionesses for hunting game had jaded the hunter in him and now he had not eaten for eight days and hunger was searing like a hot sword through his belly. Night waxed upon the land as the big feline walked seemingly aimlessly, even though his eyes were scouring the landscape for the chance of an easy meal. Darkness completely blanketed the forest. This was not a problem as his night vision was one of the best in the animal kingdom and had not faded a bit, even in his advancing leonine years.

Just then his eyes caught a glint of something dazzling, as if suspended in the air, moving at a leisurely pace far away to his left. It was shimmering in the darkness - its light almost like a mini sun; such was its dazzling brilliance. Normally jungle cats avoid light during the night. It is no good to be visible to the prey. Instincts honed over the eons had embossed this natural aversion to light and fire in the dark. But then, something else caught his eye. He could make out a faint outline of a creature moving along. The shimmering, dazzling object seemed to be dangling from the creature's neck. The initial instincts of the male lion were to move away from this creature. He and his feline kind had a grudging respect for this creature and would always take the greatest pains to avoid it. Moreover, the shining object made it even more imperative for him to slink away silently and melt into the darkness. But then his wicked hunger got the better of his animal instincts. So he began moving in the direction of the creature to investigate.

Back at the city of Dwaaraka..

$\mathcal{T}$he dark King sat pensively, his chin resting on his right palm and with his elbow on the arm hold of his throne. The sleek athletic look of each and every part of his highly toned body was still preserved in the eighth decade of his life. The beatific smile that was omniscient on his lips was missing today, and now, as he sat by himself on his throne with all his courtiers retired for the night, the brows of his frown darkened.

Times were not good for Dwaaraka, his beautiful kingdom by the sea. The land was reeling from a bitter draught that had ravaged the kingdom for a third straight season. Not a single drop of rain had fallen all this time and the populace was reeling. The only good thing that had brought cheer to him in recent times was the surprise visit by a close friend from his childhood, Sudaama, on whom he had showered a huge chunk of his own personal wealth. Of course, the dark King had also shown his largesse to his subjects by opening up his coffers, which had mitigated their suffering to a large extent.

But still the draught raged, and the dark King, blessed as he was with infinite supernatural powers to create rain even in the most barren of deserts, had bound himself by the shackles of fate and time that had been pre-programmed high up in the heavens. The *Leela* had to be played out in its entirety without a single event out of script. And the dark King had accepted this like a warrior. Yet, there was another event that had shaken him to his core - an event that had transpired in his court the previous evening.

Satrajit, a nobleman from his city, and a fervent devotee of the Sun god, Lord Surya, had returned to Dwaaraka after offering severe penance to Surya in the burning deserts to the northwest of his land. It was a herculean feat, one full year of standing on one leg right in the middle of the desert without even a morsel of food or a drop of water. During this time he had gone through a wall of hellfire; the burning heat of the day, the deadly chill of the desert night, fierce sand storms, and stings of poisonous scorpions and snakes. But he had not flinched, so lost was he in the full trance of supremely high level yoga, a level that can be attained only by the most fervent practitioners. The penance became so powerful that by the end of the year flowers started spouting up all around him in that unforgiving desert. Not only that, a brilliant ray of light descended to the very spot where Satrajit stood and brought him out of his penance.

When he opened his eyes, he saw a jewel lying on the ground shining with a brilliance that almost paralleled the Sun god. That was when he knew that he had succeeded at what he had been previously thought of as impossible; to get the Semmanthaka gem as a gift from Lord Surya. Satrajit's joy knew no bounds as he knelt in thanksgiving to Lord Surya and then he headed back to his home at Dwaaraka with the jewel proudly adorning his neck in a locket.

Such was the effulgence that emanated from the gem that the people of Dwaaraka thought it was the Sun god himself who was walking towards their city. When they saw that it was their very own Satrajit who had returned unscathed from his suicidal penance in the middle of the desert, their joy knew no bounds. Moreover, he now had a treasure that even the *Devas* coveted - the Semmanthaka gem that had extraordinary powers. One such power was that every day, it yielded *eight bharas* of pure gold. The gem, therefore, was also an answer to the economic woes currently besieging their city and this was also one of the primary reasons for which Satrajit had undertaken this penance.

But as the nobleman sat in the privacy of his home, fondly looking at the pure gold that the gem had yielded this far, the first pangs of greed and possession fleetingly whispered in his heart.

Yes, he had an audience with his dark King next day, regarding the gem. He was after all keeping the promise that he had made to everyone in Dwaaraka that if he succeeded in his brutal penance, he would personally take the gem to his King and present it to him in the larger interests of the kingdom, to help tide over the present difficult times. Now hesitation was creeping into his resolve. This gem and all the gold that was there, and the gold that was to come, would make him richer even than the legendary Kubera. How could he get out of handing the gem over to his king, he wondered.

The next day, he walked into the court of his King with the gem proudly adorning his neck. The King was enormously pleased to see Satrajit and welcomed him warmly. After small talk and pleasantries, the King came directly to the point. He pointed at the gem and asked the nobleman whether he was ready to hand it over to the royal treasury for the benefit of the people of Dwaaraka, as promised. The King also told him that the reserves in the treasury had dropped precariously and now the gold that this gem yielded was badly required to stabilize the kingdom.

Moreover, the King also promised Satrajit that the gold would only go towards the welfare of the subjects and none towards the King's personal wealth or to any of his family members. It was then that Satrajit rose hesitatingly and conveyed that he was not ready to part with the gem.

Surprised and dismayed the King tried to reason with him and so did the other courtiers. But Satrajit's resolve to hold on to the gem only got firmer. Finally, the King resigned himself to the decision and let the nobleman go back home with the gem. Before Satrajit left, the King reminded him of an appointment that Prasenjit (Satrajit's younger brother who lived with him) had with the King regarding an important land dispute later that evening. Satrajit promised King Krishna that he would make sure to remind his brother.

Satrajit's refusal to part with the gem for helping the state treasury perturbed Krishna to the core. How even the best of men changed, swayed by the dazzle of gold and precious stones was something he knew all too well. He had seen, countless times in the past, lofty ideals and promises evaporating under the lure of wealth. Even the *Devas* were not immune to this and Satrajit was after all a human being.

So lost was Krishna in his thoughts that he did not see his elder brother Balaraama walk in. A muscular giant, almost seven feet in height, Balaraama commanded an enormous presence. His body was still strong but a discernible paunch betrayed his recent decadence – his fondness for wine and other worldly pleasures. This was certainly redolent of the times soon to visit on Dwaaraka and the Yaadavas.

'Well Satrajit, for all his brutal penance and big promises, turns out to be a mere mortal after all, brother Krishna.'

'We have seen people reneging on worse in our lifetime brother, and no doubt we will see even more in the future. This refusal by Satrajit pales in comparison. We will have to find another way to bolster our treasury.'

'Well, I guess so Krishna. Anyway, it is time for me to retire for the night.'

'As a matter of fact I have a previously scheduled appointment with Satrajit's younger brother Prasenjit very soon.'

'Indeed, a very knotty issue concerning that disputed land around the temple which Satrajit and Prasenjit claim as belonging to their family and not to the public.'

'Yes brother. It is a very important matter that I have to sort out before the *mahaa utsav* next month. I will update you regarding that in the morning.' The beatific smile returned to Krishna's lips.

It was really dark now and Prasenjit walked as if in a trance. His steps were wayward due to the heavy intake of wine that he had consumed earlier that evening at his elder brother Satrajit's place. The latter had just returned from Krishna's court, proudly and possessively squeezing the gem in his right palm.

'Nobody is going to take this gem from me. It is forever mine,' Satrajit had proclaimed proudly to his younger brother Prasenjit.

'Brother Satrajit, I'm really happy for you. To tell you the truth brother, I was worried that you would hand over the gem to King Krishna.'

'I'm relieved myself Prasenjit. From now on, this legendary Semmanthaka is going to be our family heirloom. Let's eat and celebrate.'

After a sumptuous dinner, accompanied by pitchers of heavy rice wine, the brothers continued drinking and chatting for a very long time as they sat on Satrajit's bed in his huge mansion. It was then that Satrajit fondly placed the gem around his brother's neck as he gulped down another pitcher of rice wine.

'Looks good on you my dearest Prasenjit. Tonight this jewel is yours.'

Prasenjit was overjoyed at this gesture from his elder brother.

'Oh brother Satrajit. I'm overjoyed by your gesture. Let me celebrate this by taking a walk around town with this jewel on me. As you may be aware, I also have an appointment tonight with King Krishna regarding the disputed temple land. I promise to be back soon.'

'Sure brother, sure. I had almost forgotten about that. The King mentioned it to me as I left his court. But now you are dead drunk my little brother. How can you meet the King in this condition? It will be considered extremely disrespectful.'

'Brother Satrajit, you are forgetting that we are now proud owners of the immortal Semmanthaka and this means we will be richer than King Krishna himself with all that gold that this gem is going to give us every day. King Krishna cannot refuse me now even if I am dead drunk. Forget King Krishna, even Lord Vishnu in *Vaikunth* cannot refuse me. We are the richest and greatest in all the three worlds!' Prasenjit downed another pitcher.

'Ha, ha, ha, brother, you are so right. How can you not be? You are, after all, my blood. Yes we will be richer and mightier than even the gods themselves. Alright then, good night and let me know in the morning how the meeting went. That land is ours.'

Satrajit was so inebriated by this time that he fell flat on his bed and passed out. As for Prasenjit, he staggered out of his brother's house. Even though deeply intoxicated, the alcohol had not gotten to him as much as it had gotten to his older brother. As he swayed out into the night, into the streets, empty save for a few strays, the gem around his neck shone brilliantly as if it was daylight, and lit up the surrounds.

Prasenjit kept on walking. He did not even know when he digressed from his intended route and reached the outskirts of the city and entered the scrub forest surrounding it. Moreover, he had completely forgotten his royal appointment with Krishna. Darkness had fallen on the land and Prasenjit had still not stopped.

He was totally oblivious to his surrounds even as the effects of the rice wine began waning considerably. Stumbling through the dark, Prasenjit abruptly realized that he had lost his way, and more importantly, forgotten his appointment. He had strayed into the deepest parts of the forest where no human had ever entered in recent times. Prasenjit halted in his tracks and surveyed the scenery. There was nothing but scrub jungle all around.

The faraway trees looked like dark sentinels against the blackened sky. Prasenjit resigned himself to the current situation. Moreover, he was too exhausted to continue. He decided to find a safe place to spend the night and make his way back to town the next morning. As for the missed appointment with the King, he decided that it was the King who needed him and his brother more than they needed him. They held the ace card; the mighty gem that even the gods themselves coveted. He resumed his walk but halted abruptly once again. He thought he saw a shadow move on his right. He turned and strained his eyes in that direction, but could not discern anything beyond the circumference of light thrown by the gem around his neck.

When he resumed his journey, once more he perceived a shadow moving on his right, a shadow as big as a bullock. He turned once again in that direction and once again, his straining eyes could perceive nothing in the darkness beyond. This exercise was repeated a couple more times before Prasenjit began to panic, sensing that he was being stalked and that whatever was stalking him froze like a stone whenever he turned to look in its direction. A shiver of fear ran through his body. Could this be a bandit staking him out, he shuddered. Moreover, he was unarmed and alone. He once again turned and looked to his right. But there was nothing out of the ordinary to alarm him. 'Maybe it is the wine,' he convinced himself.

Prasenjit's next plan was to find shelter for the night. He spotted a tree to his left. He decided to climb the tree and rest on it for the night. He made his way up the huge trunk adroitly and then found a thick bough on which he could perch comfortably. He once again surveyed the far surrounds. Nothing moved and everything seemed calm except for the sound of the crickets. There was a dry stream bed a bit further to the left of the direction in which Prasenjit had walked earlier and it passed right under the distal end of the bough on which he was resting.

As the night wore on, Prasenjit felt exhaustion and sleep covered him like a heavy blanket. Leaning his back on the main trunk, Prasenjit closed his eyes. A steady breeze had started to blow from his right and his nostrils picked up a faint ammoniac odor. It was an odor that he was both familiar and unfamiliar with; in the sense that he had come across the odor sometime in the remote past but could not pinpoint when. Then he stopped thinking anymore and drifted to sleep.

A deafening roar that seemed to come from the very depths of hell thundered him wide awake with a wildly beating heart as the full blast of the sound hit his body and along with it, an acrid ammoniac odor. The sound came from below and the terrified Prasenjit turned his eyes downwards. The light emanating from the gem helped to clearly discern the threat below. A huge tawny creature with glowing amber eyes was slowly trying to make its way up the main trunk. The eyes impaled him and exuded a ferocity and a desire to consume him bone and sinew. It was rage fueled by pure hunger and Prasenjit was the intended meal.

For a brief moment Prasenjit was frozen with fear before he composed himself and looked for options. The choice of this tree was certainly not optimal for this situation. In fact, he was sitting on the highest bough that could bear his full weight. So, there was no use trying to find a higher and safer perch. He looked down below and saw that the beast had now almost climbed halfway. Unlike leopards, lions are not expert climbers even though they can skim up some short, stout trees when desperate. But this was one desperate hungry lion, intent on getting to its prey. The only option for Prasenjit was to move to the distal end of the bough on which he was seated. The last option of jumping to the ground and making a dash was nothing but suicidal. There was no way any man could outrun a lion.

Prasenjit slowly groped his way with trembling hands to the far end of the branch. But there was a limit to this as, beyond a point, the bough looked thin and weak. Now Prasenjit began to worry whether the lion too would get onto the bough and snap it.

It was then that Prasenjit's memories were rekindled, regarding the ammoniac odor. He had once been to a travelling circus during his childhood, and the same odor had emanated from the cages holding the lions and tigers. It was due to the high ammonia content in the urine of these cats from their ultra-high protein diet of raw flesh. The male lion had now almost reached the bough when it somehow seemed to lose its grip. As it slid down the main trunk, the raking sound of its claws was clearly audible, as the lion tried desperately to find purchase. It held itself at the halfway point for a brief while before losing grip again and jumping sideways to the ground on its left. Once again it shimmied up the trunk only to lose grip and jump back below. After the fifth unsuccessful attempt, it positioned itself below the point where Prasenjit was perched and snarled and roared, baring its massive canines at him.

Prasenjit was by now visibly shaken. But somehow he held on. His next instinct was to grope his way back to his original position at the proximal end of the bough. But he stopped himself. What if the beast attempted to climb again and was successful in reaching him? So he stayed put. The male lion now lay down on the ground and fixed its glowering eyes on him. It decided to play the waiting game.

The wind was slowly beginning to pick up and Prasenjit looked above to the skies. Dark clouds were gathering signaling rain. Within an hour, the wind become very strong and the first droplets began falling on Prasenjit's temple. 'Rain in this seemingly endless drought!! So the legend about the gem is true that it brings rain and prosperity even to the most wretched of lands,' Prasenjit marveled. The skies were now streaked with lighting and there were thunderclaps all around. Prasenjit hoped that these sounds would somehow drive the lion away from its vigil, but to his chagrin he found it still rooted to its spot.

Another titanic thunderclap followed a lightning streak and this time Prasenjit, to his relief, found that the big cat had gone. The rain reached full ferocity and the dry streambed below started coming to life. Another hour passed and the lion was still gone. But the rain and the wind did not wane in their collective intensity. The next big gust hit Prasenjit's bough with such a force that it snapped at its middle and hung precariously. Now Prasenjit dangled helplessly 12 feet from the ground, when previously, he had been another 10 feet higher. Any moment, it seemed to him, the bough would snap completely and send him crashing to the ground. He closed his eyes wondering what to do next. Consequently, Prasenjit did not see the giant forepaws of the lion which reappeared out of nowhere launch itself into the air reaching out to him. They connected to Prasenjit's body with such force that he was brought down from the bough in that single blow. One of the claws hooked on to the locket bearing the gem ripping it away from Prasenjit's neck.

The locket flew in the air in a long shiny arc and landed in the gushing water of the previously bone dry streambed. As for Prasenjit, his neck was broken in the fall to the ground. He died on impact. The violence in the skies reached a crescendo. Lightning streaks crisscrossing the dark skies were accompanied by titanic thunderclaps. One such lightning streak hit the broken branch and torched the entire tree to flames the next instant. The lion and its kill, who were just below the bough, were not spared either in this show of nature's wrath. High voltage seared straight though his massive leonine head, torching his mane and completely charring his once magnificently ferocious face. It passed through the dead body of Prasenjit too, on its way to being grounded by the earth, completely charring the carcass in the process. Nothing was left of the tree, the lion, as well as Prasenjit, except their badly charred and unrecognizable frames.

The rain continued to rage throughout the night and the streambed turned into a raging torrent cutting a swathe through the dry scrub forest. Three consecutive seasons of tormenting drought had now been broken, in this deluge from the heavens. The rushing water swept the gem locket along with it, till it reached an area consisting of a catacomb of caves. Here the locket got wedged very tightly between two rocks and there it would remain for the next few days, after the rain subsided and calm returned.

On the seventh night after the cloud burst, the locket and its fiery gem came into the sights of Jaambhav, a giant cave bear for whom these catacombs were home. An ancient being, Jaambhav had been roaming the earth since the dawn of the *Sathyayug*. He belonged to a separate species of bear; a species that walked on two legs like humans. One could say that his species was the ursine equivalent of the great apes. And his intelligence and wisdom rivaled that of the great sages; such was the vastness of his life experience over the eons. Standing on huge pillar like legs, Jaambhav was a towering 25 feet of living and breathing rock hard muscle, sinew, and bone, with not even an inch of fat anywhere on his herculean frame. He could easily uproot and carry the biggest of trees on his shoulders as if they were rag dolls, such was his strength. All the other creatures in the forest, including the king of beasts, gave him a very wide berth; such was his might, power and ferocity, if provoked to battle.

But he was also the last of his kind; only he and his family, consisting of his 1000th bear wife in succession over the centuries and a young female daughter remained on this earth. At one point in the *Sathyayug*, thousands of his kind existed, but many of them had disappeared over the centuries due to changes in the ecology of the earth. Actually, the lifespan of his species was just 250 years, but Jaambhav had a boon from Lord Brahma for a very long life that would almost stretch to the end of the *Thretaayug*. And this boon was elevated to immortality by Lord Raama himself for the immense valor with which the bear had served Raama's *vaanar sena* during the epic war with the demon king Raavana in the same *yuga*.

There was a look of awe in Jaambhav's eyes as he beheld the gem clasped in his massive ursine hand that had 20 inch long claws like steel spears. Drawing on the vast reserves of his ancient wisdom, he immediately recognized that the gem was not of this earth. He immediately took the gem to his home in the catacombs and presented it to his daughter, on whom he profusely doted. The joy of the young female bear knew no bounds, on receiving this gift from her father.

'This is a gift to us from the gods themselves my child and now this belongs to you,' Jaambhav growled in his ancient bear tongue. 'Take good care of it and never let it go out of your sight. It will bring you lots of blessings.'

'Yes my father,' his daughter let out a cubbish squeal of delight. From then on, the jewel was her constant companion and she guarded it with all her might. The light from the gem, along with the daily gold it yielded, gave the catacombs a heavenly glow from the outside.

Satrajit had a completely harried and distressed look on his face when he rushed into Krishna's court the following evening.

'O Krishna my King, my brother Prasenjit has been missing since yesterday night, the same night he was supposed to meet with you regarding the land dispute. Did he indicate in any way where he was going after he met you *Maharaj*?'

'I myself was waiting the whole evening and even the first half of the night. But your brother Prasenjit did not turn up here.'

'You are telling me that he did not meet you yesterday *Maharaj*?'

'Yes, he did not come here and in fact I was going to send my men to your home in this regard.'

'Yesterday night, after dinner, he told me that he was going to meet you. Moreover, he was wearing the gem on him as I had given it to him to wear for the night. Now I'm doubly worried *Maharaj*. Not only has he not met you as you say, he has also not returned home. Was he waylaid by bandits, God forbid?'

'Relax Satrajit. He could have gone over to a friend's place or left town for some other purpose. Regarding bandits, you know that our land does not even have petty thieves. Remember that people here do not even lock their homes when they are away.'

'I understand *Maharaj*, but this gem is so special, doubly so during these times of drought, which of course has now thankfully broken - and I attribute this to the heavenly powers of the gem. That makes it an object eminently desirable to one and all. Moreover, my brother never does anything or goes anywhere without informing me.'

'Don't worry Satrajit. I will send my soldiers to scour the town and the surrounds for Prasenjit. I'm sure that we will find him, along with the gem.'

Krishna's soldiers combed the streets of Dwaaraka as well as its surrounds. They looked in every nook and corner but to no avail. They questioned travelers who had entered Dwaaraka in the past couple of days, whether they had seen/ met any man matching the description of Prasenjit on their way in. Again, there were no palpable leads.

As one more day passed, Satrajit started to panic. He once again showed up at Krishna's court demanding an immediate audience. The King was busy with another important matter but still obliged him, taking Satrajit's predicament into consideration.

'*Maharaj*,' Satrajit rushed to the court chambers with panic writ on his face. 'I am convinced that something bad has happened to my brother. It is impossible that my brother would stay away from home for even a single day without informing me. I believe that somebody has done something harmful to my brother because of the gem that he was wearing.'

'Satrajit, you know that these kinds of crimes do not happen in our Dwaaraka. If any such incident had taken place, it is unlikely to escape the attention of my city guards. My information network also has an impeccable record throughout my reign. I'm one of the first to know if any of my subjects have come to harm. It is conceivable that your brother left the city that night under cover of darkness.'

'That is impossible my Lord. Why would he travel out of the city alone, with such a treasure in his hands, and that too unarmed?'

'Is it possible that Prasenjit had a bit too much to drink that night?'

'My brother was not drunk even though we had some wine before he left the house. He certainly was sober enough to have known where he was going. Moreover, he was on the way to meet you regarding the important business of the temple lands.'

'I was just asking because wine can foul the best of minds at times.'

That's when Satrajit lost his composure. 'That is unfair *Maharaj*,' he spoke in a stentorian tone to the astonishment of Krishna's ministers and courtiers. 'My brother is a very responsible young man and a respectable bachelor.'

'Calm down Satrajit, I was not implying anything negative about your brother.'

Satrajit bowed down his head and was silent for a while. Then he raised his head slowly and met Krishna's gaze. 'I am wondering how you knew that he had taken wine. Did you in fact meet him yesterday my Lord?'

'I just took a guess Satrajit. Prasenjit is known for his excessive fondness for wine. That's all.'

'I'm afraid my Lord that you are not telling the complete truth here.'

'What do you mean Satrajit?'

'Somehow I feel that *Maharaj* knows more about my brother's disappearance.'

'And why would that be dear Satrajit?'

'The gem itself. Wasn't my Lord very much interested in possessing the jewel?'

'You have lost your senses in your predicament Satrajit! Do you mean to imply that something wrong has happened to your brother because of the jewel and that I have something to do with it?'

'Precisely!' Satrajit was now defiant. He continued after a brief pause, 'I'm not going to say anything more in this regard. The gem is as good as lost and so also is my brother and nothing is going to come of all these discussions. I wish to leave your presence *Maharaj*.'

A wave of murmuring had now erupted all over the court. Many courtiers were appalled at Satrajit's innuendoes and the improper, accusatory tone with which he had addressed the king. Some called on Krishna to stop Satrajit from leaving and to punish him for his insolence.

'Satrajit can leave this court if he wishes and nobody shall stop him,' Krishna spoke with that beatific smile on his lips. 'Regarding the manner of his talk, it is very natural for any man to get hurt and be flustered over the disappearance of his brother. No doubt it is this frustration that has compelled him to speak in this manner. And if Satrajit suspects that I have a hand in Prasenjit's disappearance, I cannot fault him, as Prasenjit had told him that he was going to see me. So it is natural for him to suspect that I was the last person to have been with Satrajit before his disappearance. Which is why I have decided now to take it upon myself to search for Prasenjit. I will leave right away and will not return until I find the truth. In my absence, my beloved brother Balaraama will take care of the affairs of the land. All of you know how capable he is in this regard, so you do not have to worry in my absence.'

'I completely support your decision, brother Krishna,' Balaraama, who was seated to his right, interjected. 'And had you not made this decision, I myself would have ordered you, as your older brother, to immediately embark on the search for Prasenjit. This has now become a matter of honor for our family as well as the Kingdom. I also declare that I'm breaking all ties with you Krishna, till you clear your name.'

'I understand elder brother and I will do my best in this regard and will not rest till I sort this out.'

By the onset of dawn the next day, Krishna embarked on a solo search for Prasenjit. At first he went over each street of the city itself and spoke with many of his subjects, but nobody seemed to know anything. Meanwhile, rumors about the King's possible involvement in Prasenjit's disappearance snowballed by the minute. Krishna could discern suspicion and, many times, downright accusation in some of his subjects.

Krishna decided to retrace Prasenjit's possible route from his house to the palace. He stopped deliberately at many places to examine whether Prasenjit could have digressed from his path at that particular point. But nothing made any sense. It was not logical for any man to just divert from his path for no particular reason. Krishna then spoke with the guards of the palace gate and asked them whether they remembered anything out of the ordinary. At first the guards replied in the negative. However, as Krishna was about to leave, one of them remembered seeing a bright light that seemed to approach them from afar and then suddenly turn to the left and disappear among the trees. The guard thought that it was probably a big firefly and left it at that.

That's how Krishna's attention came to that long, winding, narrow, and thickly wooded path that forked out to the left just six furlongs before the entrance of his palace. This was not a path used very often and it led straight to the scrub forest to the east of the city. This path could get very lonely during dark. In previous times, the path was notorious for its bandits. Ever since Krishna had begun his rule, bandits had completely vanished. For many years, there had been no reports of banditry or even petty theft in the city. Regardless, Krishna decided to follow the path in his quest for Prasenjit.

Even though Satrajit denied that his brother was drunk that night, Krishna concluded that Satrajit may not have been telling the complete truth in order to protect Prasenjit's reputation. All along the winding path, Krishna looked for clues, but nothing seemed out of the ordinary. Now the path entered the scrub forest in earnest. Krishna kept on walking, his eyes scouring the landscape for the minutest of details.

After many hours, he reached the deepest part of the forest. Now, he realized, it was time for some divination. Endowed with superhuman mystic qualities, Krishna was godly in his powers. But he rarely used them unless the situation really warranted it. He always tried to solve problems as a mere mortal so that he could lead by example. But in this case, the trail seemed to lead nowhere. He closed his eyes and meditated at length.

When he opened his eyes, he knew the direction he had to take. At a distance of about 20 furlongs, he reached the spot where the lightning strike had annihilated Prasenjit, the lion, as well as the tree. There his eyes caught sight of a brown metallic object glinting in the sun. He approached it to take a closer look. It was a cummerbund projecting out of a heap of ash. And what was intriguing here to Krishna was the fact that the cummerbund was typically worn by people of Satrajit's class.

Then he caught sight of a huge paw with all its claws, almost the size of a man's face. It was a blackened right paw of a lion. Krishna examined it and his thoughts began racing. The small remaining burnt stump, which was the remains of the tree, next to the heap of ash then caught his eye. Wasn't there a drought breaking, huge, electrical rain storm that night? Suddenly the possibility clicked in his brain. He concluded that the stump was the remains of a tree that had most likely been reduced to ash by lightning, and if a lion had been standing beneath it, it would have combusted the lion as well.

The lion would have been charred completely except for its right paw, Krishna concluded. And then he thought about the cummerbund. Was it possible that Prasenjit was also under this tree, probably killed or eaten by the lion? Could the pile of ash also include Prasenjit? And, if Prasenjit's cummerbund was protruding from the ash, wasn't it was possible that the gem and the locket were also be buried inside? Krishna immediately went through the ash heap thoroughly, but nothing came of it. Then his eyes beheld the stream bed.

Was it possible that the locket and the gem had been ripped off Prasenjit in the attack by the lion and fallen into the streambed? Because of the heavy rains, the streambed would have been alive with running water. So, if the gem and the locket had fallen into the water, they could have been very likely washed away by the current. Krishna then decided to follow the course of the stream.

By the time Krishna reached the limpid pool of the catacombs after following the twisted course of the stream, it was dusk and getting progressively darker by the minute. Yet there was a heavenly glow coming from one of the caves of the catacombs. Krishna knew that he had come to the correct destination. He climbed the wall of rock that led from the pool to the catacombs and entered the caves. There was no need for any light here, the glow was everywhere and illuminated every nook and corner. There were gold pieces strewn all over the cave floor.

He saw a dazzle of light dart past his eyes followed by a fierce growl. Krishna's gaze instantly swung in the direction of the sound. He could perceive a bipedal she-bear cub fiercely glowering at him with her huge canines and rapier like claws. She was almost a foot taller than Krishna's own 6.5 foot frame. The locket and the gem were dangling from her right forepaw.

'So this is where he lives,' Krishna muttered to himself. 'All those rumors are true then.' For a while both of them stood their ground waiting for the other to make a move. Then came an earth shattering growl from behind. Krishna turned immediately and perceived a giant ursine silhouette standing at the cave entrance - 25 feet of pure might. The growling sound was actually words in an ancient bear tongue. They meant: Who dares to come here? Krishna understood it fully as he was a master in deciphering animal languages. He could communicate with any creature in its own language.

'My *pranaams* to you the king of bears. I know that you are the mighty invincible Jaambhav. I'm Krishna the King of Dwaaraka. I'm not here to cause any trouble, O mighty bear. I just want to take back what rightfully belongs to one of my subjects; the gem that your daughter has in her possession. Just hand it over to me and I will leave peacefully. I mean you and your family no harm whatsoever,' Krishna replied, in that same guttural ancient bear tongue.

But Jaambhav's anger went up another notch and he growled back. 'First of all, you have the temerity to enter my home and accost my family, you weak, puny human. And now you claim the jewel too, a jewel that belongs to my daughter. You have really made me angry. But I'm still willing to let you walk away unscathed. Leave immediately now and don't ever come back. Just go away you silly human.'

'I've not come here to go back empty handed, O mighty bear. This lost jewel belongs to one of my subjects and I have given my word to him that I will not return without it. Now that I've found it, there is no going back. A king has to keep his word to his subjects. Moreover, my own honor, as well as that of my clan's, is at stake.'

'You silly, insolent human! You have to be taught a fitting lesson for your intransigence. If it is the jewel that you want, then you have to go past me.'

'So be it then, O great bear. I have no problem with that.'

'Do you indeed have a death wish, you foolish human? Do you even know my strength? Here let me give you a taste,' Jaambhav picked up a huge granite boulder with his left forepaw and smashed it with a powerful blow from his right; the sound of the blow reverberated like a thunderclap all over the catacombs. 'And, let me show you what else I can do,' Jaambhav raked his claws on the granite wall of the cave and produced deep etches on them. 'This is what my claws can do to granite rock. Just imagine what they would do to the flesh of your soft throat.'

'It does not behoove you O great Jaambhav, to speak of such violence, especially to those who do not mean any harm to you.'

'But you are verily asking for this, you foolish human. I'm showing you my prowess so that you will stop entertaining any thoughts of taking me on in one to one combat. It is not too late even now. You can still leave and I promise that no harm will come to you. Just leave now.'

'I'm a *Kshatriya* warrior, O great Jaambhav and not one to turn away from a challenge. If I have to combat you to reclaim the lost property of my subject and also save the honor of my family, so be it.'

'Alright then, silly human, as you please. Don't say you weren't warned.'

'Don't worry mighty bear. I know what I'm getting into. But don't you think we need more room for this.'

'You humor me, O silly fool. Alright then, let us go to my main cave which has got plenty of room. Here, follow me.'

Jaambhav led Krishna to his main cave which was huge with a fifty foot ceiling. There was more than enough space for a one to one combat with even a giant like Jaambhav. Jaambhav's wife and daughter presently joined them as spectators.

The contestants squared up against each other. There was a quizzical look on the bear's face. The last hard battles he had were with some of the mighty demons of Lanka when he was part of Lord Raama's army eons ago. Other than that, his latest action had been when he recently killed a full grown male tiger in its prime, with a single blow to its head, when it tried to attack his daughter. Most beings avoided even crossing his path, but here was a human, very puny by his standards, who stood up to challenge him. In a way he felt sorry for this human and decided that he would use just enough force to subdue him and force him to turn back.

Jaambhav was a pure vegetarian and believed in killing only in defense and only those who sought conflict. But once roused to fury, his ferocity and aggression knew no bounds. Jaambhav crouched low and beckoned Krishna forward with his huge paws. But the wily wrestler Krishna did not take the bait and instead circled him at a distance. After being circled the third time, a bored Jaambhav charged Krishna with a terrifying growl. Krishna adeptly moved away in the last second and the bear grabbed empty air. This maneuver was repeated over and over again. Come what may, Jaambhav could not get hold of Krishna as the latter sidestepped, somersaulted, cart-wheeled, and danced around him at lightning speed. An infuriated Jaambhav then started hurling boulders and stones at Krishna but even those did not hit the target. It was well into the night when Krishna suggested a break with a blissful smile.

'O great bear, don't you need some rest; I mean we all need some rest. We can continue after the break.'

It was a big insult to Jaambhav's ego that he had not subdued his opponent so far. What he thought was going to be a very short battle had now stretched to this point; way beyond what his ego could bear. Moreover, this puny human was even suggesting a break. This enraged the giant bear even further. He charged Krishna once again, roaring in fury, but once again the latter seemed to vanish from his grasp at the last moment. When it was past midnight, a completely flummoxed Jaambhav reluctantly agreed to take a break from the action. A few minutes catching their breaths and the contestants went at it again. This time both upped the ante.

Jaambhav whirled his paws at lightning speed, as he charged in the hope that he could get a piece of Krishna. But Krishna still managed to evade him. Not only that, the human managed to jab him here and there which more than hurting the bear, pricked his ego and made him highly irritated. This continued till dawn and this time it was Jaambhav who called for a break. They resumed again and the fight went on in the same manner for days on end.

Over the course of these days, the battle spilled on to the pool where they fought above and below the waterline. Then the battle moved to the forest where Jaambhav went into a frenzy of uprooting and hurling trees futilely at Krishna. By the seventh day, the battle had moved back into the catacombs. Jaambhav was now huffing and puffing. His eyes were playing tricks on him and at times he felt that there was more than one Krishna. And Krishna taunted him mercilessly with his smile and wit. Finally Jaambhav exploded. 'You are a coward, you little human and you are not playing by the rules. If you are brave enough, just come once in my grasp and wrestle me like a warrior. Then you will see what the might of Jaambhav is.'

'Believe me, O great bear, I know what your might and valor is. But, believe me when I tell you that I haven't used my full strength either. As I said before, I have no desire to hurt you. I want to sort this out without causing you hurt and pain. I just want to take the jewel back.'

'Is that so, you foolish human. Then why don't you come and test your strength. Wrestle me arm to arm, body to body and not duck and sneak and slip around like a greasy weasel.'

'Alright, if that is what you desire, then I shall grant it to you Jaambhav.'

The two contestants squared off again and this time around their arms met and locked. Jaambhav pushed forward trying to pin down Krishna but felt a titanic wall of steel. He pushed again with all his might but could not move an inch. This shocked the bear to the core. He had not expected such strength from this puny human.

'What's the problem Jaambhav? Too strong for you?'

This infuriated the bear even more. Now he shook off Krishna and charged forward in a punching stance, his giant arms moving like pistons. But to his chagrin, he found every blow of his effectively parried by Krishna, whose arms, in turn, also seemed to move at an equal speed. Jaambhav also did his best to rake Krishna with his mammoth spear claws, but failed. Finally, he stood completely exhausted and chagrined, with drooping shoulders, in front of Krishna.

'This posture does not behoove a great bear like you Jaambhav. Is that all you've got? I expected more.'

The giant bear now completely lost it. He charged forward with murder and mayhem in his amber eyes, summoning up the last ounces of his strength from the very depths of his soul. He whirled his paws with maximum speed and strength. But suddenly, he felt his hands clamped and immovable. Krishna held them in a lock with that same smile on his lips. Then Krishna exploded in a tsunami of lightning fast one-inch punches on Jaambhav's chest, pummeling and pounding the bear. The onslaught was so ferocious that the very air was driven out of Jaambhav's lungs. The bludgeoning continued for a long time, cracking a few of Jaambhav's ribs in the process. Blood began to flow from the bear's nostrils and mouth and still the blows rained on. Blood began flowing out of the bear's ears and eyes. Jaambhav's pillar like legs buckled and giant bear collapsed on his knees and fell prone to the ground.

'I have not even used my full strength on you Jaambhav.' Krishna then walked up to Jaambhav and stood smiling over him.

'Enough, enough, enough, human! Enough! You win. I concede,' Jaambhav capitulated.

'Who are you human? Who are you? In fact I'm convinced that you are no mere mortal as no mortal has the power to defeat me in combat. Moreover, never in my life have I have ever seen my own blood spilled in combat. Not a single foe has managed to inflict the faintest of scratches on me, including the giant demons of Raavan's army whom I crushed with my bare hands in the *Thretaayug*. So I once again ask, who are you?'

'I thought you would recognize me the first time you saw me O great bear, by the strength of your devotion.'

'Stop teasing me and tell me who you are human?'

'Alright then Jaambhav. First of all rise up.' Jaambhav slowly and painfully got to his feet. His chest was throbbing with unbearable pain. Never before had he been thrashed like this.

'Now look into my eyes, O great bear.' Jaambhav leveled his face with that of Krishna and strained his bloodied eyes.

And, for a moment, he felt he was transported to another world. He could see the battlefield of Lanka and could hear the battle cries of the *vaanaras* in the background. He saw the huge demons charging towards them led by the giant of giants, Kumbakarna. Then he saw the great *vaanara* Hanumaan bringing in the huge mountain to save Laxmana. Finally, he saw the man himself, his beloved Lord Raama, as the arrow from his mighty bow seared through the ten-headed Raavana's chest and finished the wicked *asura*.

'I see you Master, I see you. *Raamaaya Raama-bhadraaya Raamachandraaya vedase. Raghunaathaaya naathaaya Seethaaya pathaye namaha. Lokabhiraamam Shreeraamam bhooyo namaamyaham*,' Jaambhav suddenly growled in ecstasy and fell prone at Krishna's feet. In a moment he had forgotten the pain and the humiliation of his defeat.

'I was such a fool my Lord, so arrogant in my strength and power that my eyes did not recognize you. And I deserve punishment for that. I now realize what you meant when you said that you did not use your full force on me. Please forgive my transgressions.'

'It's alright mighty Jaambhav. Now arise. Sometimes things are what they are and we can do nothing about them. Even the gods are helpless in the working of *kaal* and karma. In this life, I'm King Krishna of Dwaaraka, Jaambhav.'

'I had heard of your valiant exploits my Lord, and yet I could not make the connection.'

'Some things take their own time Jaambhav. Anyway, now let's get back to business. I need you to hand over the gem and its locket to me. It is lost property and does not belong to you. It must go back to its rightful owner.'

'I am more than willing to hand it over to you my lord. Please forgive my earlier foolishness and arrogance.'

'You are forgiven Jaambhav.'

'And now my lord, may I request a favor?'

'For sure Jaambhav.'

'I want you to take my daughter Jaambhavati as your wife. She now belongs to you. There cannot be a better match. Please take her back with you back to Dwaaraka.'

'A man marrying a bear is an anomaly Jaambhav, and not the norm.'

'With you anything is possible my lord. Please do not disappoint me.'

'Alright, I will take your daughter as my wife. But have you asked her what she thinks in this regard?'

'That will be absolutely no problem my lord. Long ago, she made me promise that I will get her married only to one who defeats me in one to one combat and you have just done that. Now it is time for me to fulfill my promise. Please help me out with this my lord.'

'Alright, I will take her as my wife as you desire, O great bear.'

'I'm overjoyed my lord,' Jaambhav grunted with delight.

'And now Jaambhav,' Krishna spoke at length. 'I want you to travel to higher ground in the coming years and stay there. Believe me, there is a reason for this, which will become apparent to you as time goes by. From now on, you should also remain hidden from the eyes of mortals, especially in the approaching *Kaliyug* when *adharma* will increase exponentially. You will be visible only to the lord's true devotees. Alternately, you are also free to join me on my final journey in this life, should you choose to Jaambhav.'

'Your wish is my command lord. But I still have some work left on this earth, especially during the *Kaliyug*.'

'So be it, O mighty bear.'

And thus ended Krishna's epic quest for the lost gem. When he entered Dwaaraka, Krishna went straight to Satrajit's house.

'I have mixed news for you Satrajit. I have found your gem but your brother Prasenjit is no more in this world.'

'O Prasenjit, my dear brother!' Satrajit went down on his knees and broke into a wail.

Krishna consoled Satrajit for his loss. Once Satrajit had composed himself, Krishna promptly got down to the business of narrating in detail, the events of the past few days to him.

'Forgive me my lord for addressing you in that manner in court the other day. My emotions and suspicions got the better of me,' Satrajit spoke when Krishna had finished.

'No hard feelings Satrajit, from my side. It was very natural for you to think and speak like that, considering the circumstances.'

'Regardless, it is still very magnanimous of you *Maharaj* for forgiving me. That is why I want you to keep this jewel for the benefit of Dwaaraka.'

'No Satrajit. The gem is yours to keep. Enough anguish has been caused because of this. The gem's rightful place is now with you. I have just one humble suggestion. Please try to help those less fortunate, especially during these trying times, for our state. Of course the drought has broken but we still have a lot of ground to make up. The gold yielded by the gem is not going to be of much use lying locked in your safe. Again, this is just my suggestion Satrajit. You do as you deem fit.'

'O my King, I'm disappointed that you do not accept my offer of the gem. In that case, I want you to accept my daughter Satyabhama as your wife.'

'This I will do, provided Satyabhama is willing too.'

'She is completely devoted to you my King. In fact, she has already hinted to me about her wishes in the past. Somehow I was not keen at that point of time. But now I have no reservations in this regard my lord. And yes, I will assist the state with the gold from this gem.'

Thus it came to pass, in three months' time, the marriage of Krishna to Satyabhama, who later went on to become one of his favorite consorts. The pomp and splendor of the ceremony was tempered down as the kingdom was still recovering from the punishing drought. But, the wedding was still performed with sufficient grandeur.

Satrajit was resplendent, the gem on his chest shining like a star, bewitching everyone present. But not everyone had the same eyes of admiration, especially for Satrajit and even more so, for the gem he was wearing. In those times of paucity, he looked like the heavenly Kubera himself. Moreover, the gold that the gem yielded had started accumulating and the gap between Satrajit and the rest in Dwaaraka was widening exponentially.

It was only a matter of time that his riches would overtake even the royal coffers. Satrajit had not fully followed through on his word of helping the financial recovery of the state. That was the reason why the collective eyes of the trio of Yaadava noblemen, Akrura, Kritavarma, and Shatadhanwa burned with anger and envy. Between the younger Kritavarma and Shatadhanwa, it was pure covetousness, jealousy, and a burning desire to somehow possess the jewel. Moreover, both had also desired Satyabhama and resented the fact that the lady could no longer be theirs, for this too they blamed Satrajit.

As for the gentle and just Akrura, who had been one of the bedrocks of support for Krishna during his persecution by the evil Kamsa, it was more that he resented Satrajit's initial refusal to part with the gem for the sake of Dwaaraka when Krishna had requested it. Not only that, Satrajit had even falsely accused Krishna (albeit indirectly) when his brother and the gem had gone missing. Moreover, he was not helping the kingdom as much as he really ought to as promised.

According to Akrura, Satrajit should have been punished for these things. Instead, Satrajit had now even built ties to the royal household through the marriage of his daughter and day by day his power and fortunes were on the rise. The gentle Akrura believed that Satrajit did not deserve any of these. That same night, the threesome gathered in Akrura's house and over a few pitchers of rice wine and expressed their thoughts.

'Satrajit is unfit to possess this jewel. He is a selfish man. He has not even given one ounce of the gem's gold in charity and has completely disregarded our King's advice,' Akrura spoke bitterly.

'I personally do not give a hoot whether Satrajit has given or is going to give anything in charity. All I'm concerned is that I want to make the gem mine,' Shatadhanwa spoke, completely inebriated.

'I would not mind seeing the man dispossessed of his gem either. He has become so arrogant,' Kritavarma added.

'It is not right to covet other people's property,' Akrura interjected.

'Oh come on, big brother Akrura, the man is a selfish and arrogant loser. How dare he flaunt his wealth when there is so much paucity all around?' Kritavarma got up on shaky legs.

'I have made up my mind to dispossess him of the gem. Even if I have to resort to force, I will,' Shatadhanwa's temper rose another fraction.

'But all this is just wild talk here in King Krishna's Dwaaraka. You both very well know he does not tolerate unlawful activities.' Akrura placed a calming hand on Shatadhanwa's back. 'Let's forget all this and let us retire for the night.' The threesome retired to their respective quarters for the night but the seeds of envy and rage had been sown.

In the months that followed, those seeds sprouted giant shoots that took root firmly. All that was needed now was a window of opportunity, however narrow. That window of opportunity presented itself when a messenger from Hastinaapura rushed frenetically to Dwaaraka bearing some extremely bad tidings that would sear the hearts of many in the city, especially Krishna. The Paandavas, his cousins, had been burnt to a gory death in a palace of wax. Krishna and Balaraama had to depart immediately to offer succor to the grieving kith and kin. As soon as Krishna and Balaraama were on their way, the trio of Akrura, Kritavarma, and Shatadhanwa hastily met again, this time with the intention of divesting Satrajit of his prized treasure. According to plan, they would steal into Satrajit's house in the dead of the night and remove the gem from his neck as he was sleeping. Then the trio would immediately escape east, to the holy city of Benares.

As planned the trio of Yaadava noblemen entered Satrajit's house just past midnight, covering their faces to prevent identification. They had no problem making their way to Satrajit's sleeping chambers. In Dwaaraka, none of its denizens ever felt the need for guards, even in hard times. Satrajit was fast asleep in his huge bed; the gem shining on his neck, lit his chamber bright. Ever since the death of his brother, Satrajit had become paranoid and now refused to be away from his gem even for a moment. He wore it around his neck all the time, even at night, even though the gem brightly lit his sleeping chambers. But he slept very lightly these days; even the slightest of sounds woke him and the first thing he would do was to feel for the gem around his neck.

Gold from the gem was lying strewn all over the chamber increasing the dazzle. For a moment, the threesome froze, awestruck at the sight of all the treasure. Then Kritavarma gingerly stepped towards the sleeping Satrajit with the object of removing the gem from his neck. But as he neared his target, his feet toppled a pile of gold near the foot of the bed and sent them clinking all over the floor. That was enough to wake up the paranoid Satrajit who froze in fear at the sight of three hooded individuals in his chamber.

'Give us the gem,' Kritavarma spoke in a low voice, 'I will see to it that no harm comes to you. Just hand over the gem to me.'

'No, no, no!' Satrajit stuttered and shrank back raising his arms to cover his chest. 'Who are you and why do you want the gem?'

'You have made enough gold to last many lifetimes. Now it is time for you to part with the gem and give it to needy people like us. Give us the jewel to me and we will depart in peace.'

'Are you crazy?' Satrajit raised his voice. 'This gem belongs to me. It is the fruit of my torrid penance and moreover *Maharaj* Krishna has now decreed that the gem is forever mine. So if you steal this gem from me, you are violating the royal decree. Moreover, I'm *Maharaj*'s father-in-law. He will not spare you if he finds this out.'

'Ha, ha, ha, Satrajit. Aren't you aware that neither *Maharaj* nor his brother Balaraama are in the city? And it will take some time before they return. So no one is going to come to your help. Hand over the gem.'

'No, never, never!' Satrajit rose from his bed. Kritavarma jumped forward and grabbed his hands. A struggle ensued. Shatadhanwa joined in the fray and the twosome managed to pin Satrajit down on his bed. Then Kritavarma grabbed the locket intending to rip it off Satrajit's neck. The thought of losing his gem made Satrajit summon the last ounces of his strength. He broke free and drew out the dagger that he always wore around his waist ever since Prasenjit's death. With a roar, he lunged at Kritavarma, slashing furiously. He cut the latter across his body, drawing blood. Kritavarma shrieked in pain and withdrew.

Satrajit now moved menacingly towards Kritavarma intending to inflict further damage. He had not noticed Shatadhanwa creeping up behind him. He did not even see Shatadhanwa's sword swinging towards his back, plunging through his right kidney. Satrajit staggered forward in pain, blood gushing in torrents out of his mouth, splattering Kritavarma's hooded face. Then he fell forward face down on the floor and was gone. It had all happened so fast, leaving Akrura stunned. The killing of Satrajit was not part of the plan, but it had happened. Now they had certainly earned the wrath of their King.

'My God Shatadhanwa, why did you have to kill him? You could have just knocked him out cold. Now *Maharaj* will not spare us.'

'What has happened, has happened,' Kritavarma wiped the blood splatter from his hood and removed it from his face. 'Let us take the gem and get out of here.'

Shatadhanwa removed the locket from Satrajit's body and motioned to the others to leave. The threesome departed stealthily. They picked up a few more expensive items and gold from the chamber to make it look like a robbery. However, in their haste, they forgot that Kritavarma was not hooded. It was Akrura that noticed this and elbowed Kritavarma hard in his ribs. 'For goodness' sake, cover your face Kritavarma.' He grabbed the cloth hood from Kritavarma's hand and placed it on his head.

'Ah yes, brother Akrura,' Kritavarma pulled the hood over his face. But the damage had already been done. Satrajit's niece who happened to be visiting had been awoken by the sounds of the scuffle emanating from Satrajit's bedroom, and she had come to the living quarters to investigate. As she stepped into the huge living room across which was Satrajit's chamber, she almost bumped into the threesome as they emerged from Satrajit's chamber. She swiftly drew back into the shadows to avoid detection. It was then that she recognized the uncovered face of Kritavarma.

Actually, it would have been very difficult to recognize Kritavarma's face in the darkness even if his face was uncovered. But the light of the gem had illuminated every feature of his face starkly. After the threesome had departed, she rushed into Satrajit's bedroom and let out a scream at the sight of his corpse. By the early hours of the morning, commotion reigned in the city of Dwaaraka. The murder of Satrajit was the talk of the town and Kritavarma was on the list of the most wanted in Dwaaraka. A messenger had also set off speedily on horseback to Hastinaapura, to inform Krishna and his brother about this murder.

As for the threesome, they had made good their escape from Dwaaraka without event. As soon as they had stepped out of Satrajit's house, they had made sure that the jewel was well hidden, covered by layers of thick clothing and then placed in an iron box so that its shining light would not betray them. Once they had gotten far away from the city, they decided to split. Akrura and Kritavarma headed to Benares with the jewel, while Shatadhanwa headed northwards. He would catch up with them in due time. But before they split, Akrura exacted a promise from Shatadhanwa that he would not divulge to anyone, even under the gravest threat to his life, that the gem was now in the possession of Akrura, and divulge his whereabouts.

Krishna and Balaraama rushed back to Dwaaraka when they received the news of Satrajit's murder. Almost immediately, Krishna started tapping into his efficient network of informers regarding the possible whereabouts of Kritavarma. Moreover, from the description given by Satrajit's niece, Krishna knew that there were two more people involved in this crime, even though they were not identified by her. After making enquiries, as well as by using his own powers of observation, Krishna had a fair estimate about the identity of the other two. The fact that these two were also missing from Dwaaraka confirmed his theory.

Krishna was profoundly disappointed that his beloved Akrura was involved in this. But then he knew that this gem and the copious gold that it yielded provoked dark desires in the bosom of humans and could easily corrupt even those with the noblest of hearts. Later on that day, one of his messengers informed him that Shatadhanwa had been spotted in a small town called Suta, north of Dwaaraka. Krishna and Balaraama immediately set forth on a chariot to Suta with the intention of capturing Shatadhanwa alive.

Balaraama was still not convinced of Shatadhanwa's guilt. He did not give full credence to the eye witness' account of Satrajit's murder. In his opinion, there were too many loose ends in the niece's story. Moreover, Balaraama could not bring himself to believe that noblemen of the caliber of Shatadhanwa, Akrura, and Kritavarma would stoop to such low levels as murder for gain.

When they reached Suta, they found that Shatadhanwa had already got wind of their arrival and had sped off further north on his horse. Krishna and Balaraama set of on hot pursuit of their quarry. They engaged in a torrid chase with the intent of exhausting Shatadhanwa's steed. Shatadhanwa was forced to alight from his horse and attempt to escape by foot. He immediately set off on a rocky path which could not be negotiated by chariots.

When Krishna and Balaraama reached the spot where Shatadhanwa had abandoned his panting horse, Krishna stopped, alighted from his chariot and surveyed the surrounds. It took Krishna less than a minute to hone in on the path taken by the fleeing Shatadhanwa. It was steep, rocky terrain and Krishna asked Balaraama to stay put at the spot while he set off in pursuit. It took close to three hours of painstaking tracking before Krishna had Shatadhanwa's retreating back in his sights.

'Stop Shatadhanwa, you cannot go any further,' Krishna called out. But the latter pretended he had not heard Krishna and increased his pace.

'Stop Shatadhanwa, lest I be forced to use harsher methods and believe me I will.' But Shatadhanwa broke into a run instead.

'You leave me with no alternative, O fellow Yaadava.' Krishna then summoned his *Sudarshana* discus and sent it searing through the air in the direction of Shatadhanwa. The discus overtook Shatadhanwa in no time and began circling menacingly obstructing his path. Krishna then walked up to Shatadhanwa with his trademark beatific smile.

'My dear Shatadhanwa, come to your senses. There is no escape for you from here. Come back with me to Dwaaraka to face justice, and of course, return the gem. You must also tell me where your partners in crime, Akrura and Kritavarma, are currently.'

'I do not have the gem on me and neither am I coming back to Dwaaraka with you *Maharaj*. As for the whereabouts of Akrura and Kritavarma, I have no idea where they are or what crime you are talking about.'

'Do not play games with me Shatadhanwa. I'm dead serious.'

'I am serious too *Maharaj* Krishna. I have nothing to say to you.'

'Hmm... so is that all you have to say Shatadhanwa?'

'Absolutely *Maharaj*.'

'Then I have to let my discus do its job.' Shatadhanwa did not even have time to answer. The discus sliced clean through his neck and beheaded him. Krishna then frisked Shatadhanwa's corpse thoroughly, but Shatadhanwa was indeed speaking the truth that he did not have the gem on him. This meant that it was certainly with Akrura and Kritavarma. So the next task was to find out where they had gone. Krishna returned to the spot where Balaraama was waiting.

'Did you track him down?' Balaraama asked impatiently.

'Yes and I was forced to kill him.'

'So, where is the gem?'

'The gem was not on his person. He refused to say anything in this regard. But I strongly believe that the gem is with Akrura and Kritavarma. Now we need to find out where they have gone.'

'I can't believe this! Are you telling me that you killed him for nothing Krishna? I'm deeply disappointed with you. Do you still believe the story of that niece of Satrajit who saw someone in the dark and believed it to be Kritavarma? Moreover, you have dragged the noble Akrura into this sordid affair. Both Kritavarma and Akrura are some of the finest of our clan and Shatadhanwa is not far behind. Come on Krishna, what did you achieve by all this? Now you have stained your hand with the blood of an innocent man. I also believe that you know more about the gem than you are telling me. You have a lot to answer for!'

Krishna did not reply; he merely smiled at his brother and added: 'I do not wish to say anything in this regard, O elder brother. Just that things will reveal themselves over time.'

'O Krishna, I wish I could believe you but I cannot. In fact, I will not join you on your return journey to Dwaaraka. I will go instead, to the kingdom of Videha to be with King Janaka, my very dear friend. And unless I'm convinced that you have not killed Shatadhanwa in vain, I will not return.'

'O brother, I'm deeply disappointed by your lack of trust in me. Please come back with me to Dwaaraka.'

'My mind is made up brother Krishna. Please do not stop me.'

'Alright brother Balaraama. If this is your wish, so be it.'

Thus the two brothers parted ways with Krishna heading back empty handed to Dwaaraka and Balaraama going over to Videha. At Dwaaraka too, public opinion was divided over Krishna's slaying of Shatadhanwa and various rumors and theories began doing the rounds. Once again Krishna was caught needlessly in the warp of suspicion regarding the disappearance of the gem. The march of time continued and three years passed. Balaraama returned to Dwaaraka after having a change of heart. He reasoned that three years was enough time to persuade himself that his younger brother did not possess the gem. But he was still not entirely comfortable in this regard.

The march of time continued, 52 years went by and the epic war of Mahabharata came to pass. During this time, Akrura and Kritavarma stayed put in the holy city of Benares. Akrura, stung with remorse over the killing of Satrajit, now led a life of complete austerity and forced Kritavarma to go to the forests and do hard penance. The Semmanthaka gem was indeed in his possession but he did not enrich himself with it. He had realized that the gem had the power to destroy its possessor should the possessor not have complete purity of thought and action. All the gold that the gem yielded on a daily basis, he gave away entirely to charity. But, he took great care to not reveal to anyone the source of the gold. He also persuaded Kritavarma of this, when he returned from his penance, and made him promise to abandon all desire to possess the gem.

Ever since, the twosome made Benares their home, the city had prospered enormously. Day by day, stories of its riches and splendor spread all over *Bhaarath-varsh*.

In Dwaaraka, Krishna too became aware of the economic might of Benares and was convinced that it could only be due to the effect of an extraordinary external force. All that gold in Benares surely meant that the Semmanthaka gem was certainly in that city and that also meant that Akrura was living there. Krishna immediately sent an emissary to Benares along with a message to Akrura. In that message, Krishna entreated Akrura to return unconditionally to Dwaaraka and that all would be forgiven. He did not mention anything about the gem.

An overjoyed Akrura, who was, himself, pining to return, sent back a message to Krishna that he would come back at the earliest but on the condition that Krishna pardon

Kritavarma too. Krishna sent back a message that Kritavarma was also equally welcome to return to Dwaaraka. Thus the two prodigal sons of Dwaaraka returned to their homeland within a month. Once again, Krishna did not question Akrura or Kritavarma about the gem or about Satrajit's death.

In the coming months, as Akrura resettled in the city, there was a visible improvement in the economic prosperity of Dwaaraka. Akrura continued to donate gold as he did in Benares. Now it was the city of Dwaaraka that slowly started to become the golden star of *Bhaarath-varsh*. Neither Akrura nor Kritavarma revealed the source of the gold nor did Krishna ask them about it even though he was certain that Akrura was getting the gold from the gem.

It was only during the final days of Dwaaraka, before the tsunami, that he had smilingly asked Akrura to come clean. Akrura, in turn, broke down and confessed before his King in public. He also recounted at length what had transpired on the night Satrajit was murdered, that the murder had not been premeditated and that it was Shatadhanwa who had plunged the sword into Satrajit's back, much to his chagrin. In this manner, the shadow of suspicion that hung around Krishna over the killing of Shatadhanwa was finally cleared up. A beaming Akrura then went back to his mansion and returned with the gem. He entreated Krishna to take possession of the jewel. Krishna refused and convinced Akrura to keep it in his possession and continue his monumental work of charity.

And thus ends the tale of the gem, as we all know it, from the annals of the sacred history of *Bhaarath-varsh*, Dr Baalan,' the hermit stroked his silver beard. 'As to what really happened to the gem after the tsunami of Dwaaraka; that part of the story will be revealed to you only by Guruji, whom I am taking you to see. Please do not ask him any questions regarding his past, which he has put behind him. Speak only when asked to and stick to the issue at hand, which is the quest for the gem.'

Guruji

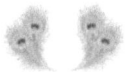

The threesome once again started out the next morning, along a narrow treacherous path. But the path thankfully did not climb and instead went into a steep descent. A bone chilling wind was now blowing into their faces, throwing snowflakes along its wake. But the brew given by the hermit was once again working like a charm, insulating their insides from the chill.

After almost two hours of trekking slowly, the hermit halted and pointed upwards. Along the left rock wall, there was a rope hanging down for a length of almost 40 feet. At the top end of the rope, they could discern a cave. There were small steps, which served as footholds on the rock face running close and parallel to the rope.

'That is where you have to go Dr Baalan and Yogi. My job ends here.'

'Are you serious? Do you expect us now to climb this vertical wall to access that cave?'

'Alas, there is no other alternative Dr Baalan.'

'I'm not some super mountaineer that I can do this. Even the fact that I made it so far is a very big miracle.'

'And that miracle may continue, doctor.'

'How so?'

'Ask your athletic young assistant to take the lead. And, of course, make sure that the flute half is secure with you. The miracle will follow.'

'Are you sure? The climb looks impossible for a middle-aged and 'not so fit' human like me!'

'Believe me doctor you can do it - and if you get into any difficulty, chant the Hare Krishna Mahaa Mantram.'

'I'll take the lead Dr Baalan. I had figured even before we left that there may be some climbing involved,' Yogi interjected. 'First of all let me tie the flute half securely to you sir.' He produced a blue nylon rope from his backpack and tied the rope between his waist and Dr Baalan's. 'This will secure you to me; in case should you slip doctor. And don't worry sir. I have some experience in rock climbing from my Australian days.'

Yogi gripped both his gloved palms on the coir rope and placed his right foot on the first stone rung. Soon he was pulling himself up and egging on a very hesitant Dr Baalan to follow suit. Dr Baalan threw his hands up in exasperation as he felt the blue nylon rope connecting him to Yogi tugging at him eagerly. The doctor finally placed his right foot on the first stone rung and held on to the rope. Slowly, with tremendous effort, he hauled himself up. Very slowly, they climbed 32 feet when disaster struck. Dr Baalan lost his footing on the slippery stone rung and dangled mid-air; his body pulling Yogi down with its full weight. Yogi, in turn, hung on desperately, with all his might. Yet, they could not prevent themselves from slipping down at least 10 feet. To complicate things further, the blue nylon rope snagged on a small crack on the rock face and dangled the doctor at an angle to the stone rungs. The doctor shuddered as he pictured the drop. A fall from here would send them plunging all the way down to the valley 7000 feet below.

'Dr Baalan, you have to disentangle the rope connecting us from the crack. Do it quickly!' Yogi grunted with effort, sweat streaming from his body. 'I'm afraid, I cannot hold on for much longer.'

'*Ayyayyo kadavule enga vandhu maatikkitome! Saadhuji*, where are you? Help!!!' Dr Baalan's eyes searched for the hermit but he was nowhere to be seen. Dr Baalan began praying fervently and now he remembered the hermit's advice. He feverishly began chanting the Hare Krishna Mahaa Mantram. Yogi, on his part, was holding on with an iron grip but his strength was steadily ebbing. From the corner of his eyes, Dr Baalan could see the stone rungs just to his left, but he had to swing quite a bit to free the blue nylon rope from the crack and get back on course.

He closed his eyes and summoned up his strength, then his scrabbling feet somehow found purchase on the rock face and arrested the slide. Gritting his teeth he placed both his feet firmly on the rock and thrust himself to the side. The first attempt did not bear fruit and so he tried again and again and by the fifth time he was completely wasted.

'You have to somehow get us out of this doctor. My hands will give away any moment. Already, my shoulders are numb with pain!'

And so Dr Baalan, gave it a go one more time, with a strength that only comes from fear of imminent death. In one brute heave that came from the depths of his soul, the nylon rope came free of the crack and his foot found thankful purchase on a stone rung. Above him Yogi, suddenly felt the blood gush back to his shoulders. He almost collapsed in immense relief as he let out a deep breath.

For a long while both of them stayed put, gathering themselves from the near-death experience. Then they recommenced their strenuous climb to the cave above. They approached each and every step with caution and it took almost another hour to pull themselves into the cave.

At first, they could see nothing inside, just dark gloom. Suddenly, the entire cave was filled with the glow from powerful flame torches. Their eyes could now perceive a man's head with matted hair and a face with a thick beard resting on a rock. His torso was lying separately nearby as were his arms and legs. There was a staff in his right hand. His body parts were completely coated with sacred ash and his eyes glowed like red hot coals. In the next instant all the parts came together as whole and the amazed duo found themselves in facing a living and breathing man with his right leg raised and placed on a rock, He appeared to be no older than 60 years of age, though Jaarra *baaba* had told them that he was over a 100. He seemed extremely lithe and fit. They could now also perceive a huge tiger lying by his left side. Dr Baalan's mouth went agape with incredulity.

'Reassembling body parts and tigers at this altitude and cold,' he muttered under his breath to Yogi.

'The separating and rejoining of body parts is one of the highest and most sublime forms of yoga. And as for tigers in the cold; they also roam the frozen tundra wastes of Siberia, Dr Baalan,' Yogi muttered back.

For a while there was nothing but silence and then the man spoke in a deep rumble: 'And yes, what you saw here was the yoga of the part and the whole, one of its highest forms. I always stay dissembled whenever I'm not interacting with another human. Keeps the ego in check.'

Dr Baalan's mouth was still agape.

'Congratulations doctor, on having made it this far successfully. Most people, with the exception of highly seasoned mountaineers, do not survive the climb. But then, you have a divine musical instrument in your possession that takes you unscathed through the fiercest of storms. Now, here you are as fated. You have got a monumental task at hand doctor, one that involves the very survival of mankind. You are the chosen one for this task.'

'Why me of all the people in this world? I mean there are much better people than me out there who have the capacity and quality to save mankind. I'm but a simple marine archeologist.' Dr Baalan replied.

'You are more than what you think you are Dr Baalan. Alas, I cannot give you the reasons. Suffice to say that you will know why in time. But let me come to the issue at hand, which is your quest for the Semmanthaka gem. It is not you or anyone else that has initiated this quest. Rather, I would say, that it was the divine forces that orchestrated these happenings and those same forces brought you here.

You are the chosen one Dr Baalan. You will not understand and believe what I am talking about until if and when you find the gem. Let me emphasize the word "IF". Because, there is no guarantee that the gem will reveal itself to you. You have to earn it from here on. But you will have help in the form of these two flute halves, one which you carry and the other which I have with me. Now the time has to come for these halves to meet but not just yet.

Remember Dr Baalan what the marks on the wild ass stallion revealed. It told you that the gateway to the gem is at a kingdom of the great temple by the sea. And very likely the seas pertain to *Bhaarath-varsh*. But the seas abutting our lands are vast. So where will you find this temple? This is where the flute halves will come to your aid. They will serve as the very beacon in this regard. In your quest for the gem you will reach a certain sacred co-ordinate, a portal where these halves have to reach as a single unit. This must be done before the next *Amaavaasya*, which is roughly 15 days from now. If you fail to meet this deadline the planet will be wracked with catastrophe. So, in a way you are on a mission to save Mother Earth. The gem is at the exact location as the portal.

You have to take the two halves with you and scour the seas surrounding our ancient land. That I will leave to you to get it done. Once you are anywhere within 5 km radius of the portal, electric energy will start radiating from the flute halves and this is the sign that they are ready to be joined as one. Do not take the flute halves out of their boxes till this happens.

After that the joined flute will act as a signal homing device and take you to the portal. I must warn you of one more thing. When electric energy starts radiating from the flute halves, other forces could get activated as well, and titanic natural calamities may be triggered. But as long as you hold pure thoughts and chant the lord's name, no harm will come to you. Dr Baalan, you can come forward now and receive the other flute half from me.

Once you place the flute in its destined final location, the gem may be revealed to you. Please note the word MAY here. That is why sincere devotion and purity of thought is essential in this venture. The desire to possess this great gem for your personal gain should never cross your minds. If greed strikes you, it will do you great harm.

Throughout the history of this magnificent gem, those who desired to possess it met with untimely and often gory deaths. That is why I forbid you from taking anyone along with you, especially someone with vested interests. You exactly know whom I mean here. My disciple Jaarra *baaba* has already instructed you clearly on this matter and I reiterate his warning.'

Dr Baalan stepped forward gingerly towards the sage, his eyes on the fierce tiger whose amber eyes seemed to bore right through him. 'Don't worry about my animal friend. He will do you no harm,' Guruji put aside his staff and reverently picked up a long rectangular box near him. He handed it to Dr Baalan.

'Go forth on your quest Dr Baalan. And you will reveal to no one anything about meeting me or about this place. Go forth with my blessings.'

Dr Baalan had a lot of questions for Guruji, especially to ask if he was the real Netaji. But they had been explicitly forbidden by their hermit guide to ask any questions in this regard. The twosome now walked back to the mouth of the cave and started preparations for their descent.

'Don't worry Dr Baalan, who I am really does not matter. What matters, and in fact all that matters now, is the quest that you are embarking on,' Guruji called out from behind.

'There goes another mind reader,' Dr Baalan muttered to Yogi.

'Actually reading people's minds is not an extraordinary feat for those involved in the quest for the divine. *Vande-Maataram*,' Guruji spoke again.

Dr Baalan looked up startled. He had not expected that particular parting salutation from the Guruji. Guruji's face was inscrutable but his lips bore a faint smile as he joined his palms in a *namaskar*.

'To repeat,' Guruji continued. 'You must proceed with haste. *Asuric* forces have shifted the planet to a different dimension and now we need the combined forces of Krishna's flute and the gem to bring the planet back to its original dimension. Of course, no living creature on this earth with any super sophisticated instrument can detect this supernatural transition. But it has happened. If the planet remains in this *Asuric* dimension, its destruction will be accelerated by all those forces that are threatening it today: global warming, climate change, and Adharma in the form of war and terrorism. And the history of humanity will end prematurely, affecting the workings of *kaal*.

But, if the flute of Krishna is brought to the exact geographical coordinates of the sacred portal, musical vibrations from the flute induced by the Lord, along with the unified field forces of the gem, will activate gravitons in that *asuric* dimension. These activated gravitons will bring back the planet to its original dimension, halting colossal damage to the earth and keeping Adharma in check. So this quest, you see, is in fact much greater than the gem.'

'Guruji, but I have a couple of questions here, with all due respect.' Dr Baalan spoke as he adjusted the nylon rope securing him once again to Yogi. 'What was the necessity for Lord Krishna to resort to all this? The flute could have been placed directly at the portal, along with the gem, by him or Shatamanyu Yaadav or Jaarra after the tsunami. And my second question is why did Krishna break his flute into two halves?'

'Very good questions doctor. In fact, I expected a man of profound erudition like you to ask this question. Had the flute been at the location where the portal is, there would have been no way it could have intervened to save Dharma at crucial junctures in the history of *Bhaarath-varsh*. Hope this answers your question Dr Baalan. Moreover, there are karmic debts that come into this equation which may be revealed to you later, provided you get to the portal in time. Keep in mind that any delay beyond this *Amaavaasya,* will lock the planet forever in the *Asuric* dimension.'

'Well, about the flute…' Dr Baalan began.

'All in good time. Do not think too much now. Many times, the answers are just staring at us in the face and we look elsewhere. Go with my blessings doctor, and remember that the Lord has always acted as a savior of this world and Dharma, and will always continue to do so.'

The twosome began their descent down the rope and the stone rungs again. They took their time getting down, but made it without any incident. Once down, they found their hermit guide waiting for them. Actually he had seemed to have appeared out of nowhere.

'Where were you *Saadhuji*' Dr Baalan asked with surprise.

'You did not need me so I had gone. Now that you are back here, I am back too, to guide you to Kathmandu airport.'

The journey to Kathmandu airport was uneventful. Soon Dr Baalan and Yogi were heading back on the flight to Ahmedabad via New Delhi.

The Second Quest

$\mathcal{B}$ack at his office in Ahmedabad, Dr Baalan relaxed with a hot cup of black tea in his easy chair. 'Where are we going to start Yogi? It is going to be like searching for a needle in the haystack, except that we have a sensor here in the form of the flute. First of all, we need to find the exact location of the portal where the gem is also located. And then too, we are not sure whether we will get to the gem.'

'I still say that we give it a shot. At least let us play our part in saving the planet regardless of whether we get to the gem or not.'

'That is a quite a noble motivation indeed Yogi. Let's do it. I suppose we can execute the search methodically within 2 kilometers from the coastline here.'

'We are assuming that the gem is still in or around Dwaaraka coast because that was its last location as mentioned in the *Puraanas*. And it may be very well buried under the seabed following the tsunami.'

'Quite logical Yogi.'

'But let us also note the fact sir that there are other great temples by the sea in this land.'

'Yes, we have great sea temples like Puri, Tiruchendur, Mahabalipuram, Kanyakumari etc. to name a few all along the coastline of this ancient land. These are the known ones and there are countless relatively lesser known and smaller coastal temples. But once again, the gem is very likely in Dwaaraka.'

'Give me some time to ruminate on this Dr Baalan. For now, let us relax.'

'Yes, I badly need to rest Yogi.'

Yogi then proceeded to shut himself in the lab for the next three days. On the fourth morning, he burst through the lab door with palpable excitement.

'I now have strong reasons to believe that the portal and the gem could also be outside of Dwaaraka. Remember what Netaji told us as we departed his cave: that the answers could be staring at our face and that the lord has always acted as a savior of this Earth as well as Dharma. Well if the gem is going to be very important for the saving of the planet from the *asuric* dimension, then it is quite likely that the Lord had saved the gem from getting inundated by the tsunami that finished his city. It is quite possible that he made arrangements to get the gem out of Dwaaraka. Now this line of reasoning is a strong probability, Dr Baalan.'

'Hmmm…quite possible Yogi. The jewel could have moved out of Dwaaraka before the tsunami even though there is no mention of this anywhere in the *puraanas*. But I guess we could take a calculated chance.'

'Therefore, we will conduct a meticulous search along the coast line beginning from Dwaaraka Dr Baalan. We will keep within 2 kms of the shoreline and scour the entire shoreline of this country.'

'That sure sounds to be a logical and methodical way of doing this. But somehow I feel that it is not going to be as quick as we would like it to be.'

'Let us be optimistic sir.'

'That aside, there is also another sticky issue. The issue of keeping Stalin in the dark on all of this. As I told you earlier, I'm not at all comfortable with what I see as a clear breach of contract from my side. It pricks my conscience very badly.'

'Sir, let's be practical here. I understand your feelings, but we had better keep Mr. Malhotra out of this as we have been explicitly warned to do so by the holy men. We have seen and experienced enough to believe that there is substance in what they are telling us.'

'I agree with you Yogi but once again we have to give Stalin the slip and this time for close to 10 days'

'If at all we get the gem we will have to hand it over to Stalin as per our contract with him. But how do we convince him that the gem is fatal to those who want to possess it?'

'I think I have the answer to my problem right here, in what you've said just now. In a way I will be only protecting my client if I keep him in the dark about what we are going to do, even though I am violating my professional commitment to him. If I bring him into this, he will do everything possible to get possession of the gem and that would only serve to destroy him, according to the legend.'

'This means sir, we have to proceed with stealth from here on. I suggest that we start from the Gulf of Kutch, hugging the coast and move slowly southwards towards Dwaaraka. This means we will even enter the Cambay Gulf. Let us also remember that the coastline north of the Cambay Gulf is part of present day Pakistan, which was part of our land before 1947. But given that most Hindu temples have been looted and destroyed in this part of the world, I do not see much reason that the gem would be in that direction. Therefore, the northernmost boundary of our search will be the Cambay Gulf. Let me now see if I can hire an inconspicuous fishing trawler where we can stay low profile.'

'As you say, but I feel that we should start from Dwaaraka itself and proceed northwards all the way to the Gulf of Kutch and then double back. That way we can thoroughly scour the area Yogi.'

'Good idea, sir. Let me get on this right away.'

Within a couple of days, Yogi arranged for an old rust bucket of a trawler owned by a potbellied middle aged fisherman called Ishaan. The plan was to start from Dwaaraka and head northwards hugging the coast. They would also dress like fishermen to avoid unwanted attention, and certainly to avoid getting noticed by Malhotra, whose submarine yacht could possibly be in the region.

In three days, near the end of their two week break from Malhotra, they began their task. Ishaan was waiting for them as planned at an abandoned jetty 5 kilometers south of Dwaaraka. Yogi broke a coconut on the jetty, burnt incense and camphor, and invoked Lord Ganesha - *Om Shree Ganeshaaya namaha* - before he and Dr Baalan stepped aboard the trawler. Subsequently, they proceeded northwards slowly, keeping their eyes open for any sort of electrical energy emanating from the flute halves. But they drew a blank even as they reached the temple shoreline and continued northwards. They drew a blank all along the gulfs of Cambay and Kutch. Once they reached the northernmost part of their planned route at the Gulf of Kutch, where they almost touched Pakistan's maritime borders, they stopped and decided to turn back. It was here that trouble courted them.

While still well outside of Pakistan's waters, a bit north of the entrance of the Kori creek, a shiny black speck materialized in the seas to their northwest and began growing very fast every passing minute. It was a small vessel manned by three heavily armed men.

'*Rukho*,' one the men yelled across the water in Urdu as the vessel came within 20 meters of their trawler. 'We are the Pakistani coast guard and we want to know what you are doing in our waters.'

Dr Baalan threw a puzzled look at Yogi and then at their boatman Ishaan. 'Pakistani waters my foot!!! What's more they don't look like any coast guard,' he exclaimed.

'We are still in our waters sir, but very close to the disputed Sir Creek line. There is a maritime dispute going on about this between Bhaarath and Pakistan. This sort of thing happens all the time here. And you are right; they could just be small time pirates. Say nothing. I will handle it. Sometimes, these fellows are only looking for money. Just leave it to me.'

'We just came here fishing and we were just about to turn around and go back. We intend to cause no trouble,' Ishaan yelled back in Hindi. But these assurances fell on deaf ears and the vessel continued to advance, finally came to halt at touching distance. One of the armed men immediately jumped into their trawler with catlike efficiency and stood menacingly in front of the now trembling Ishaan.

'I want to see some identification,' he demanded gruffly. In the next instance, the other two armed men also jumped into the trawler.

'Who are these people with you?' the first armed man demanded pointing at Dr Baalan and Yogi.

'They are my fishing partners, *mai baap*,' Ishaan visibly cowered. The armed man eyes bored into the twosome.

'They don't look like fishermen, at least going by their looks and skin. Something is not adding up here. I want to see some ID.'

'*Mai baap*, we do not want to cause any trouble and we are turning back. If there is something that we can do, please tell us,' Ishaan folded his hands pleadingly and for the next half an hour, a discussion raged back and forth between him and the armed men. The voices of the armed men were growing more stentorian by the passing minute.

'Why should we do anything?' Dr Baalan suddenly exploded in English, losing his cool. 'I do not think that we are in their waters. It is they who need to identify themselves. Let them go back to their god damned, basket case of a country, before our own coast guards come here and kick their behinds.'

'Well, well, well! What do we have here?' one of the armed men exclaimed in English, turning on Dr Baalan. 'So you do speak good English,' the armed man now came forward stood very close to the archeo. 'Seems to me that you people are here on some sort of spying expedition. Confess at once - or else, we have ways to make you talk.'

'We have nothing to tell you and we are not spies. We have better things to do than spy on your god forsaken country. Just go your way and we will go ours.'

'You have a very loose tongue and you will pay for your insolence, trespasser!' The armed man shoved the barrel of his gun hard into the doctor's abdomen. Dr Baalan crumpled to his knees in pain.

'Tell me what exactly you people are doing here or you will really feel the pain. This was just a trailer,' the armed man took another step towards Dr Baalan with his gun raised. What followed next was just a blur. A fist pounded straight into the head of the armed man, dropping him instantly, then two more kicks sliced through the air taking the other two armed men in lightning succession and propelling their bodies straight out of the trawler into the water with a mighty splash.

'My God Yogi, you really have some moves,' Dr Baalan was filled with awe and he completely forgot the pain in his abdomen. 'Wing-chun Dr Baalan. Comes in handy at times,' Yogi winked at Dr Baalan. He quickly lifted the prone man by his armpits and dropped him into the sea. Then he looked at the equally stunned Ishaan and nodded his head, 'Let's get the hell out of here before more of them show up!'

'*Jee mai baap*,' Ishaan was more than willing to oblige. The trawler now made a U-turn and headed southwards. The rest of the journey to Dwaaraka was uneventful.

'Well Yogi, other than that adventure with the mad Pakis, we have drawn a full blank. In fact, I half expected our target to be within this area. Now doubts are creeping into my mind whether all this is indeed for real,' Dr Baalan sounded frustrated.

'As I have reasoned earlier, there is a possibility that the gem left Dwaaraka before the tsunami. Therefore, let us keep on going southwards Dr Baalan. There are other great temples by the sea in this land.'

'I wish I was as optimistic as you are Yogi.'

'It is hope that drives great discoveries Dr Baalan.'

'Oh come on Yogi. I believe in evidence more than hope. But let's continue, I guess.'

They travelled slowly going down the western coast and were treated to some spectacular views as the sun set in the Arabian Sea. They were now skirting Maharashtra. The night was slowly setting in when Ishaan decided to set anchor. The seas were calm and a yellow moon was hanging low in the sky. Ishaan brewed some hot tea and then they had a simple dinner consisting of hard *roti* and *dhal*. Then they slept in the rickety, old cabin as the trawler slowly undulated with the gentle waves. At dawn, they journeyed once again southwards. They swept past Mumbai and then Navi Mumbai and down the verdant Konkan. Still nothing happened.

Their pace had dropped to a lazy crawl over the waters of the Arabian Sea, skirting the Mangalore coast. Another two days passed by. The skies over the land to their left (as they headed southwards) had turned crimson with tongues of orange flames streaking it, signaling daybreak. Dr Baalan sipped tea from a tin mug as he soaked in the tranquility and enjoyed the cool breeze blowing in steadily from the land. Three sea gulls were cackling merrily over the trawler, keeping pace with it, so that it seemed as if they were suspended stationary in the air.

Yogi, seated across the deck from Dr Baalan, was going through some notes in his diary as he too sipped tea. It was as tranquil as it could get and yet Dr Baalan was perturbed. His eyes had spotted something vaguely the previous evening in the waters behind them. He had noticed something following them, maintaining a steady gap between itself and the trawler. But his straining eyes could not clearly make out what it was as darkness had set in over the waters. He went into the cabin and fetched his binoculars, but by the time he got back, whatever object he thought he had seen had vanished.

'Good morning, sir,' Yogi beamed.

'Good morning Yogi,' Dr Baalan responded absentmindedly. He continued to gaze back at the seas to his west, lost in thought.

Yogi rose up from his seat and strode across the deck to Dr Baalan. 'Sir, is something bothering you? Anything I can do?'

'Nothing Yogi. I thought I saw something in the waters behind us. At first I thought it was just some debris, but then debris does not follow you at the same pace and that too for a long while. From far away, it looked like a head of a killer whale. But killer whales do not keep their heads out of the water surface for stretches of time. They bob in and out. By the time I could fetch the binoculars from the cabin to get a better look, the object had vanished.'

'Interesting sir, this could also be a dolphin. Often these mammals follow fishing trawlers looking for some jettisoned tidbits. Other times, these mammals are known to do it just out of curiosity.'

'I'm positive that it looked very much like a killer whale and not at all like a dolphin. What intrigues me is that killer whales are not often sighted in these waters.

'It could be a transient hunting on its own or a resident cut off from its pod that lost its way in the high seas. Anyway, whatever it is, it looks like it has gone.'

'Yes indeed Yogi,' Dr Baalan smiled at his assistant and wondered how Yogi had this unique quality of calming things and people around him.

Late in the afternoon, they ran into a flotilla of fishing boats returning to the land after a successful fishing stint in the high seas. The fishermen, were in high spirits as they had netted some high value catch. As they drew nearer, one of the fishermen waved his hands at Ishaan. They seemed to know each other from before. The fishing boat now drew parallel to their trawler and Ishaan began chatting away as the vessels slowed down to drift speed.

'Sir, these fishermen want us to join them on shore. They are going to have a grand celebration at their fishing village after their very successful fishing foray. There's going to be lots of food and drink. You know how fishermen are when it comes to the bottle!!'

'Of course, we would like to join them for refreshments. Why not? But I'm not in the mood to drink today and Yogi does not drink, nor do we eat non-vegetarian food,' Dr Baalan replied.

'That should be no problem at all sir. You will be pleasantly surprised to see that the fishing villages of today are a far cry from what they used to be even a decade or two ago. Now there's lots of affluence and one almost gets everything there. I'm sure that my fishing friends will take care of you sir.'

'Alright then, let's do it.' Dr Baalan gave it a thumbs-up.

In another hour, they had drawn anchor somewhere south of Mangalore and then jumped on one of the fishing boats to head to the fishing village. Ishaan was right indeed. The fishing villages had everything a modern housing society would boast of: HD TVs, broadband connections, cable, latest cars, and plush houses with latest furnishing. Wow!! was all Yogi could say. They were hosted in a posh house belonging to the head-fisherman of the village. The vegetarian food they were served was par excellence and they also had copious glasses of apple juice. As the evening advanced into the night, the juice became laced with Russian rum unbeknownst to them. This made them dizzy and drowsy as the night wore on. Finally, the twosome lay down on the cool beach sand and fell into blissful slumber under the stars, enjoying the cool land breeze. As for Ishaan, he had gone on a complete bender and passed out in the front yard of his host.

The dream was as vivid as it could get... The giant, glistening, golden coiled body undulated with sounds of deafening thunder and streaks of blinding lightning... Then a great reptilian face appeared in his field of vision. Its eyes glittered like pink diamonds and its forked tongue slithered in and out of its mouth like a streak of fire. Each time, it seemed to Dr Baalan that this kiss of fire was getting closer and closer, almost to within a whiskers' range of his face. The accompanying HISSSSSSSSSSSSSSSS sounded to him like a powerful industrial air hose at its maximum setting... 'What a strange, surreal dream!' Dr Baalan wondered as he came awake blinking at the night sky. He felt disoriented as if he had ranged far beyond the stars. He looked at his watch. It was around 1am. Lulled by sound of the sea, Dr Baalan drifted off again. This time he slept dreamlessly........

The eastern skies were glowing red when Dr Baalan slowly stirred awake. The sound of the waves and the seagulls were sweet to his ears. It has been ages since he had slept like this. Suddenly, he felt the singeing cold of metal on his neck.

'Wake up my dear doctor.' A familiar voice boomed into his ears and startled him into alertness.

'What the hell...' Dr Baalan rubbed his eyes and stared at the tough grizzled face that looked at him, steely eyed. 'Stalin?'

'Mother-lode *da puttar*, doctor. It is your client Stalin whom you seem to have forgotten, or should I say, forsaken. By the way, I hope you had a great time last night. The fishermen did not invite you by chance. I pre-arranged it; so also the spiking of your drinks.'

Stalin Malhotra fiddled menacingly with the gleaming barrel of the shotgun in his hands. 'My dear doctor, you seem to be running away from me, quite in violation of the rules of the contract between us. I really did not expect this from a man of your reputation.'

'I can explain Stalin.' Dr Baalan clasped his hands in apparent regret as his eyes slowly caught sight of his client's submarine yacht slowly breaking surface behind their trawler. The vessel truly looked magnificent in the gold hue of the early morning light.

'She sure is a beauty isn't it? And I really wonder why you wouldn't prefer this luxury trawler over that rust bucket. Why doctor?'

'I'll explain, but please take away the gun. It is making me very nervous and believe me you would not be needing it.' Dr Baalan cleared his throat.

'Alright, alright. But let us cut the crap. Tell me doctor, what are you hiding from me?' Stalin activated the safety-catch and threw the gun aside.

'I can explain all of this Mr. Malhotra. Give me five minutes of your time and everything will be clear to you,' Yogi's voice interjected. 'There is a reason why we had to exclude you so far and why we will have to continue to exclude you from here on.'

'No Yogi, I have had enough of this hide and seek business', Dr Baalan intervened. 'Let us come clean here. I have never been more disgraced in my entire career. Stalin is absolutely right. We have violated the terms of our contract by keeping him in the dark and now we owe him an explanation and an apology.'

'But we have been forbidden from involving others...' Yogi protested.

'To hell with all this. From here on, Stalin is with us all the way or this quest ends here.'

'Dr Baalan speaks sense, don't you think so Yogi? And it would behoove you well to listen to him. I don't take broken deals lightly in my line of business. The last person that tried this trick in the deserts of Namibia got all the bones in his body rearranged and fed to the spotted hyenas of the Namib. Mother-lode *da puttar,* we are all gentlemen here, especially my dear Dr Baalan, and I will not need to go those unpleasant extremes. What do you say sir?'

'Yes, you are completely right Stalin. I do apologize profusely for all of this. But first you have to listen to our part of the story then you will understand why we had to keep you in the dark all this time.'

'Ok doctor, shoot! I'm all ears. But let me make it clear that I have no time for cock and bull rigmarole. I hope I can expect the full truth from a gentleman like you.'

Much to Yogi's displeasure, Dr Baalan sat Stalin down and narrated the whole sequence of events, right from their being summoned by the holy men at the Rann, to their consequent sojourn to the frigid heights of the Himalayas, followed by their time on the trawler to the point where they were intercepted by Stalin.

'Incredible... but I have my doubts,' Stalin boomed rolling his eyes backward.

'You have to believe me, Stalin, especially after some of things that I have seen and experienced. Everything that I have told you is nothing but the truth.'

'Then show me the flute halves.'

'Yes we have it with us but you cannot have it. In fact, you cannot even touch it.'

'Why not?'

'The legend says that one has to be pure of thought and intention if one was to hold them even for a few seconds.'

'That makes me even more curious to behold it.'

'Alright then Stalin, since you insist on it. Don't tell me later that you weren't warned!'

'I like to take chances in life. That's the kind of attitude that has gotten me to where I'm today - a very successful treasure hunter with an enviable hit rate.'

Dr Baalan led Stalin to the trawler with Yogi following close behind. Once on the vessel, he carefully walked towards one of the casings containing the distal flute half and gingerly picked it up.

'The flute half is inside Stalin.'

'Open it, I want to take a good look.'

'It cannot be brought out now, else will jeopardize the quest. Remember I told you that the halves cannot be exposed to each other until it is time. Please understand Stalin. It is in your own good interests.'

'Ok doctor.' Stalin had a sour look on his face.

'Thanks for understanding Stalin.'

'By the way, where is the other half, doctor?'

'Over there,' Dr Baalan pointed to the other casing at the other end of the trawler.

'I want both these delivered to my yacht. If I'm not getting the gem, I'm at least taking these trophies home.'

'Cannot do it till we finish our quest,' Yogi said firmly. Stalin Malhotra glared at Yogi with irritation writ large all over his face. He turned to Dr Baalan, 'Seems to me doctor that your good assistant is getting out of line. Mother-lode *da puttar,* he had better learn to speak to me with more care.'

'I'm sorry Stalin, I apologize on his behalf,' Dr Baalan shot a look of disapproval at his assistant. 'At the same time, I must say in all sincerity that my assistant has a point and that we must complete the search on this very trawler. Let's not make any changes at this juncture, having come this far. Sure, the yacht is a great option, we do not know what may happen if we take the flute halves there. However, you are welcome to follow us in your vessel.'

'Alright, alright, but I will not tolerate any nasty surprises. You do not want to see my dark side doctor, and neither does your over enthusiastic assistant. On second thoughts, I will stay right here with you on this wretched rust bucket and my yacht and men will follow closely. Once again I warn the two of you - no surprises…or, mother-lode *da puttar,* the consequences will be fatal!' Stalin Malhotra caressed the gleaming barrel of his gun.

'Be our guest sir and I hope that we end up with something remarkable.'

'I hope so too. Once again, regardless of what else happens, those flute halves are mine. No way am I returning empty handed, especially after the way you have dealt with our contract.'

'Agreed sir,' Dr Baalan heaved a visible sigh of relief.

Yogi had now become laconic and was staring into the horizon with a discernible frown. Eventually he composed himself and turned around with a smile. 'Let's not waste any more time. Let's get going.'

Hare-Krishna

$\mathcal{B}$y late evening, the trawler was on the move again, sailing southwards. Dr Baalan stood on the deck with Stalin Malhotra.

'Stalin, I wanted to ask - did you or your men in your yacht sub observe anything strange in the waters, the day before?' The two were sipping hot tea prepared by Ishaan.

'What do you mean doctor, can you be more specific?'

'I thought I saw a killer whale in the water following us. At least it looked like that. It was following us for a long time. I was intrigued because you do not find them much in these waters. But before I could get a closer look, it was gone.'

'Ah… you did notice doctor. It was certainly a killer whale but not the real one. It was our bionic robotic camera shaped as a killer whale which was tracking you.'

'Oh…that explains it Stalin. But at least I was partly right in my observations.'

The fishing trawler chugged on at a moderate pace with Stalin Malhotra's yacht following it a distance of a quarter of a nautical mile. Stalin was continuously in touch with his vessel over a walkie-talkie and made sure that both vessels were in visual sight of each other at all times. They had just skirted the northern tip of Kerala and the waters of the Arabian Sea looked magnificent.

It was late noon and the visibility was crystal clear for miles and miles across the water and so also the waters close to the coast. At dusk the skies put on a show of varied hues of purple, red, yellow and orange as the sun ebbed into the distant horizon to their west. The advent of darkness was sudden and soon the stars and a crescent moon appeared on the skies. It was dinner time and they dropped anchor. So did the yacht behind them. Stalin suggested they go over to the yacht for dinner. The dinner was ultra-five-star with a banquet and drinks of mindboggling variety. After the meal, they rested for a while before going back to the trawler. Once again they started moving southwards.

It was past dawn when they drew near Kochi, sighting its harbor on their southeast. There were no plans to call port so they sailed past it in a couple of hours. As they sailed southwards, the seas became rough. There was a strong gale force wind that blew in from the west. It was so strong that the men on the trawler took shelter in the makeshift cabin. The submarine yacht following them went underwater, avoiding the choppy surface. Regardless, it kept pace behind them. A steady southward current now pulled them faster as they headed towards the coastline of Aalapuzha and thence on to Kollam and Trivandrum.

They reached the northern edge of Trivandrum near Varkala, in the small hours of the morning. A crescent moon had now risen in the sky and the waters were shimmering silver. The seas had become calm once more and soon they were skirting the iconic Vikram Sarabhai space center and the Thumba rocket launch pad. At around 4am they had sailed past Shanmukham beach at the southern end of Vallakkadal. It was then that it all began.

There was visible static in the air and then blue sparks began to fly between the two flute halves. In the darkness of dawn, the sparks made a great arc.

'I think it is time Dr Baalan.' Yogi motioned towards him.

'Yes, I think it is time for the marriage,' Dr Baalan hurried towards the proximal half. The static current was intense even as he reached out towards the half with his hands. Then he closed his eyes and meditated on the HARE-KRISHNA Mahaa-Mantram. He gingerly opened the rectangular case containing the half and pulled it out. His full body shook with the energy emanating from the half as he walked towards the other half housed in its case at the opposite corner of the trawler. Stalin Malhotra, who was taking in all this, now excitedly radioed his yacht to break surface.

Dr Baalan slowly reached out to get the distal half out of its box. The surging energy current had reached another level and now it looked as if Dr Baalan was convulsing. But the archeo held on. There was a ruby red glow all over the place radiating from the flute halves and the sparks flowing between them resembled lightning streaks. Then Dr Baalan took both the halves in each of his shaking hands and brought them together.

There was titanic thunderclap of a sound when both the flute halves joined to become whole. And then it seemed like the sea started to churn and the trawler began going round and round its central axis as if stuck in a whirlpool. Faster and faster it rotated and the foursome on deck held on tight to whatever fixed objects their hands could get a grip on. Suddenly Ishaan just rocketed out of the deck in a high arc, plunged into the dark waters and was gone. The remaining three huddled together in trepidation.

[And somewhere in that other dimension, the giant snake had now risen up in full hood; its pink diamond eyes glowed hot and its fierce hisses threw flame streaks from its great mouth and sent them rocketing high up all the way into outer space. This in turn stimulated mighty

bursts of solar flares from the Sun that licked past the planet's stratosphere and ignited mighty auroras - a super electromagnetic solar storm, the likes of which the planet had never experienced before. It completely wiped out all electric grids across the globe and plunged the entire planet into an electrical blackout.]

Dr Baalan held on to the flute, his lips chanting the Mahaa-Mantram and Yogi also followed suit. Then there was another thunderclap of sound, a mighty flash, and the next moment, Stalin's yacht, which had just broken surface on his order, violently lurched forward. Its front deck sloped down and the back deck rose into the air.

'My billion dollar baby!!' Stalin roared through the din. 'NO, NO, NO, this can't be. It's my life's work and passion.' He then held his walkie-talkie to his mouth. 'Dive deep and get as far away from this area as soon as possible…NOW!!!!' his shouts crackled through the walkie-talkie.

Suddenly Stalin lost his balance and skidded all the way to the far side of deck and flipped over. But at the last moment, his hands gripped the side of the trawler and he clung on desperately, his body submerged by the sea below his waist. Even a very strong man like Stalin was helpless against the might of the sea and it was only a matter of time before he was swept off.

'Help me!!!' Stalin screamed.

Yogi immediately rushed towards Stalin somehow maintaining his balance and held out his arm. But he stopped an inch stop away from grabbing the latter's desperately outstretched hand.

'I will help you sir, provided you drop all thoughts of possessing the gem as well as the flute. You have to promise me that.'

'Mother-lode *da puttar,* you are asking for the impossible!'

'No, you must promise.'

'Just give me your hand man, I promise to think about it.'

'No sir, you must promise now.'

'OK, OK, OK... I promise.'

'I can't hear you.'

'OK I PROMISE.'

'PROMISE WHAT....'

'I PROMISE THAT I WILL DROP ALL THOUGHTS OF POSSESSING THE GEM AS WELL AS THE FLUTE. NOW HELP ME WILL YOU!' Stalin bellowed at the top of his voice.

In the next instant, Yogi grasped Stalin's hand and heaved with all his might. Stalin somehow managed to roll into the trawler and lay flat on his back on the heaving deck.

'Mother-lode *da puttar*, that was real close....' Stalin covered his face with his left palm. 'I owe you one Yogi, for sure.'

'You do not owe me anything sir. Just stick to your promise.'

'Ok, ok, ok... I will.'

'You sure will not change your mind later sir.'

'I have my code of honor and pride too Yogi, as unbelievable as it may seem to you.'

'That's all I wanted to hear sir,'

Abruptly the spinning stopped. There was another thunderclap and everything around them seemed to freeze in time. In the next instant, a wormhole opened up in front of them and they felt an enormous tug as the flute pulled the threesome into the opening. For the next few moments, they floated through the wormhole. The world outside the portal had now frozen in time. They floated for almost 3 kilometers till they found themselves in front of the main sanctum of the iconic Shri Padmanabha temple. The wormhole snaked twenty feet underground in front of the main sanctum and brought them to a giant door set in a vault. Two giant portraits of cobras adorned the door.

'So glad you made it here finally,' the hermit guide who had taken them to Netaji's cave in the Himalayas was standing there with a *tamboor* around his neck. He was looking even more radiant and his long matted hair was tied in a bun behind his head. Also, his beard was gone. 'Salutations from Naaradh, the humble servant of Lord Padmanabha,' the hermit continued.

'The great Naaradh of our Hindu lore?' Dr Baalan gasped.

'*Naaraayan, Naaraayan* Dr Baalan, I'm the very same Naaradh. And now you have brought the flute successfully to its portal, which is located inside this vault. You may be wondering how this slightly inland temple is a temple by the sea. In ancient times, the precincts and the lands of this great temple encompassed a huge area and its western boundary stretched all the way to the coast. By the grace of the supreme Lord, you have successfully negotiated many an obstacle and now you are here just in time. This vault is not one of those legendary six vaults of the temple that you humans have in modern times designated as A, B, C, D, E, and F. They only contain earthly treasures which have no meaning for the Lord.

This seventh vault in front of us is the secret of all the secret vaults of this great ancient temple and even the King of Travancore does not know of its existence. This vault exists in a separate dimension in space and not in the usual physical reality that the eyes of mortal perceive and experience, and is the source of all those earthly treasures in the other six vaults. The great *Naaga Paasa* Mantra is holding the doors shut and no force in the three worlds can pry them open. So it is time to call for assistance,' Naaradh closed his eyes and clasped his hands. Suddenly there was an electrifying raptor cry and a brilliant flash of golden light. A huge golden eagle with fierce ruby red eyes and mighty sword-like talons appeared in front of Naaradh and bowed its head.

'*Naaraayan Naaraayan.* Salutations O mighty Garuda, you are the only one who can open these doors as per the Lord's orders. The time has come now. Please oblige O mightiest of eagles.'

The bird raised itself, turned to face the vault, spread its colossal wings and tapped the door seven times. The next instant, the two giant cobras on the door vanished and the door opened with a loud creak. The light from the raptor as well as the flute illuminated the vault interior.

'Remember that one has to have the purest thoughts and intentions before entering this vault. It is a must,' Naaradh spoke at length. The threesome - Dr Baalan, Yogi, and Malhotra now entered the vault followed by Naaradh. The great eagle stayed put outside the vault door. The inside of the vault was empty. They could distinctly hear the sound of sea waves thudding in the distance. That sound was overlaid by sounds of distant roaring emanating from a nearby pillar. The roaring became progressively louder and nearer as the moments passed. Finally with an earth shattering growl, a fierce creature broke through the pillar. Standing in front of them was a golden, fifteen foot tall, half man half lion with huge canines and diamond talons.

'*Naaraayan Naaraayan.* This is *Ugra-Narasimha*, one of the *Amsaas* of Lord Padmanabha. He is guarding the inside chamber. As per the Lord's *Leela*, he played the part of that lion that killed Prasenjit, for whose death Krishna was falsely accused. Naaradh bent down deeply in *pranaams*. 'Mercy on us O mighty *Ugra-Narasimha*. We are here on a divine mission. We beg you to kindly give way. And then he prayed in Sanskrit

> '*Shreemad akalanka paripoorNa shashikoTi*
> *Shreedhara manohara saTaapaTalakaanta |*
> *Paalaya krupaalaya bhavaambudhi nimagnam*
> *Daityavarakaala narasimha narasimha'*

The half lion half man roared once again as he shrank back into the pillar; the sounds of the roars began receding and finally faded away.

'*Ugra-Narasimha* has given way to us, for now,' Naaradh said. Now they could see another door at the far wall of the chamber. Naaradh led the trio towards the door and then turned towards them.

'Now I have something of great significance to reveal to you Dr Baalan. You were none other than the great Akrura in your previous birth.' Naaradh continued.

'My God…. This is becoming more mindboggling by the minute!' Dr Baalan exclaimed.

'*Naaraayan Naaraayan.* Remember Akrura, what the Lord told you before the great tsunami swallowed up Dwaaraka towards the end of the *Dwaaparyug*. Close your eyes and go back in time Akrura,' Naaradh reached out and placed his right hand on Dr Baalan's head. The instant the hand touched his head and Dr Baalan closed his eyes, he felt an explosion of radiance within his mind. Then he saw the blissful face of Krishna standing in front of him in royal splendor, in his palace.

'My Akrura, you know how dear you are to me,' Krishna spoke in that beatific voice. 'I have called you here for a matter of utmost importance. The end of our *yug* is upon us. The Yaadav race and all of us will soon be wiped out. That is our destiny and we cannot override it in any way. Before all that happens, I want you to do something for me, dear Akrura.'

'Command me my Lord,' Akrura bowed.

'I want you to hand over the Semmanthaka gem, which is in your possession. The gem does not belong to mankind anymore, especially after I have departed from this earth as ordained. I cannot take the gem with me because it will be needed here on Earth for the workings of *kaal*. Alas, humans cannot be trusted with this gem because it can stoke and elicit the darkest compulsions in them. I know the gem is very dear to you. But the time has come Akrura to part with it.'

'Under normal circumstances I would have found it very difficult to part with the gem. It has become an extension of me all these years and I cherish it with the last drop of my blood because it has helped to do humongous charity all these years. But you have opened my eyes my Lord and I completely agree with you that the gem could fall into unsuitable hands after our time on this earth. I shall immediately comply with your wishes.'

Akrura had then rushed to his home, brought back the gem and handed the Semmanthaka to Krishna in total secrecy. 'It has all come back into my memory O great Naaradh,' Dr Baalan folded his hands in veneration.

'Actually, it does not matter to me now whether I get to the gem or not, O great sage,' Dr Baalan continued. 'By your grace, I was able to once again see the face of my Lord and this is more than enough for me. I'm actually ready to leave with a full heart. If I could just go the main sanctum of this great temple and have *darshan* of Lord Padmanabha, I will be eternally grateful.'

'*Naaraayan Naaraayan.* Exalted thoughts indeed Dr Baalan. The quest has indeed ignited your *Janmaantar vaasana,* the thirst for the real truth.'

He then beckoned to Yogi and then pointed to the flute in Dr Baalan's hand. 'The exact coordinate of the portal is yonder. It is time for you, Yogi, to play the tune that Lord Krishna taught you. Only the acoustic vibrations from that tune can help the flute set in place.'

'Lord Krishna taught me??!' Yogi reeled in surprise.

Naaradh reached out with his right hand and placed it on Yogi's head. 'Go back in time Yogi to the month before the mighty tsunami of ancient Dwaaraka and let your soul remember that you were none other than Kritavarma in your previous birth. Now play the tune the Lord taught you.

In his mind's eye Yogi could see vividly a magnificent courtyard in front of a great palace. Peacocks and deer and other songbirds abounded everywhere and then he could see his king Krishna sitting under a tree beckoning him with a smile. Krishna started playing his flute and all the birds and animals rushed towards the Lord and gathered around, enthralled.

'My dear Kritavarma, it is time for me to teach you this tune that can even enthrall birds and animals and make them your captive audience. You have requested me several times to teach you some of my magic tunes. Well, I am pleased with the way you have evolved spiritually in all the years since you fled Dwaaraka with Akrura. Hence I'm teaching this very special tune to you. Watch my fingering patterns and lips very closely. You are already an accomplished flute player; so learning this tune will not be difficult. But you must pay close attention to the nuances and reproduce it exactly. One day in the very distant future, maybe in another life, you will need this very tune.'

'Yes my King. I will try my best,' Kritavarma answered back reverentially. Krishna played the tune a few more times and demonstrated the nuances, the high and the low notes and their periods. He handed his flute to Kritavarma, who began trembling as the energy current from the flute surged through him. But one wave of Krishna's hand calmed him down and he was ready for his music lesson. It took Kritavarma 108 full repetitions before he could play it exactly as Krishna did.

'*Naaraayan Naaraayan.* Now come back Kritavarma - Yogi and play the exact same tune that the Lord taught you. When I say exact, I really mean EXACT,' Naaradh's voice brought Yogi out of his trance. 'Do it my son without asking any questions.'

Yogi reverentially picked up the flute from Dr Baalan. Once again the energy currents from the flute surged through him. Yogi closed his eyes and meditated on the Mahaa Mantram and the shaking stopped. He then put the flute to his lips. The next couple of minutes were pure magic as Yogi produced one of the most bewitching, ethereal tunes. It was completely out of this world. The bliss that Yogi felt all over his body was divine to say the least. So lost he was in ecstasy that he had completely forgotten about the quest...*param dhrustva nivartate...* At first, nothing happened. Then the flute slipped out of Yogi's hands, wafted through the door and was gone.

'*Naaraayan Naaraayan.* The mission is complete and the flute has gone to its proper place by the mercy of the Lord,' Naaradh rhapsodized.

The next instant, the door burst open releasing a bluish golden brilliance that shone with the light of a thousand suns. Humongous energy currents surged out of the colossal chamber in front of them. Dr Baalan, Yogi, and Stalin felt their breaths driven from their bodies and found that they could not move a muscle. It was as if a great force from the chamber was pressing down upon them.

'Do not attempt to move forward. Once again meditate on the Lord with the purest of intentions, if you wish to see anything at all,' Naaradh's voice resonated through the vault.

Dr Baalan closed his eyes in deep meditation, his lips chanting the Mahaa Mantram. Then he slowly opened his eyes. The splendor of the cavernous chamber put the greatest of riches to pale. The chamber was filled with mighty blocks of gold everywhere. In its center was a raised platform on which lay coiled a humongous snake with eyes of pink diamonds. Its one thousand heads, in full hood, fanned around the entire chamber like a giant umbrella. Its ruby tongue of flame wafted in and out of its great mouth. And its mighty hiss seared through the walls of vault. There were streaks of blinding lightning and sounds of deafening thunder as its coils moved.

Dr Baalan gasped in amazement as he recognized the serpent from his vivid dream. And there, on top of its central head was the greatest of gems that the earth would ever know. THE SEMMANTHAKA. True to its lore, it shone like the sun. For a moment, the lightning, thunder, and hissing stopped and the chamber filled with the bewitching sound of the flute; the same tune Yogi had played, except two semitones higher and with more nuances and improvisations. They could discern a dark blue silhouette of a magnificent face, flute at his lips, behind the giant serpent's head for a few seconds before it disappeared.

'*Naaraayan Naaraayan.* Behold the jewel that you three came in search for, Akrura, Kritavarma, and Shatadhanwa. Yes Stalin, you are indeed the reincarnation of Shatadhanwa,' the voice of Naaradh spoke. 'That great snake you behold is none other than the king of serpents, Aadhisesha, who, as we all know, bears the weight of this Earth and who incarnated as Lord's Krishna's elder brother Balaraama. The day before the great tsunami, Krishna requested Balaraama to immediately leave for the south along with the gem and rest in this very place in his primal serpent form as its protector, away from the covetous eyes of humans. Moreover, the Lord selected this great temple because it would remain unmolested by the many invaders who would ravage and plunder our land and its many temples later in the *Kaliyug*.

The Semmanthaka was originally a *Naag Mani* formed from the hardening of Aadhsesha's excess unused venom over millions of *yug* cycles. Unlike his ill-tempered, demonic siblings - Vaasuki, Takshaka, Manasa and other, lesser snakes, Aadhisesha never found much use for his venom and thus it kept on accumulating at a high and concentrated rate and was transformed into a *Naag Mani* of extraordinary powers. It was loaned to Lord Surya as a boon by the Lord. And Surya, in turn, endowed it with its mystical powers of matter creation from ether and transformed the gem into a *Surya Mani*.

The trifecta of the gem, the great snake, and Krishna's flute has to work in PERFECT sync and coordination for the Earth to come back from the *asuric* dimension. The music from Krishna's flute will activate the gravitons needed for this transition and create a worm hole through which Aadishesha will carry the planet. In normal times, Aadishesha acts a shock absorber for our mother Earth. Without him, there would be severe tectonic instabilities. The transition from the *asuric* dimension will need all his mystic powers and he will have to rely on the original *Naag Mani* powers of the Semmanthaka to guide him properly through the entire transition.

As for your epic journey here, you three still had unquenched karmic attraction for the gem and that is why you have reincarnated in your present births to settle residual karmic debts. These karmic debts were used adroitly by the Lord to bring his flute to the portal and save this world.' Naaradh turned to them: 'Now your part is done. *Naaraayan Naaraayan.*'

The door now snapped shut sealing the great chamber once more.

'*Naaraayan Naaraayan.* All of this is the Lord's *Leela* in which you have played out your respective parts. *Bhoolokam* will now begin moving out of the Asuric dimension back to its original dimension. It will be a slow and protracted process taking years. But now it is time for all of you to return to your present earthly lives. Leave, and do not ever attempt to come back. Remember your oath of secrecy. Breaking it will rain down all kinds of calamities on this planet. Alas for you Shatadhanwa - Stalin, you cannot possess the gem in this life too. The strings of desire once again scythed your heart at the sight of the great gem and all that gold. But you have to once again remain empty handed, my son. Even before this present birth of yours as Stalin, your unquenched desire for the gem made you a pawn in the hands of the *asuric* forces in their goal of locking this *Bhoolokam* forever in their dimensional prison. But the power and will of the Lord turned out to be stronger. *Naaraayan Naaraayan.*

And now to answer the question that Dr Baalan posed Guruji at the Himalayas as to why Krishna broke his flute into two halves... The answer is that: left as a whole, Krishna's flute is a tempting musical instrument for even any mortal with the purest of intentions. But this is no ordinary flute and random playing on it can send undesirable gravitational ripples into space and time and affect the workings of *Srusthi* and *kaal.* Only the Lord can play this flute without any causal effects, or someone to whom He delegates the power and authority to do so. So he made sure that the flute would be unplayable until now, when it was really needed.

And once again, I advise all of you to leave immediately, as I have commanded before. Without the protective aura of the Lord's flute, it is extremely dangerous to remain in this vault as the highly temperamental *Ugra-Narasimha* will return. He does not take too kindly to the presence of mortals in this chamber because mortals are always swayed by greed and other *tamasic* forces.' Even as Naaradh spoke, they could hear a distant roar emanating from the same pillar once again, growing louder progressively.

'Move, now! *Naaraayan Naaraayan,*' Naaradh urged the awestruck threesome, who were unable to even utter a syllable.

Another surge of energy and the threesome - Dr Baalan, Yogi, and Stalin found themselves pulled out of the door of the vault. The great eagle was still standing guard and then, with a high pitched shrill, it spread its great wings and disappeared. The vault doors slammed shut and the portrait of the two huge cobras reappeared on the door. The wormhole once again sucked them in and then Dr Baalan blacked out.

Finals

'Where am I?' Dr Baalan woke with a start. He found himself lying in a hospital bed. Yogi, who was standing next to him, placed a reassuring hand on his shoulder.

'Relax sir. Glad to see you back in your senses.'

'What happened Yogi?'

'You had passed out sir, on the trawler.'

'My God Yogi! Did all that really happen? I mean, you also bore full witness to all that transpired with us. Please reassure me that it was all real. It feels like a surreal dream!'

Yogi did not respond, just smiled and put his index finger on his lips.

'Ah… I get you Yogi.'

Yogi once again nodded with a smile.

'By the way, what happened to Stalin? Is he OK?'

'Yes and no, sir.'

'What do you mean? Is he alive?'

'Well he is and he is just in the adjacent ward.'

'I want to see him just now,' Dr Baalan sat up with a start. 'Take me to him Yogi.'

'Sir, you need to rest.'

'No Yogi, I'm OK. Please take me to him. I insist.' Dr Baalan got off the bed and stood up.

'OK sir, since you insist,' Yogi led Dr Baalan to the adjacent ward. Stalin Malhotra was sitting on one of the corner beds.

'Stalin, how are you?' Dr Baalan rushed towards him. But there was no response from Stalin. He just stared blankly ahead, like a statue.

'Stalin! Stalin!' Dr Baalan waved his hand at the former's face. But there was no response.

'He has been this way since the time he was brought here from the trawler.'

'Oh my God! Now that you mention that rust bucket, what happened to Ishaan?'

'He is fine sir. He was found floating in the sea, buoyed by a log of wood and was rescued by another fishing boat. He was a bit dehydrated but he is OK now and has gone back to his trawler.'

'Thank God, he is fine Yogi. I do feel extremely sorry for the way things have panned out for Stalin however…. What about his yacht?'

'It seems to have disappeared without a trace. And search operations have been hindered too. Power shut downs have occurred all over the world. Almost everything everywhere is now running on backup generators. There have also been a string of big natural calamities in different parts of the world.'

'IncredibleYogi, I don't know what to say. But in our cotext, the loss of the submarine yactch is another devastating blow in store for Stalin, when he emerges from his present state. Look, the fairest thing we can do by him now is refund the advance he has given us for the contract.'

'I concur,' Yogi nodded. 'I also have an announcement to make Dr Baalan. I have decided to go off on my own from here on. What I actually mean to say is that I need a lengthy break from marine archeology.'

'My God Yogi, do you really mean it?'

'Yes sir. I have made up my mind.'

'It will be tough to lose you. But at the same time, I completely understand and Yogi, go with my good wishes, though I am sorry to lose such a good archeologist as my right hand. I hope that the time you spent with me was worth it.'

'If I say that it was also a deeply spiritual journey that would be an understatement. I'm lost for words here.'

'Same here, Yogi. Every moment I spent in your erudite and exemplary company was worth it for me. You are not only a talented archeo; you are also a good human being. It's been a privilege knowing you. You are the son I never had.'

'I can echo these same heartfelt sentiments to you sir. Thank you for everything.' The twosome hugged tightly and shook hands vigorously.

'Before we part Yogi, please tell me; in fact reassure me, that it was all real and not a dream.'

Once again Yogi just placed his index finger on his lips and smiled.

Epilogue

Two months later…

Stalin Malhotra had not yet recovered fully from his state of shock. Recently, his closest kin had brought him to an Ayurvedic center near Guruvayoor for treatment. There, he partially recovered, to the extent that he could walk with support. But he would never spoke a word again, for the rest of his life.

The old Jaarra *baaba* could no longer be found in the underground cavern at the Rann. According to the *pujari* Radheshyam, the *baaba* had left for the Himalayas on being summoned by his Guruji, who was now soon to depart the mortal realm. He had told the old priest that his work on this Earth was over and that he would never return.

Ishaan was still scrapping by and running his rust bucket up and down the Gulfs of Cambay and Kutch.

Dr Baalan packed his belongings in various boxes. All his professional stuff was labeled, ready to be sent to his former student, Parameswaran, who worked for the ASI. He had tried to contact Yogi, as he would have liked him to have some of his books, but could not locate him. Dr Baalan had also sold off all his properties and the money from the sales; he converted to bundles of cash, which he stuffed into a canvass bag. He then tonsured his head, save for a *shendi* at the back.

A one way ticket to Mumbai and he was soon walking straight into the main sanctum of the grand temple of the International Krishna Society. There he emptied all the cash into the main *hundi*, closed his eyes in prayer, and contemplated on the idols of Radhe-Krishna in front of him in the main sanctum.

'I expected this to happen eventually, but did not expect it to happen so soon,' a familiar voice brought him out of his trance.

'Yogi!' Dr Baalan was pleasantly surprised.

'Welcome sir. So glad that you are here.'

'I'm glad that you are here too. I did not expect it.'

'About five years back, I had already taken *deeksha* sir. But, around last year, I was summoned to get back to *samsaara*, to my original profession of archeology and join you on a divine mission.'

'My God Yogi! So you were already in the know.'

'Yes, you can say that sir.'

'And who was the one who gave you the summons?'

'That I cannot say sir. I'm bound by oath.'

'Alright, but at least humor me this once. Please reassure me Yogi that all that happened was real. The events are already starting to fade away from my brain as if it were all one big dream.'

'Put that question to yourself and you will get the answer. Tell me, why else a man like you would be here after giving up his entire earthly possessions and also the profession he loves so much and which brought him so much fame and honor. By the way sir, aren't you supposed to be in New York today to receive the prestigious Dr David Livingstone award from the International Archaeology Federation. But you are here instead as an aspiring monk. Why is that Sir?'

'To seek further answers Yogi.'

'Well then sir, that is your journey and you have to find your own way from here on to that higher realm, to that higher state of the senses, to that greatest of all treasures more effulgent than a trillion suns. As the verse of the sacred Gita avers - *param dhrustva nivartate*...' Yogi smiled and walked away.

Dr Baalan once again looked at the main sanctum and closed his eyes in prayer.

HARE KRISHNA HARE KRISHNA KRISHNA KRISHNA HARE HARE

HARE RAAM HARE RAAM RAAM RAAM HARE HARE

[This entire narrative is for me nothing but an ode to Krishna as well as Bhaarath-varsha. Krishna consciousness and patriotism are not mutually exclusive. The author]

About the Author

The author is a Professor of Pharmaceutical Chemistry at a reputed Pharmacy college in the South. He has published many scientific articles in his field as well as many well received articles in the field of higher education. He has also authored popular articles, blogs, and short stories on a variety of topics. Prior to this work, he has published four works of fiction. Other than writing, the author has a passion for music and Vedic Ghanam chanting.